M000190278

PRAISE FOR
R. FRANKLIN JAMES

THE RETURN OF THE FALLEN ANGELS BOOK CLUB

"A wonderful thriller, loaded with twists and turns and red herrings that will leave you guessing all the while you are flipping pages to find out what happens next."
—Vic's Media Room

"I found this third book just a bit darker than the previous two, which suited me well…. The two storylines are well fleshed out and Hollis is a character that you can't help but feel close to. *The Return Of The Fallen Angels Book Club* is well crafted, the writing is top-notch and you can see just far the author has come from her first book. The confidence in writing shows every step of the way."
—Mystery Sequels.com

STICKS AND STONES

4 Stars: "Readers are sure to be captured by this plot-twisting, exciting mystery. It is a real page turner and I certainly am going to keep reading this series."
—Cyclamen, Long and Short Reviews

"Who knew a simple nursery rhyme could be so dangerous? Someone knows. Someone has all the answers Hollis seeks.

You'll want to keep turning the pages to see if Hollis survives long enough to uncover the truth."
—I Love a Mystery Reviews

"*Sticks & Stones* is a great read, a fun legal mystery about a great researcher who really knows her stuff.... There was even a light romance, which did not overpower the plot."
—Mystery Sequels

The Fallen Angels Book Club

"Hollis is a character you sorta warm up to, you have to get past her cool exterior and suddenly you realize you REALLY like her and care what happens to her. "
—Bless Their Hearts Mom Blog

"R. Franklin James' new book has everything a reader could ask for in a good mystery: intriguing plot, fascinating characters, and a few shockers thrown in along the way."
—Shirley Kennedy, romance novelist

5 Stars: "Although I had my suspicions of one character, the solution to the mystery surprised me. And that, my friends, is the mark of a good mystery."
—Self-Taught Cook Blog

"A fast paced plot with many twists coupled with a smart and determined protagonist make this a most enjoyable read."
—Kathleen Delaney, author of the Ellen McKenzie mysteries

"The author manages to reel the reader in with her delightful storytelling and likable characters.... a great first book that lovers of the old-fashioned detective genre surely will appreciate!"
—Fenny, Hotchpotch Blog

"A satisfying, clean mystery with several twists that kept me guessing, and also left me anxious for the next book in the Hollis Morgan Mystery series."
—W.V. Stitcher

"I love a good mystery and this is one of the better ones I have read in awhile. A fun story for sure!!!"
—Kathleen Kelly, Celtic Lady's Reviews

"The story line was interesting, as were the characters.... I really liked the author's way of writing.... If you love a good murder mystery, you should get a copy of this book."
—Vicki, I'd Rather Be at the Beach Blog

"This book allows the reader to take part in the investigation; I felt my suspicions sift as each new clue was revealed. This is a remarkable, well-rounded mystery and I HIGHLY recommend this to anyone who enjoys crime fiction."
—Heather Coulter, Books, Books, and More Books

"This first book written by Ms. James is a winner for anyone who enjoys a clean mystery which will keep you guessing until the end about 'whodunit.'"
—My Home of Books Blog

"This book is full of murder, mystery and of course mayhem. Thoroughly entertaining and a fast read, I can't wait for the next book in the series. Excellent debut novel, Ms. James!"
—Tammy & Michelle, Nook Users' Book Club

"This is R. Franklin James' debut novel, a fact which I find hard to believe. She has created a character I love in Hollis Morgan, and a great plot .... I'm going to follow the series and R. Franklin James. I've found a winner."
—Views from the Countryside Blog

"Highly inventive… a wonderful thriller. The tension mounts as Hollis becomes the target of the killer, putting her life in great peril."
—Vic's Media Room

"The author … does a excellent job of creating a story line that's both realistic and suspenseful. There was never a dull moment. I really look forward to reading more from this author."
—Heather, Saving for 6 Blogspot

"A delightful read. It certainly contained mystery, murder and mayhem…. Like any good mystery, there was a mystery within a mystery and I found [Hollis'] exchanges with the older folks at the center refreshing and decidedly touching…. The reader could feel Hollis's fear with each event and her determination to clear her name. Very well written and very well thought out! Well done, Ms. James, well done!"
—Beth, Art From the Heart Blog

"An enjoyable first book in the new series featuring Hollis Morgan. Hollis is a good heroine as she is smart, determined and resourceful."
—Barbara Cothern, *Portland Book Review*

The Trade List

The Trade List

A HOLLIS MORGAN
MYSTERY

R. FRANKLIN JAMES

**CAMEL
PRESS**
Seattle, WA

CAMEL PRESS

Camel Press
PO Box 70515
Seattle, WA 98127

For more information go to: www.camelpress.com
www.rfranklinjames.com

All rights reserved. No part of this book may be reproduced or transmitted in any form or by any means, electronic or mechanical, including photocopying, recording, or any information storage and retrieval system, without permission in writing from the publisher.

This is a work of fiction. Names, characters, places, brands, media, and incidents are either the product of the author's imagination or are used fictitiously.

Cover design by Sabrina Sun

The Trade List
Copyright © 2016 by R. Franklin James

ISBN: 978-1-60381-219-1 (Trade Paper)
ISBN: 978-1-60381-220-7 (eBook)

Library of Congress Control Number: 2016932438

Printed in the United States of America

For Leonard

Acknowledgments

⚓

I HAVE SO MANY ANGELS supporting me.

The list would start with my publisher, Camel Press. Catherine and Jennifer, you are the absolute greatest.

To the best critique group ever: Kathleen Asay, Terri Judd, Cindy Sample and Pat Foulk, whose patience and skill keep me motivated.

To Michele Drier, Linda Townsdin, Sonja Webster and Penny Manson, for reading my manuscript and providing perceptive comments.

To Susan Spann, thank you for our breakfast talks and your eagle eye.

To Tim Hallinan and Ritz Naygrow, I hope you enjoy your namesakes' roles. Your caring friends and family were successful bidders benefiting Authors On the Move.

To Joyce Pope, Geri Nibbs, Patsy Baysmore, Anna Dever, Vanessa Aquino and Barbara Lawrence, for all the things you do, thank you for being there.

CHAPTER ONE

THE SUDDEN VIBRATION IN HER purse caused Hollis to jump. Glancing down, she noticed she had received a text, but she couldn't make out from whom. It would have to wait. Judge Morris's probate court was notorious for taking a short docket and stretching it out to fill a day.

She checked the time and took a deep breath. If things didn't speed up, she was going to miss lunch with John. At this rate her afternoon office appointments were in jeopardy as well. The attorney in the case ahead of hers was still plodding through Morris's questions, even after he pointed out they'd already been addressed in the file sitting before the judge.

She'd been looking forward to sharing a midday break with Detective John Faber, but he would understand. Her boyfriend had broken enough lunch dates with her. She reached for her phone, but before she could read the text, the bailiff's voice boomed out over the room, calling her matter. She slipped the phone into her briefcase and rose to speak.

Five minutes later she paused in her presentation. "Your honor, in summary, this is a routine probate matter with no one left to contest. I have located the single beneficiary, who could not travel to the court today, but is aware of these proceedings and has no objection." She came forward and handed the court clerk a sheet of paper. "I have an affidavit from the beneficiary stating such."

The court clerk stamped it in and passed it to the judge.

Morris painstakingly turned the pages of the filing, stopping to take a sip from a mug on top of the dais. Hollis leaned back in her chair, counting to ten. She made it to twelve.

He peered up at her as if he wore glasses balanced on his nose. It had to be a carryover habit, she thought, since he now wore contacts.

"Very well, Ms. Morgan, everything appears to be in order," he said. "Probate in the Matter of the Estate of Abner K. Johnson is approved and may proceed for filing with the County Clerk."

Hollis's smile was sincere. "Thank you, your honor."

She scrambled to get her briefcase and files out of the way for the next attorney, a young man who misguidedly felt he had to rush up to the table. She jogged down the steps to the parking lot and decided to make a run for lunch. If all the traffic signals were in her favor, she'd only be ten minutes late.

Closing her car door against the chill, she took out her phone to text John that she was on her way. The phone vibrated in her hand and her eyes caught the brief message waiting for her: *Sorry, babe, can't make it. c u at home.*

Clearly lunch wasn't in the cards.

She pulled out of the parking lot and headed for the office. Fortunately, Dodson Dodson and Doyle—or Triple D, as its employees fondly referred to it—was located in downtown Oakland a few blocks from Jack London Square, and a couple of blocks from the courthouse. Moments later, she was entering the firm's lobby.

"No calls, but George wants to see you as soon as you get in," Tiffany, the receptionist, whispered as she removed the ear bud from her ear. She motioned she had a client on the other end.

Hollis gave her a tiny wave and headed to her supervising attorney's office.

"Good morning, George, Tiffany said you wanted to see me?"

George Ravel was aging badly. Despite his trice weekly workout at the gym and daily morning meditation, he carried a small paunch and his face had a pallor that screamed stress. Self-consciously, she smoothed back her shoulder-length auburn hair. She'd been running around all day, and for all she knew she had mascara smudged under her eyes.

"Have a seat. How did it go this morning?"

"Piece of cake." Hollis chose the high-backed red leather chair in front of his desk. "I sat around for an hour longer than it took for my ten minute item to be heard."

"Morris?"

Hollis smiled and nodded, waiting to hear why she'd been summoned.

"I want to talk to you about a new client." He reached across his desk to a stack of folders and removed a sheet from the one on top. "Zoe Allen is a seventy-eight-year-old widow who has a travel consulting business. She also teaches a seniors' yoga class and volunteers at an animal shelter."

"Impressive," Hollis said.

George ran his hand over his thinning hair. "Yeah, she sounds like a marvel all right. Evidently, she and her husband came to Triple D about seven years ago to revise their trust and update their wills. Avery Mitchell handled the paperwork. I wasn't at Triple D, and you were … you were …."

"In prison?" Hollis offered.

Her time in Chowchilla Women's Facility in Central California was memorable for a number of reasons. It was undoubtedly the second lowest point in her life—the absolute lowest being when her ex-husband shrugged and turned his back on her as she was escorted to prison for a crime he'd committed. As it was, it took years to get over the betrayal, but now she was grateful for the character-building time served.

"Uh, yes, anyway, they moved to Southern California and retained the Coronado Legal Group in La Jolla near San Diego, and it was that attorney who contacted me personally about three weeks ago, indicating that the husband had died some months before and she wanted to return to our firm. Zoe Allen had moved back to San Francisco and changed her will to recognize a new beneficiary." George gave a light cough into his fist. "Then, this past weekend I was asked to meet with her because … because she was dying and wanted my … help with implementing her will. Because there could be a perceived conflict of interest, I couldn't help her. In fact, I'd like you to handle the particulars."

"Okay, but a conflict? Who's the new beneficiary?"

"Me."

"Er … you?" Hollis blinked surprise. "Just how large is this estate?"

"Large." George grinned sheepishly. "Millions large."

"Oh, my God, George. You're kidding me. How did you know her? No, wait, can you adopt me?" She laughed.

George waved his hand. "Very funny. I'm sure it's clear to you why I can't work with the Allen estate."

"Sure, *that* I understand. I take it she's a distant relative?"

George handed her the file. "She's my birth mother."

"Birth mother," Hollis repeated and opened the folder. "You were adopted? When did you find each other?"

George said nothing but stood and walked over to the window. From where she was sitting, Hollis could see the scattered sailboats on the bay. Not wanting to interrupt his thoughts, she for once waited patiently for him to provide the story. He finally turned back toward her.

"I was fourteen when my parents told me I was adopted." He reached under his credenza to a small refrigerator, pulled out two bottles of water, and put one in front of her. "The teen years are not the best time to hear that your birth mother gave

you up. But my parents loved me, and they waited for me to …
to get my head around the idea. Meantime, they had to put up
with me acting out throughout high school."

Hollis opened the bottled water. She had to resist the urge
to take notes.

"When I was getting ready to start my junior year in high
school, my dad told my mom that he and I were going on a
camping trip. You'd have to know him to understand, but he is
the kindest, gentlest man on earth. I knew he'd had enough of
my ways, but at the time I didn't care. Well, instead of camping
in Yosemite, we went to the worst streets of Oakland and San
Francisco. One night we stayed in a homeless shelter where
he read me the riot act, and then he took me to Santa Rita
Jail where one of his friends was a deputy sheriff. Scared me
straight. It was the four-day 'camping trip' from hell."

Hollis gave a small laugh. "I know it's not funny, but George,
I cannot see you at Santa Rita at all."

"And you won't see me there." He grinned. "After that, I got
my life together in a hurry. Fast forward almost thirty years,
and like I said, a few weeks ago I was contacted by her attorney
with the Coronado Legal Group. He said he represented my
birth mother, she was very ill and was anxious to meet me."

"That must have been a shock."

George raised his eyebrows. "You have no idea." He ran
his hand over his head. "You see, I never had any interest or
curiosity about finding her. As far as I was concerned, Bill and
Kathy Ravel were my parents."

Hollis looked at the clock on George's desk and grimaced.

"George, can you stay late tonight? I want to hear the rest of
the story, but I've got a two o'clock I need to get ready for. You
can finish bringing me up to date then."

He waved at her. "Go. There's not much more left to tell," he
said, composing himself. "I can stay until six, and then I have
to go. I'm babysitting the kids so my wife can go to class."

"I'll see you at five if not before." Hollis grabbed the trust file and dashed out of the room.

She finished with her last client by four, made herself a cup of tea, and proceeded to go through George's file. While there were a few pages provided by Triple D, including the original trust, the majority of the paperwork was supplied by the Coronado law firm. She scanned through the birth certificate, the formal adoption papers, and the client correspondence.

Zoe, now living in San Francisco, had been married for fifty-two years to Howard when he died seven months ago in Southern California. The money was largely Howard Allen's, and he left it all to his wife. Upon the death of her father, she'd also inherited a modest sum that had been kept as her separate property. According to the attorney's letter to George, Zoe never told her husband about her youthful indiscretion that had produced a child. But after he was gone, she'd asked the Coronado firm to locate her son so they could reconnect.

The lawyers hired an investigator who did the research and located George Ravel.

Hollis put the file down and thought about George's numbed recounting of his reaction when he heard from his birth mother ... and the details of her bountiful estate. She smiled at the irony of it all. She'd always preferred to think—no, *hope*— she was adopted rather than accept the reality of her cold and judgmental birth family. Sighing, she wondered how George's life would change and headed to his office to find out.

"Listen, I had a great family." He leaned back in his chair. "My real mother and father raised me to be the man I am today." He paused with a slight frown. "To finish up our earlier talk, I'll give you the short version; I was contacted by Zoe Allen's attorneys. I met with her three weeks ago, and then again last weekend, and we ... we visited some more." He paused, pointed to the phone and continued, "I just got a call that she passed away last night."

"George, I'm so sorry," she mumbled and shifted in her chair. He was silent for a long moment.

"Yeah, well, at least I got a chance to meet her before … before she died." George cleared his throat. "I can't judge her. She did the best she could; she said … she said her husband would never have married her if he knew … if he knew about me. So …."

To put him at ease, Hollis asked, "How was it to meet her for the first time?"

He shook his head like a dog shaking off water. "It was like a chapter was closed. I don't have to wonder anymore." He looked down at his watch. "I've got to get going. Do you have enough background to start the process?"

She matched his curt, all-business tone. "Not a problem. I'll contact Mrs. Allen's attorneys and get it done."

George retreated to the paperwork on his desk. He looked up as if he were going to say something else but changed his mind.

BACK AT HER DESK, HOLLIS opened her cellphone to retrieve messages that had piled up over the day. There were at least a half-dozen.

She scrolled back to the beginning. Gene Donovan had called to say that he was going on vacation and not to call back. Hollis smiled. Gene was a fellow ex-felon and a founding member of the Fallen Angels Book Club. His abrupt manner turned off some people, but she enjoyed goading him. Three of the remaining calls were from potential clients, and one was from a current client who just remembered he hadn't told her the complete truth about his assets.

But it was the last message, a text from a "Private Caller" that caused her to swallow deeply. "I got her routine down. She's in my sights. She's dead whenever you say."

Private Caller.

Was the message meant for her to read? Or was it about her?

She scrolled through recent messages for clues: nothing. She hit reply.

Caller Unknown.

She shivered and stared at the phone.

HOLLIS WAS RELIEVED TO SEE John's car parked in the driveway when she got home. The text message had shaken her.

He kissed her hello and was getting ready to turn back to a stack of papers on the kitchen table he'd been working on.

"John, I need to talk to you."

He frowned up at her. "You look upset. What happened?"

She held up her hand to reassure him. "It may be nothing, but I got a text today and it's pretty alarming if it's what I think it is."

She could see his shoulders release some of their tension. But he still wouldn't take his eyes off hers.

"Tell me. No, show me the text."

Hollis reached into her purse and pulled out her phone. After a moment of scrolling she handed it over to him. He read the message.

He scowled and slowly shook his head. "I know where you're going with this, but it doesn't necessarily mean dead, dead—human dead. Maybe they're hunters and they're talking about an animal. You know the sender?"

"No, not at all."

"I know it's a private caller, but they have your cellphone number. They could have dialed blind …" Handing the phone back, John responded to his own suggestion, "… but that's going to be a long shot. It's more likely that you're on their call list and they clicked the wrong name."

She puckered her forehead. "I don't know any hunters."

"Do you know any killers?"

"Very funny." Hollis flashed him a weak smile. "But just supposing it is a murder in the making—who should I contact?"

He folded his arms across his chest. "I would start with the San Lucian Police. They'll take a report and handle it themselves or refer you to the right agency."

Hollis sat down and leaned over the table. "John, can you call? After that matter with Jeffrey Wallace's death, they think I'm crazy. One of the officers called me the Typhoid Mary of San Lucian."

John started to laugh heartily and didn't stop until he reached for a paper towel to wipe the tears from his brown eyes. "Oh, that's a good one."

She was serious; over the past months she'd been pulled into enough homicide investigations to make her wonder if she was becoming a murder magnet. Fortunately, the police grudgingly gave her credit for assisting them.

John ran his fingers through his thick wavy hair and took a deep breath. "But sorry, hon, I can't. Besides they're going to want to talk with you." He patted the papers on the table. "As it turns out, I got home early because I've been given a special assignment, and I have to leave first thing in the morning."

Hollis suppressed the urge to whine and pulled herself together. Ever since John had started a new career with Homeland Security, these 'special assignments' were becoming less special and more common.

"Oh, John, not again. When will you be back?"

"This time it shouldn't take more than a few days." He reached for her hand. "I'll be back in time for our dinner with Mark and Rena."

"You better, or Rena will kill me. I promised we would go over the details for the wedding." She chuckled. "It's amusing seeing Rena with her sophisticated air and aloof model looks giving in to commonplace panic."

"I like them both; they make a good couple."

"Just see that you're back on Friday."

Hollis was grateful John would be gone only until the end of the week, but she wasn't ready to let go of her request. "Well, then you would be doing me a big favor if you would just make the first contact with the police," she insisted.

Although his face showed sympathy, he wouldn't budge. "You know, whoever I talk to now won't be the person you have to give the report to later. You'll still have to meet with an officer." He leaned back in the chair and smiled mischievously. "Besides, I heard that Mosley's gone."

Hollis cocked her head. Mosley had been her chiding nemesis during Jeffrey Wallace's murder investigation. He'd treated her like a nuisance and whenever possible tried to discredit her findings. It wasn't until she forced him to acknowledge her contribution to a case solved that he muttered a "thank you." But John was right; Mosley was the reason she didn't want to contact the police.

"Gone, where?"

John's expression held a glint of deviltry. He evidently could hear the relief in her voice. "He took a position in San Jose. His mother is elderly, and the family wanted him to be close by."

Mosley has a mother? Hard to imagine.

"That's great news." A smile crept across her face. "I'll contact Stephanie. Even though she works in the forensic lab, she'll know a good person in the department for me to approach."

"I thought that might cheer you up," John said.

CHAPTER TWO

SINCE JOHN HAD LEFT AT the crack of dawn, Hollis got to the office early, but even so, she wasn't the first one there. One of the attorneys—head bent over his computer keyboard, sheets of paper and open books on the floor—had clearly been at work for some time. She wondered if he'd ever gone home last night. Triple D had a way of drawing out the high achiever gene in its attorneys, almost to a negative.

As she passed through the lobby, she caught just the barest hint of light as the sun eased over the Oakland hills. She usually took the time to pause and reflect, but this morning she hurried past the beauty of the San Francisco Bay to her office. She and Stephanie had agreed to meet at ten this morning.

She flipped through the work in her in-box. George had given her a couple of cases with impending deadlines; she would get them out of the way before she had to leave for her meeting.

CLEARING THE CASES TOOK A little longer than she anticipated, making Hollis almost fifteen minutes late for her meeting with Stephanie.

She slid into the booth a little breathless. "I'm sorry, I had to finish—"

Stephanie waved her hand. "No need to explain. You're always on time and I'm usually the one who's late, so I figured something held you up. Besides, I brought reading with me." She pointed to a small stack of reports.

Stephanie Ross and Hollis had been friends for what seemed like forever, but it had been less than five years. Stephanie had come to Hollis's aid any number of times, and would still recount the time she "took a bullet" for her.

Attractive but not beautiful, Stephanie had a lively personality that registered in the character lines in her face and almost made her pretty. Her dark, caramel-brown hair framed even darker expressive brown eyes that couldn't help but reveal her intelligence or her impatience with superficial people.

She and Hollis ordered coffee from the waitress, who went away with a promise to return for their order. Hollis pulled her phone out of her purse.

"Take a look at this," she said, handing it over to Stephanie.

Stephanie glanced down and then frowned. "Now I see why you called me last night. The message looks worse when you see it on the screen." She handed the phone back. "I arranged for you to see Detective Warren at eleven thirty. He said he could take your report but this type of thing doesn't come under his jurisdiction ... or expertise. He's going to turn you over to one of the sheriff's tech guys."

Hollis swallowed. "Will you come with me to meet the tech guy?"

Stephanie looked at her curiously. "What's bothering you? You've never asked me to tag along before."

Hollis turned her head to glance around the room. "You know the text could be interpreted as coming from a murderer who could have me on their call list, or ... knows me, or ... or I could be the intended victim."

Stephanie just looked at her. "So, you want me there to hear what Warren has to say? You think you'll be too overwhelmed?"

Hollis nodded.

"All right, I'll come with you to meet the tech guy. I can't take the time to sit with you and Warren, but you don't have anything to be concerned about with him anyway. You won't have any problem with him; he doesn't know *you*." Stephanie smiled pointedly, took another sip of coffee, and stood. "But now I've got to get back to work. Hey, if John's working tonight, why don't we get together?"

"John's away on assignment but we could get together even if he were here." Hollis could hear the strength returning to her voice. "I'll have to let you know later about tonight. I have tons of work in the office and a new case that looks like it might be a real kicker."

THE DOOR OPENED INTO JIM Warren's small and windowless office about five feet from the front of his desk. He continued to tap rapidly on a keyboard for a few minutes before final looking up at her over the monitor.

"Ms. Morgan? Good, you're on time. Take a seat; I'll be right with you."

Hollis moved the files nestled in the only chair onto the floor and sat down.

Jim Warren was short and stubby. He wasn't fat but his torso reminded Hollis of half a candle or maybe half a sausage. His face was stubby too, with features appearing scrunched together like crumpled paper, as if they needed to be smoothed out. He reached across the desk with a thick hand to shake hers and turned back to finish an email.

"Now, sorry for the delay," he said. "At Stephanie Ross's insistence I squeezed you in." He gave her a slight smile. "First, let me call up the intake form and then you can tell me your story. Everything is electronic so I can do this online."

After a moment he motioned for her to proceed.

"I appreciate your taking my incident report so quickly,

but I don't have much to say." She reached into her purse and pushed her phone over to him. "This says it all. It is the reason I'm here."

He glanced down at the phone and read the message. "Okay, start from the beginning. Where were you when you got this?"

Hollis recounted the circumstances and noticed he entered the time and day in the report and typed in the exact message.

When he was finished, he said, "There's not much I can do. I'll get this over to the sheriff's office before I go to my next meeting. They'll assign someone to investigate."

"Do you know how long it will take?"

He scrunched his features even more. "Ah, it'll probably be today. This doesn't sound good. They'll want to get on it. Give me your information and you'll be contacted."

Hollis handed him a card.

"Oh, and you might as well look into getting another phone. They'll want to take this one."

It was a little after twelve o'clock before Hollis got back to the office. Immediately she went to work on the case files in her inbox. She'd hoped to have heard from Zoe Allen's Coronado law firm, but they hadn't returned her call.

From time to time she stared at her cellphone, resting on top of her desk. She used it for work as well as personal calls, but some attorneys in the office had three phones: work, personal, and backup. Probate law didn't generate the clientele who required a lot of conversation and Hollis had felt comfortable with just the one phone, at least until now.

She worked through the afternoon and was grateful for the uninterrupted span of time, but by four o'clock when her phone rang she grabbed it with anticipation.

"Ms. Morgan? I'm Detective Daniel Silva with the Russell County Sheriff. I've received your report from the San Lucian Police. I was wondering if we could meet today or first thing in the morning?"

"This afternoon would be fine. Where are your offices?"

He paused. "My permanent office is near Livermore." She could hear him working a keyboard. "But tell you what, why don't I meet you at the San Lucian station? I have to leave shortly for a meeting in San Leandro. The station is not far from there. What do you say we make it six o'clock?"

When they hung up, Hollis drew in a long breath. She quickly tapped in Stephanie's number and told her about the appointment.

"Not a problem," Stephanie said. "I'll meet you there."

IF THE STATION DAY OFFICER was surprised to see her twice in the same day, he didn't raise an eyebrow. Hollis took a seat in one of the plastic chairs that lined the lobby wall facing the door. There wasn't a lot of activity, and after only a few minutes, a tall muscular man strode purposefully in and walked over to the reception desk. Hollis couldn't hear the conversation, but moments later he walked over to where she was sitting.

He removed his sunglasses. "Hollis Morgan? Daniel Silva." He reached out to shake her hand. "I got out of my session a little early. Why don't we get started? I've reserved one of the spare offices for our meeting."

Hollis rose to her feet. Daniel Silva had a deep commanding voice that reminded Hollis of a news anchor's. He towered over her five foot three frame, and while he didn't look to be more than in his mid-thirties, he had a paternal air. He led her to an office through a secured corridor.

"I … I've asked a friend to sit with me," Hollis murmured, looking back toward the lobby.

He smiled. "You mean like having someone sit with you to hear your medical diagnosis?"

Hollis laughed. "Yes, I guess so." He'd put her at ease, and she felt her calm returning. "We can get started. Stephanie will be along in a few minutes."

He pointed her to a chair at a small round conference table.

He pulled out a slim file and took the seat opposite.

"First, why don't you let me see your phone? Have you deleted any messages, either text or phone, since you got the text?"

Hollis handed him her phone. "No … I didn't know what to do."

He gave her a small smile. "Of course." He read the message and then began scrolling through her directory.

The door opened and Stephanie, looking breathless, was let into the room by a uniformed officer.

"I'm sorry I'm late. I got caught in evening traffic." She slipped into the chair next to Hollis, putting her tote and jacket on the remaining seat.

Hollis introduced Silva to Stephanie, and she and Silva exchanged greetings. Stephanie's demeanor underwent a subtle change. He was an attractive man, so Hollis wasn't surprised that Stephanie had noticed.

Silva returned to scrolling through the phone. A few minutes later, his head still down, he said, "You were right to bring this to our attention. Before I comment, what do you think? Do you know anyone who could have sent this message?"

He still hadn't looked up from scrolling through messages. Hollis realized that it must appear as if she never cleared her inbox.

Hollis reflected before she spoke. "No, absolutely not. I don't have any friends or clients who would be sending anything like that. I … I don't know why I got it in the first place."

He gave her a protracted look. "Don't you?"

"What do you mean?" Hollis heard her voice rise and after giving him a long look, she forced herself to take a deep breath. "I guess you mean that it's likely … or at least there's a chance that I know the sender."

There was silence.

Stephanie cleared her throat. "Detective Silva, is there a way to find out who sent that message?" She spoke quietly, giving Hollis time to collect herself.

Silva shrugged. "It would help if Ms. Morgan could narrow the field for us. That way we could cross-check her recent call list with calls made to her number."

Stephanie nodded. "That makes sense. Are you able to triangulate all her 'Private Caller' calls backward to their source?"

Silva smiled. "Very good Miss ... I'm sorry, Miss ...?" He paused.

With a blush, Stephanie replied, "Miss Ross."

"Miss Ross, that's exactly how it works, except that in the interest of time, if Ms. Morgan could reduce the numbers we have to research, it would save time and money."

Hollis shook her head. "But I don't know—"

"Ms. Morgan, as a matter of procedure, I ran a check on you. You're an ex-conand before you protest," he went on, raising his hand to avert her response, "I know you received a pardon. But not only did you spend time in prison, you continued to associate with other ex-felons."

"It's a book club, for God's sake." Hollis didn't even try to modify her volume. She ignored Stephanie's hand on her arm.

He looked down at his file. "Yes, a book club of ex-felons."

"Are you telling me that you can't help me because my pool of friends is suspect?"

"No, what I'm telling you is that I'm going to obtain warrants to access the phone records of your friends. I want to eliminate your ex-con acquaintances first. I would appreciate it if you didn't give them a heads up."

Hollis slumped back into the chair.

Great.

Stephanie cleared her throat. "Detective, here's my contact information in case you can't reach Hollis. Can you tell us what comes next?" Stephanie slid her business card across the table.

"I'd like to keep the phone."

"I'll need to get another phone," Hollis protested. "And I'll need to transfer my call list."

Silva said, "It would be better if you went to the phone store and told them your phone was stolen. Or that you simply want a new phone. I don't know what kind of access you have."

Hollis straightened. "But my contact list ... there's no way I can re-create it. My clients ... friends, and family."

"I'll remove the SIM card but I would still like to have the phone to review your call histories." He looked at her. "Tell you what, I'll do a data dump of all the numbers with names on your SIM card. You can pick up the printout in a couple of days. You'll have to re-enter everything, but it's better than nothing."

Stephanie leaned in. "Does she have a choice?"

Silva gave her a small smile. "No." He took out a pen and scribbled something on a piece of paper that went into his file. "This is now an official investigation. I'll be getting back in touch with you as soon as I start delving into your contacts list."

Hollis and Stephanie gathered their things. Hollis turned back to Silva as he held the door open for them to pass.

"If it's me—I mean if the intended victim is me—then what happens if ... if ...." Hollis couldn't finish her sentence.

Silva's expression was stern. "Then I had better find the murderer before he or she finds you."

Hollis and Stephanie finished giving their pizza order then turned back to their drinks.

"You were shameless, Stephanie." Hollis shook her finger in reproach.

"What?"

"Here I am facing a possible death threat and you're flirting with the detective." Hollis took a sip from her wine. " 'Will you be able to triangulate the calls' .... Please, give me a break."

Stephanie smiled sheepishly. "You're right, maybe I did get a little carried away. But you have to admit he's cute."

Hollis shrugged and grinned. "Yeah, he's not bad looking

at all." She twirled her glass on the cocktail napkin. "It was a good thing the phone store was still open. I couldn't go a day without a cellphone. As it is, I'll be scrambling trying to remember phone numbers."

"It's only for a day or two." Stephanie reached over and patted her hand. "Once you get the contacts printout …."

Hollis pulled her hair back. "I know. I know that. But there's the bigger picture that someone I know might be a murderer. Ace Detective Silva thinks it's one of the Fallen Angels, just because we're easy suspects." She looked around the busy eatery and turned with a worried look to a silent Stephanie. "There's one thing he's going to find out real quick …."

Stephanie looked up, waiting for her to finish her thought.

Hollis continued, "All of the Fallen Angels block their identification information and have the readout of 'Private Caller,' even me."

CHAPTER THREE

———∾∾———

SINCE ALL HER CLIENT FILES contained contact information, the next morning Hollis was able to begin the task of entering the data into her phone. She had just put in the last number when her desk phone buzzed.

It was Tiffany, Triple D's young receptionist.

"Hollis, you have a caller on the main line, a Charles Allen," she said with her usual competence and clicked off.

Hollis reached from near the top of the stack of files in front of her and opened the Zoe Allen file. She hit the key to connect the call.

"Mr. Allen, this is Hollis Morgan. You're calling about your mother's trust?"

"Stepmother, and that's right. The family wants to meet with you. My stepmother was a fool, and judging from this recent shot, she might have been crazy as well." He paused and lowered his voice. "That said, we want to meet with you to discuss the matter."

Hollis took a deep breath. She'd have to remind George that nothing was ever really simple. "Mr. Allen, you sound upset. Your stepmother just passed away and you may need time to … to grieve. If you want to talk about the trust, the Coronado Legal Group are the ones—"

"Look, those attorneys just want to charge us by the hour. Besides we already met with them yesterday," Allen growled. "We would rather meet with Ravel, but he just gave me some bull about having to speak with his attorney, and he gave us your name."

Hollis looked up to the ceiling just as George popped his head in her door. He mouthed "Allen?" And at her nod he took a seat in front of her desk.

Hollis turned to her wall calendar. "Mr. Allen, when would you like to meet?"

"Do we have to come there?"

I don't make house calls.

She tried to keep the snap out of her voice. "Yes. Do the family members live in the Bay Area?"

"Half do, and half live in the San Diego area. Even though we told him we weren't going to pay for him to sit around, our attorney wants to come and listen," he muttered. "And we were hoping you could come to San Diego."

Half … how many are there?

"No, I can't come to San Diego," she repeated for George's benefit, "but I can arrange a Skype call in an affiliate's law office in San Diego for those members who live there. The rest can meet here in our offices."

Charles Allen hesitated. "Well, I guess so, if you make all the arrangements."

Hollis and Allen agreed that the following Monday would be suitable. He gave her the name of their attorney and agreed to contact her if there was a problem. She would contact him with the location of the Skype call.

She hung up the phone and looked at George.

"Thanks."

He shrugged. "I tried to get here before Allen got you on the phone." He crossed his legs. "I should have guessed that she …

my … my mother had more family. It's clear they don't want to share."

"George, I've got a message from Zoe Allen's attorneys. We're supposed to speak later this morning. How big is her estate? You said millions, but how much exactly?"

"I don't know. I didn't think to ask for an accounting," he said grimly. "I'd just met my birth mother, and now she's gone. Besides I'm that much of a lawyer to know that once I heard I was a beneficiary I didn't want to engage the Allen attorneys in a conversation until I had all the information."

Hollis sighed. "Good idea. Let's get together after I speak with Simon McDermid. He's a managing partner with the Coronado Legal Group. It must be a big account if he's sitting in."

"I read it the same way." George stood. "We'll talk after your phone call."

Hollis's phone rang right on the hour. She waited for their firm's receptionist to connect her.

"Ms. Morgan? This is Simon McDermid. How are you this morning?" His voice was booming and crisp. He had her on speaker phone.

"Fine, thanks, and yourself?" Hollis smiled. She could play the socially correct game.

"Well, actually not so good. I'm here with my colleagues Tim Hallinan and Kevin Larkin. They're the senior attorneys who oversee the Zoe Allen estate. It appears we may have a problem."

Hollis stiffened. "What problem is that?"

"Your client is claiming he is the sole beneficiary to the Allen estate." McDermid gave a harrumph. "Mrs. Allen has stepchildren and grandchildren who also deserve beneficiary consideration. It is a problem that will need to be dealt with because right now the situation is unsatisfactory to all parties."

Hollis hesitated. The battle lines were starting to take form.

"I see," she said. "My first thought is that Mr. Ravel is not claiming to be the sole beneficiary; he *is* the sole beneficiary as stated in the trust. Second, he is the acknowledged birth child of Zoe Allen, and it is my understanding that she had the mental capacity to do what she wanted with her money."

She could hear forced chuckles of laughter from the three men.

"Ms. Morgan, may I call you Hollis?" McDermid didn't wait for her response. "Zoe Allen was a charming, beautiful, and fascinating woman. I'm sure she would have liked you. But the money she inherited was made by her husband, Howard. Howard had two children from a previous marriage when he married Zoe." He chuckled again. "He didn't marry her for her brains—"

"Mr. McDermid, may I call you Simon? I think I know where this is going. I really think I need to read the language in the original trust before we speak again." Hollis hoped she was keeping the irritation out of her voice. "Also, are you aware that I have been contacted by Allen family members who want to speak with me directly?"

There were muffled murmurs on the other end.

"Ms. Morgan, this is Tim Hallinan," another voice said. "I'll be direct. The Coronado Legal Group became the attorneys for the Allen family after they left your firm and moved to San Diego. We handle the entire family's legal transactions. However, after Mr. Allen died, Zoe Allen went outside the firm to another law office to have changes made in her pour-over will, and had we known, we would have advised her against it."

Hollis leaned back in her chair. Now the situation was clear. A pour-over will is used to capture all assets or special bequests not already in the trust, to be added at the time of the death of the individual. The combination of the trust and pour-over will ensures that the trust remains intact and all recently added assets are passed to the beneficiaries according to the trust. In Zoe Allen's case, she outlived her husband and was the last trustee. She took the opportunity to specify her son as her sole beneficiary. Hallinan was right about one thing: Zoe probably hadn't realized the implications for the other heirs.

Hallinan was quoting different sections of the Probate Code. He paused, and then said, "As far as speaking directly with family members, can you tell me which one contacted you?"

"Charles."

There was an acknowledging murmur.

This time McDermid responded, "Charles Allen is a good man—impatient, but a good man. I will speak with him later about our conversation."

"Ms. Morgan, Tim Hallinan again, we'd like to have some idea of your thinking about what we've just discussed."

Hollis made notes on a pad.

"Mr. Hallinan, you have me at a disadvantage. As I said, I have not read the original trust, though I do have a copy of Zoe Allen's will that you sent my client. I did not know there was another firm involved." She kept her tone friendly. "Why don't we speak again after you've sent me the original trust and the contact information for the attorney who wrote her revised will?"

"Of course," he said. "You realize that as usual time is of the essence. The family is quite upset. How long do you think you'll need?"

Hollis smiled to herself but said out loud, "Only as long as it takes."

LATER, SHE GAZED BLANKLY OUT her office window, re-running the Coronado call in her head. The call with the Allen attorneys had taken a different turn than she anticipated and she wanted to think things through before she brought George up to date. Also, she'd hoped to go over the Allen case and a couple of other files with her paralegal, Penny. Penny was excellent at taking initiative and reading Hollis's mind. She would arrange the Skype call and do the background research on the Allens.

It was a few minutes before she noticed her message light was blinking and she hit the replay key.

"You have three messages," said the mechanical voice.

She picked up the first message.

"Hey, honey, it's me. I'll be home tomorrow evening. You don't need to pick me up from the airport, I'll get a ride. If I don't call you tonight, I'll see you tomorrow. Love you."

She smiled. John once told her that since he started working for Homeland Security, he'd never felt more energized and excited about a job. It also had positive fallout for their relationship. When he was out of town, he made sure she knew how much he cared about her.

She pushed to listen to the second message.

"Ms. Morgan, Detective Silva. I'd like to speak with you today as soon as possible. Please call me when you get this message."

She looked up to see George standing in her doorway.

"Who's Detective Silva?" he asked and sat down.

"Don't ask. It's not about work." Hollis put the phone back in its base. "I was going to come to your office to go over the Coronado call. Can you give me about five minutes?"

He stood. "Sure. I'm anxious to hear how things went."

"I'll be right there." Hollis gave him a small smile as he left and pushed the button for her last message.

"Hollis, this is Gene. I postponed my vacation. We need to talk … in person. I've got to run an errand, so call me before you leave for home."

She frowned. Gene sounded mildly stressed and that was unlike his usual "let them eat cake" attitude. She'd be sure to call him later.

First, Detective Silva.

"Ms. Morgan, thanks for getting back to me. I have your printout here. Hopefully it should help you recreate your contact list into your new phone. Perhaps when you come to pick it up, we can talk a bit. I'd like to update you where we are with the investigation."

Hollis flipped through the files on her desk. "It will have to be later in the day. Will that work for you?"

"Not a problem. Let's say four o'clock."

She made a note and an alert in her cellphone.

Hollis and George sat on the overstuffed sofa that filled the alcove in George's office. Hollis was reluctant to tell George about her threatening text. It wasn't work-related and he was preoccupied with his new family and improved circumstances. But by the time she finished this thought, she knew she was rationalizing—George would be concerned and would want to know what was going on. Still, she was still trying to figure out things for herself. She would tell him later. Right now, he was going to be anxious enough when she briefed him on her call with the Coronado lawyers.

"So, if I understand you correctly … you think Zoe Allen's trust or will is going to be contested?" George's eyes narrowed.

"Oh, I'm almost certain it is," Hollis responded. "I put McDermid and Hallinan off by saying I couldn't talk with them or advise you until I read the trust. So they are going to send an overnight copy."

"What's your next step?"

She looked down at her pad of paper. "First, I agreed to have a Skype call on Monday with Charles Allen, who I verified is your stepbrother. I don't know what he talked with you about, but he said he was also speaking for all the other beneficiaries. I'll know more about them after the Skype call. Then, I'm going to contact the attorney who drew up Zoe Allen's new will. His office is in Berkeley. Hopefully, I'll learn what all the fuss is about from your end of things." She straightened. "George, what do you think about meeting with your … your relatives in an informal setting, maybe over dinner, and just getting to know each other?"

"Maybe so, but I'd like to have an idea of the language in the old and new trusts myself. And I'd really like to read Zoe Allen's new will." George rubbed his hand over his thinning hair. "I didn't want it to be like this."

Hollis kept her face blank. She didn't want him to know that she didn't have a good feeling about George's newfound family.

ANTHONY GRUEBER HAD A SONOROUS voice with slight tremor. Hollis had reached him at his office, and after five minutes of small talk, felt her patience running dangerously thin, especially when despite her best efforts to get to the point, he appeared to be taking a second pass at the weather.

"Mr. Grueber, I know you must be busy, and I have an important meeting coming up in a short while." She looked at her wall clock. "As I said, I am representing George Ravel, who is the beneficiary in Zoe Allen's trust. I'd like to talk with you about your client. What can you tell me about her? How long have you been her attorney?"

He chuckled. "Miss Morgan, I'm old school. I don't like talking business over the phone. Are you available for lunch?"

"Why yes, but it will have to be a late lunch." She quickly perused her to-do list. "Where would you like to meet?"

"There's a little café in Berkeley on Fourth Street, Maud's. Do you know it?"

"I've never been to Maud's, but I know the Fourth Street neighborhood. I can meet you there at one o'clock."

BERKELEY'S FOURTH STREET DISTRICT WAS located not far from the marina's edge. It had been a rundown industrial area in the '80s, but an enterprising developer, along with Berkeley's own creative artists, had turned it into an upscale outdoor boutique with an intriguing potpourri of shops, art studios, cafés, and gourmet stores. During the day, jazz bands played free concerts for shoppers. Without a doubt, Fourth

Street added even more mileage to Berkeley's aura of charm and middle class consumerism.

Hollis hadn't been there since law school. She hadn't made time and had forgotten about it after she started working for Triple D. She smiled as she drove past the varied store fronts and pulled into the parking lot of a small white clapboard building with a unassuming sign that said: Maud's Café. She would have passed it by, had it not been for the nearly block-long line of customers waiting patiently to get in.

Walking up to stand behind the last person in line, she frowned with concern that they would be seated anytime soon, and she didn't see anyone resembling an attorney. She should have remembered her college days at Cal, when one never went anywhere without a book. Most of the patrons were reading newspapers, books, or swiping their tablets, obviously well prepared for an extended wait.

She jumped when she felt a tap on her shoulder.

"Miss Morgan?"

A nebbishy little man, about her height with snow-white hair, was dressed in khaki slacks, striped polo shirt, and navy corduroy jacket. He carried a cloth briefcase and wore an engaging smile.

"Yes, I'm Hollis Morgan. Mr. Grueber?"

He nodded, and pointed to the rear of the building with a deep maroon cane. "Come on. We don't have to wait in this line. I know the owner. They know we're coming."

Hollis grinned. "Thank goodness. It looks like a popular eatery."

His limp was noticeable, and Hollis guessed it was his hip that had given way. Even so, he moved quickly enough that she had to almost run to keep up.

She stayed behind him when they reached the rear of the restaurant. There was outside seating and the section was full of customers chatting and laughing. Grueber went through a side screen door that opened onto a narrow passage obviously leading from the kitchen. When they came to a doorway, he poked his head around the corner and waved to someone Hollis couldn't see.

"Come this way," he directed.

They entered into the open area of the café where about twenty wooden tables, covered with plaid tablecloths, filled the room. The sound of an active coffee grinder overlay the "mmm" murmurs of satisfied eaters, and the smell of recently baked goods combined with the lure of fresh deli meats went straight to Hollis's nostrils. As they weaved their way in and around the tables, her stomach growled. There wasn't an empty seat, except for one table in the far right corner behind a half wall covered with event posters. Grueber stepped aside and let her slide into the booth.

"Wow, Mr. Grueber, I'm impressed." Hollis raised her eyebrows and laughed. "Can you get me into the French Laundry?" The last time Hollis checked there was a three-month wait to make reservations for the five-star restaurant near Napa.

He chuckled as he put on a pair of horn-rimmed glasses and said, "Maybe."

Hollis blinked rapidly. "I was just kidding, but … really?"

He looked her in the eyes. "I never kid."

They settled into their seats, and a moment later a server wearing jeans and a black t-shirt with MAUD printed in bold white on the front handed out menus and glasses of water. Hollis only needed to glance at the menu before making her choice. Anthony Grueber just put it aside, and as soon as he did, the server was back to take their order.

"The usual," Grueber said.

"A tuna sandwich, please," Hollis ordered. This was the item she used to test the excellence of a neighborhood café. If she could get a decent tuna sandwich then it was likely everything else would be pretty good too.

As soon as he was gone, Grueber put his case on the table,

pulled out a yellow legal pad full of notes and flipped it to the middle. "Now, let's get started. You were asking me about Zoe Allen."

Hollis quickly brought out her pad and handed him her business card. "I'm representing George Ravel. He's a senior attorney with our firm, but for reasons of conflict he has asked me to oversee the processing of the Allen trust. As you already know, he … he never had a relationship with Zoe Allen. He knew he was adopted but never connected with his birth mother, and from what I understand, for reasons of her own, she never sought him out until recently. When you contacted Mr. Ravel, he had no idea she was living in the Bay Area."

"She was living in San Diego and moved back to San Francisco when her husband, Howard Allen, died two months ago," Grueber said. "She asked the Coronado lawyers to locate him, and when she got his contact information, she asked me to call him."

Hollis made a note. The server came with their lunch. Pen in one hand, Hollis took a bite of her tuna sandwich with her other.

"Oh my goodness, this is delicious." She dabbed her mouth with a napkin.

Hollis's obvious pleasure made Grueber smile. "Good." He closed his eyes briefly when he took a bite from his grilled cheese sandwich. "As I was saying, shortly after her husband died, Zoe Allen asked me to amend her trust and revise her will to make her firstborn son her sole beneficiary and sole trustee. She died before she could execute an updated trust, but her new will is still valid." He took another bite, clearly relishing the taste.

He continued, "Zoe never forgot the child she gave up when she was an unwed teen. Unfortunately, she did not think Howard would take the news well. He was not an easy man to live with, or know, and that's why she never told him about her son."

Hollis peered at Grueber. "So let me understand … when Triple D's Avery Mitchell drafted the original trust, the couple was living here. Zoe continued to keep her son secret from her husband, thereby leaving the Allen family to assume they were the only beneficiaries to the estate."

"Correct. Howard had just hit it big with an electronics patent and they moved to San Diego, but up until then, Zoe's small inheritance from her parents was filling financial support gaps." Grueber took a bite from his sandwich. "Miss Morgan, Howard Allen revised the trust at least three or four times after the Dodson, Dodson and Doyle work. Unfortunately, he was a smart but vindictive man and was continually taking his children, selected charities, and his other relatives in and out of his line of beneficiaries like a pin ball machine. That was one reason for the delay in updating the conditions in the trust: the rest of the family raised objections and couldn't agree."

He paused to take another bite of his lunch. Hollis had finished her tuna sandwich and debated ordering another.

She gave him a moment to chew. "I take it Mrs. Allen went along?"

"Zoe Allen is … was one of the kindest, warmest and most loving people you could ever know," he said in a wistful tone. "Yes, she went along. For some reason I could never fathom she loved Howard, at least in the beginning. Then, I think, after so many years together in a certain lifestyle, she just stuck by her marriage vows."

"She would just wait him out."

His eyes met hers.

"No, it was more than that. She was grateful to him for marrying her and giving her an escape, even though he didn't know why he had her allegiance." He wiped his mouth with a napkin and pushed his plate away. "Arnold had two children from a previous marriage, now adults—Rosemary, Ned and Charles. They have six children between them and then there are a few nieces and nephews who were named specifically in the trust and given bequests in his will. However, since theirs was a revocable trust, everything went to Zoe as the executor and trustee. When she ... she passed ...." He choked up and tried to cover it with a small cough.

Hollis looked away. "You cared for her, too?"

"I was with her when she died. Before she asked me to prepare a new trust, I hadn't seen her for many months. I'd been ill myself and out of the country. She'd had a bad heart for years. She was so happy to have been reunited with her son. It was as if ..." his voice drifted. "It was as if she was ready to say goodbye to life."

Hollis said nothing. He hadn't really answered her question. Grueber picked up where he left off.

"Upon Howard's death, the estate automatically reverted to Zoe for her life. They both had wills and they specified that their joint estate would transfer in trust to Charles, Ned and Rosemary. Then, as I said, after Howard died, Zoe had me change her will in favor of her son. She left intact her husband's latest designations of beneficiaries, but she rewrote her pour-over will and related language in the trust to give her half of the estate at the time of her death to her son. Howard's beneficiaries would share in the other half."

"Let me guess: they're not the sharing kind."

"Not one little bit. In the previous trust Charles, Ned and Rosemary were joint beneficiaries to the entire estate. Howard had assumed Zoe would pre-decease him. Why he thought that, I couldn't tell you, except he was arrogant that way. So when he died first, Zoe became sole heir."

The server returned with the check, which Grueber initialed and turned face down.

"Mr. Grueber, just how big is the Allen estate?"

"As of market close yesterday afternoon ... about twenty million dollars before taxes."

Hollis paused mid-air with her mouth partially open.

"Ms. Morgan, all documents are in order. Zoe called me

last week to tell me that she'd re-written her will by hand and had two friends as witnesses. I would have drafted it formally myself except … like I said, I wasn't available. Still, the will is valid and has all the required legal language."

He adjusted his glasses on the bridge of his nose, reached into his case and took out a modest-sized file.

"Here are her original and revised pour-over wills and a copy of the current trust with Howard." He pushed the papers across the table. "Here is a copy of Mr. Ravel's original birth certificate and a letter of acknowledgement from Zoe."

"A letter of acknowledgement … why would she need to do that?"

Grueber rubbed his chin. "I know, I know, we have the birth certificate and adoption papers, but I think she did this more for Mr. Ravel or maybe to quiet Charles, Ned and Rosemary, than for any legal necessity."

Hollis glanced at him with understanding.

He gathered up his briefcase and sweater. "This is a lot to absorb. Read over all the papers and let me know if you have any questions." He put his glasses in his pocket. "I … I have to return to Canada for another surgery. I'm not as young as I look." He gave a false chuckle. "My daughter is old enough to be your mother. Anyway … there's a good chance this may be our last meeting, Ms. Morgan. I'm only going to be in the Bay Area for a short while before I leave again."

Hollis realized how disappointed she was to hear this news. Two hours had passed and she had thoroughly enjoyed his company.

She put her pad and pen away in her briefcase. "Well then, I'll read through everything as soon as I can. Would it be all right if I touch base with you tomorrow? I want to make sure I'm ready for the Allen clan on Monday. Is the number you gave me earlier still good?"

"Yes, you can reach me there or here."

"Here?" Hollis questioned.

"Yes, here." He grinned.

A man with a slim build and apron had come to stand next to their table. He had pale blue eyes, curly black hair, and thick eyebrows. He was already in a battle with five o'clock shadow at three o'clock. He reached out to vigorously shake Grueber's hand. Tilting his head at Hollis, he beamed a smile, then turned back to Grueber to give his shoulder a squeeze.

"Tony," he said. "When did you get back? One of the servers told me this morning you wanted your table for a meeting."

Grueber's cheeks had turned deep pink. "I got in a few days ago. Ms. Morgan, this is my partner, Ritz Naygrow. Ritz, Ms. Morgan is an attorney and now a Maud's tuna sandwich believer."

Hollis shook his hand and smiled. "He's right. This was the best tuna sandwich I've ever tasted. If you ever need legal advice, I'll work for tuna sandwiches."

They laughed.

"Nah, no offense, but I got the best lawyer as my partner in the café." He gave Grueber a look that was just short of adoration.

Seemingly embarrassed, Grueber reached for his cane and clumsily rose from his seat. "Well I've got to take care of some business." He squinted at Ritz. "I'll see you later so we can wrap up that minor matter."

This time Ritz's face flushed, but he only nodded. He gave Hollis a "nice meeting you" goodbye and returned to the kitchen. Hollis stood, put her tote on her shoulder, and picked up her briefcase. They walked out to the parking lot. This time Grueber's stride was much slower.

"Mr. Grueber," Hollis said, "it was very nice meeting you. I'll read the material and get back to you tomorrow. I … I hope everything goes well with the surgery.

"I want to finish this thing up for Zoe first. So, I'll be around." He smiled with a glint of mischief in his eyes. "Thank you, and call me Tony."

He was moving toward his car, but then he seemed to recall something and turned back to her. "Ms. Morgan, I may want you to handle some legal work for me and Ritz. Let me think about it and we can talk tomorrow when you call."

Hollis grinned. "You can call me Hollis, and I will be glad to assist you if I can."

He gave a long look, then got into his car.

HOLLIS WAS STILL SMILING TO herself as she waited in the police station lobby for Silva to call her back into his office. To make sure she was on time, she had driven straight there from Berkeley. Silva came to the double glass doors and waved her into a long hallway. They entered an interview room and sat across from each other.

Silva handed her a computerized report. "Your contact list."

"Thank you." She put the pages in her tote. "What were you able to find out?"

"This is an ongoing investigation, and I can't discuss details, but we agree with you that there may be something to the message," he said in a flat voice, his hands folded together on the table.

A shudder went through Hollis.

"Ah … what kind of something? I mean, am I in danger?"

"Is there a reason why you should be?"

Hollis was starting to feel irritated. She wasn't willing to play guessing games with Robocop. "No, there isn't. Look, did you find out anything or not?"

His demeanor relaxed. "You're right. I'll cut to the chase." He picked up a pad of paper and read his notes. "Seven numbers were flagged in our screening net. Four belonged to your book club members, two are from phones with current service, and one is from a toss-away phone."

She blinked. "Wow, that's pretty good for just twenty-four hours."

"Maybe you won't have to write us off after all." He wasn't

smiling, but his eyes had a teasing gleam. He looked at his notes. "Here's where it gets tedious. We're still going to follow up with all screened calls, but the toss-away we can't do much about. We're just going to have to wait for him to contact you again." He glanced up when he heard her stifle a groan.

Hollis grinned sheepishly. "I just dread the thought of getting another one of these messages."

Silva paused, assessing her. "Unfortunately, unless you do, or until we discover a victim, there is little more we can do here. This whole thing could be something completely innocent."

She shrugged. "All right then, I guess I won't take up any more of your time."

"At this point all we can do is wait."

"Great." Hollis stood by the door and looked at him glumly. "Wait for a murder."

CHAPTER FOUR

D ESPITE SPENDING MOST OF THE night inputting her
phone contact numbers, Hollis woke early to go to Triple
D to read the material Grueber had left with her. She still
debated whether to contact the Fallen Angels and let them
know about the pending investigation of their calls. In their
place, she would want to know, but she was an attorney now,
and disbarment or a fine in her first year could end her career.

That morning, she was the first one in the office. After
turning on the lobby lights, she headed for her office. Tiffany
had left a small stack of pink slips on her desk from the previous
afternoon. Hollis quickly glanced through the messages and
surmised that other than callbacks for a couple of possible new
clients, the rest were easily put off until later in the day.

For the next hour she swiftly went over George's adoption
papers and Zoe Allen's will. The Coronado Legal Group's
draft new trust had never been executed; Zoe died before
the quarrelling Allens could reach agreement and it could be
signed. Hollis noticed that the heirs fared much better in Zoe's
new proposed trust, drafted after Mr. Allen died. It was clear
that Zoe meant to deliberately leave her half of the estate to

her unclaimed son, allowing the other half to be shared by the Allen clan. But half wasn't whole. She was looking forward to putting all the pieces of the puzzle together after she got the draft documents from the San Diego attorneys.

She was startled when the intercom buzzed on her desk phone. She hadn't noticed it was already after nine o'clock.

"Hollis you've got a caller on our main line, a Mr. Donovan. Can I transfer?" Tiffany said.

"Yes, thank you."

Hollis hesitated before answering. "Gene, I'm sorry I missed you yesterday, but I was running from meeting to meeting. I thought you were going on vacation?"

"It was a 'staycation,' but it's on hold now," he said, rushing his words. "Look, I don't want to take a lot of time. There's a newsroom rumor that inter-enforcement personnel is assigned to the San Lucian Police Department … and your name was mentioned."

She swallowed. Gene worked for his brother's newspaper. This wasn't the first time his uncanny "nose for news" sniffed out a story in the making. Gene's partner worked in police dispatch and Hollis often thought it had to be a match made in news heaven.

"I can neither confirm nor deny."

"Oh, you're cute. Don't be evasive. Give me a break, Hollis Morgan, you owe me. Remember that last client of yours who wanted a place to get away from her family? Didn't I take the time to look up viable locations?"

Hollis protested. "You sent me to look in the special edition of the travel section."

"Okay, bad example," he said.

"Still," Hollis teased, "you're right, I do owe you for all your past good deeds, and I may need a favor. Can you come here for a sandwich lunch? I've got a ton of work and I'm under deadlines."

"Deadlines I understand. Sure, I can be there around eleven

thirty. I'll even bring the sandwiches." Gene paused, "Give me a hint. What's going on?"

"It would be better if I talk to you in person. Perhaps we can do an information exchange." Hollis debated whether to say more. "Give me another hour."

"See you at twelve thirty."

SHE GLANCED AT THE STACK of documents on top of her desk and picked up the phone.

"Mr. Grueber … Tony, I read through all the documents you gave me, and other than the emotional upheaval for the Allen heirs, I think everything is in order," Hollis said, the phone propped up between her right ear and shoulder. "I can take it from here."

There was a sigh. "That's what I wanted to hear. If you didn't realize it already, Zoe had a special place in my heart. Many years ago … well, I'm going to stop myself here. I tend to ramble."

"I understand. It's unfortunate the new trust was never signed, but the will is valid. I still want to see what San Diego is sending me, but I should have their package this morning. Unless it's different from what I suspect, I'll contact the Coronado Legal Group and let them know our position. Then I'll meet with George Ravel to see how he wants to go forward."

"Wonderful, wonderful," he said. "The follow-up is in good hands. Let me know the court date for the filing of the will to update the old trust. I thought I would be returning home soon, but it appears I may have to stay longer."

"Good, maybe we can have another tuna sandwich together," Hollis said warmly.

"Hollis, why do you want to spend time with an old man like me? You're a charmer, but I bet you get told that a lot."

"Actually no one has ever told me that. I—"

She was interrupted by George's appearance in her doorway. His lips were drawn in a thin line and his cheeks were flushed.

"Tony, I have to go, but I'll get back to you as soon as I get the hearing date."

She returned the phone to its stand.

"George, what's wrong?"

"An injunction. Zoe Allen's will can't be processed until I provide a request letter of intent." He slapped the form on her desk.

Hollis frowned and started to skim the pages. Her eyebrows shot up when she read the basis for the filing.

George continued to speak, "What kind of law manipulation is this? What's a request letter of intent?" He dropped down into a chair. "The Allens are implying that the will was fraudulently drafted." His voice rose. "I don't have to respond to this."

"George, calm down. We've been down this road before with other clients; it's just that this time ... it's your turn." She was still reading the cause of action section.

"Your words don't give me comfort."

"Well, they should. If you weren't taking this personally, you'd realize this isn't a lawsuit, it's some kind of bogus slow-it-down action. Obviously they don't want to take the time or money required for the formal court process. I can't believe an attorney drew this up ...." Her voice drifted as she turned the pages, looking for the stamp from a court clerk.

George snatched up a page and scanned down its contents. "You're right. I bet they did this without advice or assistance from their legal counsel."

"Great, kitchen table lawyers ... still, they may not realize they're showing their hand," she said thoughtfully. "Okay, let's sum up the situation. In addition to the millions your mother left you, you've also inherited a bunch of greedy step-relatives who have no intention of letting you have a piece, let alone a sizable piece, of their pie."

"Yeah, that's what I figure."

"Let me make a copy of that injunction." She paused. "This could get very expensive. We need to nip it in the bud. There are too many attorneys involved on their side."

"Are you trying to tell me in a subtle manner I may have to settle?" He ran his hands over his balding head. "Well, I'm not ready to yet. I just met my mother, and now she's gone. I just discovered I have an inheritance, and now it's threatened. I need to step back and think things through without overreacting."

"I agree."

"Er … ah … tomorrow is Zoe Allen's funeral. I'm going to attend." He looked at her with resolve. "Then I'm taking my family to visit my parents over the weekend. We'll leave right after the funeral and get on the road. Do you have things covered until Monday?"

"You can count on me. I shall be a benevolent queen."

He smiled with gratitude in his eyes.

GEORGE'S ABSENCE ON FRIDAY GAVE Hollis some breathing room. John was due back in the evening and it was more than likely he wouldn't want to see her leave for work first thing in the morning. She used the remainder of the time early in the day to clear her desk of a couple of cases and return calls. Tiffany came in an hour later with the overnight delivery from San Diego and Hollis turned the documents over to Penny to add to an ever-expanding file.

She glanced at the time. Gene would be arriving soon, but before she could finish the thought, Tiffany buzzed her with news of his arrival.

"I put him in the small conference room."

HOLLIS AND GENE EXCHANGED HUGS.

He looked handsome in his charcoal-gray slacks, V-neck black cashmere sweater, red silk tie, and gray shoes. Hollis was pleased with her new ability to assess the quality of garments, developed after much coaching from her friends Stephanie and Rena to raise her fashion sense, especially after her exposure to mundane prison garb.

"You're looking well," he said, taking a seat nearest the window overlooking the city.

Hollis said. "I was thinking the same thing about you." She folded her arms across her chest. "All right, what's on your mind?"

They traded smiles. They were of the same ilk, anxious to get to the point.

"The scuttlebutt around the department is that, based on information you gave them—I understand it was your cellphone contacts—county sheriffs are checking into the background of some of your associates, namely the Fallen Angels Book Club."

His knowledge of Silva's inquiry was no surprise; there was very little she could get past Gene if he was engaged. She also knew that, despite the directive from Silva, it would do little good to attempt to divert Gene from pursuing his hound's scent, once he was on a trail.

"You've got to keep this quiet, Gene." She leaned over the table. "This is not for any type of attribution, or blind hint, or whatever you newspaper people call a 'tease.' In other words, it stays in this room."

He held up his hand. "Hey, I get it." He did an air cross over his heart.

Hollis briefly recapped the text and her conversation with the police. "So, they've got my phone and they brought this special tech guy in to look into my contacts."

Gene's cheeks were slightly flushed. He didn't look her in the eye, but got up to stand with his back against the window, arms crossed his chest.

"I take it they have my number and that of all the Fallen Angels?"

She nodded slowly. The Fallen Angels consisted of a small group of ex-felons brought together by their mutual parole officer to form a book club. They were avid readers and articulate informal book reviewers. Except for one brief period, they had met monthly, and their time together was informative as well as entertaining. As varied in backgrounds and personalities as they were close, they'd bonded through a shared traumatic life experience. They'd even combined their individual skills to solve a nasty murder a few months back.

"You weren't going to tell us?"

"Detective Silva gave me a directive. Even so, I wanted to see where the investigation was going. If it looked like any of us were really threatened, I would have disobeyed him." She got up to stand next to him. "I couldn't risk Richard's paranoia or Michael's guilty look giving away my advance notice."

Gene gave her an uncomfortable stare, his lips forming a thin line. He re-took his seat.

"Fortunately my newspaper colleagues, after I earned their respect, gave me a pass and seem to withhold judgment against my brother for giving an ex-con a job." He leaned in. "I take it they're getting warrants to look into our contacts and recent calls?"

"I don't think so. I don't think they could justify looking at everyone's phone. When I met with Silva he said the only thing they could do is wait for the murder to happen."

"Oh, I doubt that," he said. "I'll bet he'll find a judge who will sign a warrant. But at least none of us were convicted of a homicide." He gave her a tight smile. "So, who on your contact list is a murderer?"

"That's what Silva asked me." Hollis didn't smile back. "Not funny this time, Gene. I feel frustrated because I can't stop a murder or … stop anyone from murdering me."

"You don't really think …." He couldn't finish the sentence. He reached to take her hand. "Let me see this printout of yours."

"It's at home," she said. "John's been out of town but he's due back this afternoon. I need to bring him up to date with what's been going on. Let's get together next week."

He frowned. "I've got to go out of town for a week. And next week, it could all be over … I mean …." He avoided looking at Hollis. "You know what I mean."

"Yes, I know what you mean." She sighed. "Look, John will probably want to go into the office tomorrow afternoon. Come here at three o'clock. I'll have it with me."

HOLLIS WAS FINISHING UP A legal summary breakdown of Zoe Allen's trust and will when Tiffany poked her head in the doorway holding a bulky envelope.

"Here's another package that just arrived by messenger. I didn't know if you were waiting for it. I already stamped it in," she said, putting the package in Hollis's outstretched hands.

"Yes, thank you." Hollis glanced at the sender. "It's from the same client." She paused. "Tiffany, I'm representing George in a matter that involves his family and it's getting more complicated by the hour. On top of that there's a … a case I'm working with the police and I need to be able to screen my calls. Can I forward my phone to your desk?"

Tiffany waved her hand nonchalantly. "Of course, it's been quiet. You don't get that many calls."

Hollis cleared her throat. "And Tiffany, when it looks like my messages are accumulating, give them to Penny to screen first. I'll let her know about our arrangement. She can likely take care of a few of the routine ones."

"Got it."

After Tiffany left, Hollis pulled out the papers that filled the envelope. She wondered what second thoughts the Allen lawyers had about sending the documents in the first bundle. It would be interesting to find out if the attorneys knew what their clients were up to. She portioned out the pages and began to add notes to the summary she had started. Two hours later her attention was jarred when Tiffany buzzed her.

"Hollis, it's John, shall I transfer?"

"Please." She smiled. "Well, hi there, stranger! How was the trip? I missed you."

"Ah, that's what I want to hear. I missed you too," he said. "The assignment was tiring but productive. I'm at home. How long before you can join me?"

"I can leave in an hour."

"Good, see ya." He clicked off.

She was still smiling as she ended the call, remembering how she'd resisted entering into their relationship—or any relationship, for that matter. Her fear of trusting any man after her ex-husband's betrayal almost kept her from one of the best things that had ever come into her life. John was there for her, with love, with caring, with security, and slowly she'd let down her guard to give and trust again.

Hollis stopped by her paralegal's office and went over the message handling. She could tell Penny was pleased to get an assignment where she could exercise initiative and use her own judgment.

"Not a problem, I don't mind screening your calls," Penny said. "Most of them I'm comfortable handling and anything complicated I can run by you."

Reassured, Hollis prepared to leave for home.

NOT LONG AFTER, SHE WAS curled up with John on the bed with her back to his chest.

"You know I love making love with you, but this is one of my second best favorite positions," she murmured into the arm that hugged her chest.

"Cuddling?"

"Hmmm. I feel protected and protective at the same time." She nuzzled his arm.

He gave her a gentle squeeze.

"John, do you know what I would like more than anything else right now?" She ran her fingers lightly across the hair on his arm.

His hand rubbed her leg and he pressed his cheek against the top of her head. "What?"

She turned to look him in the eyes. "Chinese food."

He laughed and pushed her away.

Fortunately, Dragon Fortune Chinese Restaurant was familiar with their order, since they ordered the same thing to go, every week—Basil Chicken and Beef with Oyster Sauce. By the time the food was delivered they had made love one more time, showered, and were waiting in the kitchen for the delivery man to ring the doorbell. After he left, they scarfed down the food, accompanied by tea for Hollis and beer for John.

"Ah, it feels good to be home," John said sprawling contentedly on the sofa.

Hollis, straightening the kitchen, called out, "So, tell me about the trip."

"No, you come here and tell me about that text you received." He patted the space next to him. "What did the police say?"

She sat and recounted her discussions with Silva, adding his conclusion that all they could do now was wait.

"I don't like it," John said. "Who's this guy, Silva?"

"He's a consultant with the sheriff's office."

"Can I see the printout they gave you?"

Hollis went upstairs and returned with the pages. "I've got all my numbers re-entered. But I haven't had a chance to see if any of them jumps out."

John flipped through the pages. "The ones without names … the area codes are all local, except for …." He scanned the rows. "Except for about a dozen. Can you eliminate any?"

She looked at him and pointed. "This is one of the Fallen Angels—he lives in Marin County. He moved to another city, but he never changed the number. The rest are clients."

"So the police didn't give you back the numbers they questioned." John tapped his chin, deep in thought.

"No," Hollis said, "but they showed them to me, and I memorized the four I didn't know."

"Of course you did." John chuckled. "Write them down for me. Let me see what I can find out."

Hollis laid the printout on the table. "It's getting late. How about I do that in the morning? Let's go to bed."

He grinned. "Yeah, let's go to bed."

CHAPTER FIVE

B Y THE TIME THEY GOT up and were ready to leave the house, Hollis was glad she had prepared to write off the morning. She didn't arrive in the office until almost noon and went immediately to Penny's office.

Triple D had a hierarchical office design. Moving quickly to the area that once held her own former paralegal office, she passed to the windowless offices situated along the interior corridor. In contrast, the managing partners took the corner offices overlooking the Bay and Golden Gate Bridges. The senior attorneys occupied the large corner offices facing the hills. All the other attorneys were allocated the space in between, and the associate attorneys got small window offices with a downtown view. Rank did make a difference.

When she reached Penny's office, Hollis stood in the doorway. "I came by to see how things were going. Anything pressing for today?"

Penny Martin was a down-to-earth professional. While many in the firm thought her humorless, Hollis enjoyed her dry wit and quick mind.

"Here's a log of your calls and how I handled them." She

handed over a single sheet of paper. "Regarding today, Gene Donovan called and asked to change his appointment to two o'clock. You had a call from a new client, an Olivia Shur, who was extremely anxious to see you today. I ordinarily wouldn't have scheduled her, but she was extremely agitated. So I gave her Donovan's three o'clock slot."

Hollis looked at the list. "Olivia Shur ... I don't know her." She wrinkled her brow. "In probate we don't usually get a lot of clients in a hurry."

Penny looked up. "Funny."

After she left Penny's office, she went to the copy machine and made seven copies of her phone printout. Returning to her own office, she finished the case work started from the day before; then, a cup of tea in hand, she stared at the printout numbers she'd memorized and copied.

She knew she had a deductive personality and as much as possible, capitalized on it. She picked up the phone and punched in the first "Private Caller" number. A robotic voice answered, without stating who it represented, and she was asked her to leave her name. She hung up without responding. Then a thought occurred to her and she scrambled for a pen and began pulling out files. Some moments later she raised her head.

"Gene Donovan is here." Tiffany poked her head in the doorway. "I put him in the same room as yesterday."

Grabbing a pad of paper and the printout, she entered the conference room and gave Gene a perfunctory hug. She paused with the printout in her hand and said, "I thought about it this morning, and I'm not going to give you a look at the whole printout." She raised her hand, palm up, at the frown on his face. "I admit, I should have let you know beforehand, but I just realized that ethically I can't. There are clients here who are entitled to confidentiality, and I am bound to that expectation."

"So this was a wasted trip." He picked up his keys.

"Hold on. I went through all the phone numbers of my

clients that I didn't initially recognize, and then I went through client files to eliminate those. Once I did that I came away with four numbers whose caller ID said 'Private Caller.' Here they are." She handed him the note paper.

Gene peered at the numbers. "Well, I guess the trip wasn't completely wasted," he said wryly. "Don't get me wrong ... I do understand and appreciate your caution. So what ideas do you have about these callers?"

"Remember, the police have this too. But you and I both know there are back channels out there that could provide an answer." She pointed to the last number. "This one was a throw-away phone. Don't give it a lot of time."

He glanced down the sheet and nodded. "Now, don't take this the wrong way, but if I help you out, would you be willing to give my paper an interview?" It was his turn to hold up his hand. "I know how you feel about having your name in the paper, but I can better justify spending *Herald* money if there's an exclusive at the end."

Hollis suppressed a shudder. "Please don't ask me to give an interview." She closed her eyes. "All right, if you come back with some solid information—and we both know what that looks like when we see it—then I'll provide a brief ... I repeat, brief, statement."

"Hollis ...." He shook his head.

"And the background you need for an exclusive."

"Deal."

HOLLIS'S OFFICE WAS IN DISARRAY after taking out client files to search for phone numbers to compare with the printout. With a new client due, she had to scramble to return everything to its rightful place. When three o'clock came, there was no buzz from Tiffany, and at three thirty Hollis went out to the lobby.

"A no-show?" She asked Tiffany.

"I guess. She hasn't called to cancel."

"Hmmm ... well, that gives me some free time. I'm going to

make a quick run to the mail room. I'll be right back."

"Say hi to Vince for me."

Triple D shared its mail distribution room with the rest of the anchor tenants in the building. The dark corridors of the basement were a maze but ultimately led to an open space of linear tables topped with white plastic postal boxes.

A cheerful voice greeted her. "Hey, Hollis, what a surprise! What are you doing down here?"

Vince Colton's smile caught her off guard. For over a year she'd waited to see him smile without prompting. To look at him now, you'd never recognize the former junkie and homeless youth. His blond hair was clean and thick with a healthy sheen. He had put on weight, which suited his lean frame. But more than anything else, his dark brown eyes were clear and focused.

He looked happy.

"I had a free moment." She stood near the Triple D counter. She knew better than to give him a hug. "How's it going?"

Vince grinned. "School is great. I think the night program is better than classes during the day. I should be finished and ready for a transfer next year at this time."

"That's great," she said. "Are you making friends? Any girl friends?"

He face turned beet red. "Aw, Hollis … no, I don't have a girlfriend. I don't have time for a girlfriend."

She gave him a doubtful look. "You know, Vince, it's okay to have a girlfriend. It's okay to have fun. You don't have to be serious all the time to get through life."

His eyes turned cold, and she took a step back. "What's the matter?"

"You haven't asked me about my mother."

She took a deep breath and said with dread, "How's your mother?"

"She's back inside, this time for bad checks and possession." He turned his head away. "You know, I can't get mad at her. We were doin' good. We got that apartment I was tellin' you about and I was able to bring food in the house, but … but I wasn't able to support her habit."

Hollis reached out to touch his arm. He jerked it back.

His voice sounded flat. "She lasted for about a month out of rehab. Then I saw her with the same dude she'd hung out with before she went in, and I chased him away." He rubbed his hand over his head. "You see, she didn't want to steal from me. She didn't want to sneak and take my money. She was so happy I was goin' to community college. She didn't want me to mess that up. So … so … so she …."

"Shh, I understand." Hollis said, unable to keep the dismay out of her voice. "Is there anything I can do?"

"Nah, she's actually better off in jail. I go see her once a week. She won't let me come more often than that." He turned and began to sort the stack of mail at the other end of the counter. "I gotta get back to work."

"Vince …" she began. Finally she said, "If you need me, I'll be here."

She went up to the lobby, but instead of returning to the Triple D offices, she walked out into the sun. She needed air. There was a homeless person walking toward her, his hand outstretched. She dug into her jacket pocket.

"I'm sorry, this is all I have with me." She gave him a couple of quarters.

He didn't seem to hear, or perhaps care. He took the coins then moved on to the person behind her.

She found herself walking toward Jack London Square, her mind racing faster than her feet moved. Finally, she looked around her and saw how the water in the bay sparkled in the glare of the sun. She sighed at its beauty.

There was nothing she could do to save Vince from the pain of dealing with the cards life had dealt him. The best way she could help him was to show no pity and catch him if he stumbled. That's what saved her.

She walked back slowly to the office. She again passed the homeless person holding out his hand.

"I don't have any more money."

He didn't seem to hear and just looked past her.

Hollis stopped at the reception desk.

"Where'd you go? Before you ask, no word from Shur," Tiffany said. She handed her a couple of messages. "You know, we should charge clients when they don't cancel an appointment."

"First, she's not a client, and second, we offer an hour consultation for free."

"It's still irritating." Tiffany picked up the ringing phone.

Hollis went back to her office. She was looking forward to the weekend with John, but she would use the next hour to prepare for the Monday conference call with the Allens. Tiffany had arranged for the Skype hookup in the firm's main conference room and let Hollis know that there would be three of them on the transmission from this end. The other six, in San Diego, would meet and call in from an affiliate law office Triple D used from time to time.

As a professional courtesy she contacted Tim Hallinan from Coronado to ensure he was aware of and would agree to the upcoming conversation with his clients. "I appreciate the notice, Ms. Morgan," he said with some condescension. "I plan on being there, just to listen. To save them legal fees I have promised the Allens I would not participate."

Hollis was surprised, but she'd had difficult clients before, too.

Finally she was ready for the weekend.

WHEN HOLLIS TURNED THE CORNER onto her street, the sight of an empty unmarked car in front of her townhome caused her to freeze. She drove past, and about a block away pulled over to park, keeping the car sighted in her rearview mirror. Taking out her phone, she punched in a number.

"Hey, what's up?" John said.

"Are you at home?"

"Not yet," he said. "Don't get mad. I won't be much longer." He paused. "Hey, where are you? You're not home either."

"I'm on my way. I'm almost there." She looked at the figure coming from the side of the house and getting back inside the car. "Don't forget we're having dinner with Mark and Rena at seven."

"Check the house phone messages. Mark and Rena cancelled. Christopher came down with the measles."

"I'd rather have a quiet evening at home anyway. Love you." She clicked off.

She didn't know why she didn't mention the detective's presence to John. But she did know she needed time to process, and to find out why herself. She pulled into the driveway. Detective Silva approached her before she reached the steps to the front door.

"Ms. Morgan, sorry to interrupt your evening, but may I ask where you've been?"

Hollis frowned. "At work, why?"

"Have you been there all afternoon?"

Oh, no.

"Yes, why?"

He continued to ignore her questions. "Did someone see you?"

"I'm not answering any more questions until you tell me why you're asking them." She reached in her purse for her door key.

"Ms. Morgan, do you know Olivia Shur?"

Hollis paused and frowned. "The name … wait, yes. She had an appointment to see me this afternoon. Why?"

"An Olivia Shur was found dead in her car at a gas station. She had a note with your name and number next to her on the front seat."

CHAPTER SIX

———∞———

SILVA LEFT HOLLIS MULLING OVER the news of Olivia Shur's death and amazingly, her unknown connection to the murder. By the time John arrived home, she was no closer to understanding, and when she briefed him about the visit, his jaw tightened and his face went expressionless.

They went out to dinner, saying little. Since living with John and learning more about him, Hollis knew he was working through the incident and its implications in his head. He would speak to her when he came to some conclusion. In the meantime, their polite conversations replaced the hard issue they weren't ready to face.

The weekend breezed by, and on Monday morning, Hollis noticed John's attitude had shifted and he seemed resigned. He motioned her to sit at the kitchen table and jumped right in.

"You're sure you don't know her?"

"John, I've racked my brain … I even Googled her," Hollis said, frustrated. "I don't know anything about her, and I definitely don't know what kind of legal work she wanted."

She got up and moved into his lap, where John held her in his arms. Hollis didn't want him to worry, but he would anyway, just as he didn't want her to get involved, but she was anyway.

"I'm making time to see Detective Silva and find out what's really going on." He looked her in the eyes. "I don't want you getting involved."

"Too late, I am involved. She was coming to see me."

"Okay, okay, don't get *more* involved." John glanced at the clock on the wall. "I've got to get going. What time is your meeting with Silva?"

"One o'clock," Hollis said. "He's coming to my office this time. I've got a big conference call to prep for and two other cases that have to get out today. If he wanted to see me, it would have to be on my turf."

"Ooohh, tough lady." He pulled her close. "Promise me you'll tell the police what you know, and then back off and let them take care of the investigation."

"Promise."

THEY WERE SPREAD OUT AROUND the large oblong table in Triple D's main conference room. The video screen monitor showed a room full of people clearly talking, but the sound was not on.

"Can I get you some water, or coffee?" Hollis made the offer to Virgie Allen, then turned to her two sons. "Charles? Ned?"

They all shook their heads, no.

Virgie Allen was Howard's sister. From her imperious manner, Hollis could tell she considered herself to be the matriarch of the family. In her seventies, she was tall and heavyset, with thinning brown hair worn in a page boy and eyes heavily made up with green eye shadow and two sets of false black lashes.

Charles and Ned reminded her of Tweedle Dee and Tweedle Dum, if they were terrorists.

They wore hostility like an aura. Both overweight, they were each about four inches shorter than their mother. Charles evidently was the older and spokesperson for his brother. They wore the same outfits in different colors. But it was their eyes that held Hollis's attention. They were a pale green, almost yellow, deep set in somewhat puffy faces.

"When are we going to get started?" Virgie asked, her head down as she plowed through her oversized Coach bag. She pulled out a small container of lotion and rubbed it into her hands.

Hollis pointed to the screen at the end of the table. "We're all set up on this end. As soon as your family members are in place in San Diego, our screen sound will come on."

She stared at the four agitated people on the monitor waving their arms and pointing at each other; she was glad she couldn't hear the ranting.

"Turn the sound on now," Ned wheezed.

Hollis turned her gaze heavenward. "I can't from here," she said. "They have to do it on their side. They may not want us to hear them getting ready."

Charles nevertheless insisted, "Turn it on now."

Hollis bit her bottom lip and reached over to turn up the monitor's volume. Nothing happened. The assistant on the other end had already installed the monitor so the people on the other end could be seen but not heard until they were ready. Now there was a cluster of six people standing around the table, apparently in heated discussion.

"Turn it up," Virgie ordered.

"Mrs. Allen, I can't turn it up. They have to allow us to hear them. I can turn on our volume access, that way they'll hear us, but we still won't be able to hear them."

"Do it," she said.

Hollis raised one eyebrow. She pushed the sound button and motioned to Virgie that she could start speaking.

"Mavis," Virgie yelled unnecessarily, "what is going on over there? You're using up our time with this attorney."

All of a sudden the gesturing on the screen stopped and everyone turned to the screen. Hollis could tell they were responding but hadn't turned on the sound.

"Hello, this is Hollis Morgan. We can see you but we can't hear you. You'll need to push the blue button at the bottom of the screen."

She sighed as family members pushed every button but the blue one. One of the younger women mouthed unheard words and shook her head in frustration.

Hollis snapped, "Go get the receptionist."

After a brief moment, Hollis vaguely recognized the middle-aged woman who entered the room showing the same frustration Hollis was feeling. "Muriel, can you get everybody set up on your side and show them how to turn on the volume?"

Muriel gave a thumbs up and pushed the blue button. "Hi Hollis, it's good to see you. Can you hear me okay?" She looked back over her shoulder at the group standing silently behind her. "I tried to tell them about the blue button but they were … preoccupied. Do you need me for anything else?"

"No, I can hear you fine. I think we can take it from here. Thank you."

On screen, a man wearing a three-piece suit and horn-rimmed glasses directed the three women and three men in the room to take a seat. There was a muffled shuffling of chairs as they did as he said. Hollis noticed the women sat on one side, the men on the other.

Horn-rimmed Glasses spoke.

"Ms. Morgan, I'm Tim Hallinan, attorney for the family. As we discussed on the phone, out of the family concerns to limit costs, I will not be taking an active part in this meeting. However, I have cautioned them not to come to an agreement until we speak offline." He took a seat out of the frame of the screen.

Hollis tried to conceal how smug she was feeling. "Certainly. I didn't realize we were discussing an agreement," she said. "Perhaps if members could briefly introduce themselves it will help me understand who's there."

"Eleanor Allen Paige," a small woman dressed in sweats called out. "Virgie is my mother and I'm Charles's sister."

Not Ned's?

"Paula Allen." A blonde rotund woman dressed all in black even to the triangle-shaped hat on her head, spoke. She reminded Hollis of a caricature of a nineteenth-century widow. "I'm married to Louis."

"Hi, I'm Louis. Howard was my great-uncle." Looking to be in his twenties, he was a good-looking man, fit and dressed like a banker. "I hope this doesn't take long, I've got to get to another meeting."

Hollis could hear what sounded like a murmur from Hallinan in the corner.

"I'm Patrice Dune, Howard's niece," said a young woman at the end of the table. "I'm just here to show support."

"Okay, well last but not least, I'm Harold Dune. I'm married to Patrice." He had a broad smile on his face. His light brown hair and thick glasses gave him a friendly aspect. "Hey, Aunt Virgie. Hi, Charlie, hi Ned."

"Don't call me Charlie."

Hollis began to roll her eyes, then stopped herself. Making an effort to appear indifferent, she said, "Okay, let's get started. Like Louis, I have a meeting after this one."

"I'll talk first," Virgie announced. "Your client, Mr. George Ravel, is trying to undermine our family's inheritance. It's our legacy, and we're not going to let that happen."

"That's right, Aunt Virgie," Louis called out. "We don't know what this Ravel's up to, but he can't come in and steal our money."

Hollis held up her hand. "All right, I understand your point. Is there a reason for this meeting?"

There was another murmur from the corner.

"Umm, yes." The speaker was Charles.

He pulled out a sheet of paper from a briefcase Hollis hadn't noticed he carried and pushed it across the table. There was silence in the Triple D conference room, and silence from San Diego.

She scanned the paper and tapped it with her pen.

"This says you want George Ravel to give back his inheritance and become a secondary heir after Charles and Eleanor, along with the eight cousins." She crossed her arms over her chest. "What are you trying to accomplish?"

"This is money my father made, not that Zoe woman he married after my mother," Virgie said.

Hollis shook her head. "That's not true. He was married to Zoe Allen for over fifty years. I did some research. Zoe came from a wealthy family in her own right. She used her money to jumpstart your father's business after it began to flounder. She has no other living family members."

"Oh, so that's how he's going to steal our money," Louis said, throwing a pencil down on the table. He muttered, "The will is not even valid."

A "sh" was uttered by a few and another murmur came from the off-screen corner of the room. Hollis took note of Louis's comment and thought that Hallinan was probably unable to contain himself by now.

Hollis cleared her throat and straightened in her seat. "Look, as I said before, I understand where all of you are coming from. However, I cannot decide anything this morning, so let me discuss things with Mr. Ravel. You can imagine how he must feel just discovering his birth mother and—"

"Please, we don't care how he feels," Charles protested. "But I agree, this meeting is getting us nowhere."

"Let me discuss your, er, request letter with Mr. Ravel. When I have an answer, who should I communicate with? Mr. Hallinan? Charles Allen?" Hollis asked.

Virgie, Ned, and Charles exchanged looks. In the monitor the San Diego table had gone into a loose huddle.

Hollis stood. "I'll give you some privacy. Just wave at me— I'll be in the lobby."

She closed the door behind her with relief. Tiffany glanced at her, barely able to hide a grin. A few moments later Charles was waving her in.

"Ms. Morgan, you may contact me directly. Is that okay with you, Virgie?" Tim Hallinan asked.

Virgie shifted her frame in the chair. "Yes, doesn't make sense to be a penny wise and a pound foolish," she said. "But we want to know everything that's going on."

Charles piped up, "And we want your special rate."

Good grief.

Hollis made a sympathetic face. She almost felt sorry for Hallinan.

WHEN EVERYONE WAS GONE, HOLLIS walked hastily back to her office. She wanted to write up notes from the Allen meeting so she'd be ready to discuss the event with George later that afternoon. But there were more pressing matters—she wanted to get ready for Silva.

During lunch, with one hand holding a sandwich and the other on the keyboard mouse, Hollis searched Triple D files for the name Olivia Shur. There was nothing. Shur must have been a referral. She wished she had her phone number. Shur had declined to give it to Tiffany when the appointment was set up. Without a number she couldn't compare it to the phone printout Silva had given her. As it was, it appeared she'd have to wait for Silva.

She didn't have to wait long. He was early.

"Thanks for coming to my office." Hollis handed him a bottle of water from a tray on her credenza.

Silva, wearing a suit without a tie, carried a thin briefcase.

He took out a pad of paper. "It's close to my next meeting over in the state building." He pulled out the printout and pursed his lips. "Ms. Morgan, as I told you earlier, Olivia Shur had your name, phone number, and a business card on her car seat. Knowing the issue you had with your phone, we automatically checked for Shur's number. She was one of the 'Private Callers.' "

Hollis rose from her chair and stood looking out the window. She was listening and taking it all in, but she had no idea how Shur had gotten her name. The woman had her business card … someone must have given Hollis as a reference.

She faced Silva. "How many calls came from that number?"

"Three."

"How long were they?"

"Two were one minute." He paused. "The third was for just under three minutes."

Hollis leaned over the table. "Maybe she was going to leave a message and decided not to. I'm telling you again, I don't know her."

Silva said nothing but pierced her with his gaze. Motioning for her to return to her seat, he said, "Can you think of a reason why she would want to meet with a probate attorney?"

Hollis was about to say something sarcastic, but bit her tongue. She said, "No, of course not." She rubbed her forehead. "Detective Silva, who was Olivia Shur?"

He hesitated a long moment. "I'm going to have to ask you to come down to the San Lucian Police Department after work today. I've got to get to my meeting, and it would be more productive to talk there."

Hollis gave him a small smile. "I see, at the police department in an interview room?"

Silva stood gathering his items, not hearing, or more likely, not answering.

"You look like you've had a rough day," George teased.

"You have no idea." Hollis flopped down in a chair in front of his desk and put her feet up on a leather foot stool.

She quickly went through the events of the Allen clan conference call. She hadn't mentioned the mystery text or Olivia Shur to George, but she was rethinking that choice now it was clear the firm could be involved. Still she would wait a bit longer, until he wasn't so preoccupied with his own issues.

He swung his chair away from her. "After the funeral and over the weekend I thought about this a lot. Zoe Allen may have kept me a secret, but she never forgot me. I could judge her but I don't want to take the energy. I had wonderful parents and a great childhood ... she gave me that." He paused. "It would have been nice to know my birth mother, but those weren't the cards I was dealt."

Hollis stayed silent. She could tell he was still formulating his thoughts.

"My family wants me to take the money. It would make our lives a lot easier. Hell, it would completely change our lives. But after what you just told me I ... I can't accept it as is. In all good conscience ...." He shook his head when Hollis started to object and held up his hand. "It's a twenty-million dollar estate. After taxes what's left will amount to thirteen, fourteen million. I'm willing to give up half."

Hollis realized little would be accomplished by arguing. George could be bull-headed when he latched on to the moral thing to do.

"All right, George, I'll communicate your wishes, but why don't you go home and sleep on it? I agree with you, seven million is quite a bit of cash, but it's still your mother's money. You're her only blood relation. As you said, you could receive fourteen million after taxes."

"I'm not going to change my mind."

"I'm not asking you to. I'm only saying that since I can't get in touch with the attorney for the Allens this evening, I'm going to have to wait until tomorrow anyway. It will give you a chance to go home and tell the family what you've decided." Hollis stood and went to the door.

George nodded. "I'll tell them."

"George," she hesitated, her hand on the door handle, "do you know of any reason why Zoe Allen's will wouldn't be valid?"

"No, why?"

"Just a side comment one of your friendly relatives made." She paused in the doorway. "I'm saving time to talk with Tony Grueber. He seems like a nice guy. I think he had a crush on your mother."

George bowed his head.

Back in her own office, Hollis snatched up the pink message slip taped to her monitor. It was from Silva, canceling their meeting for today. However, she had a choice of two time slots for tomorrow: ten a.m. or two p.m.

She wanted it over with, but she wanted to be more prepared first. She would go in the afternoon.

CHAPTER SEVEN

———— ～～ ————

THE NEXT DAY HOLLIS WAS deep into editing a brief when her phone rang. She mumbled a greeting.

"Well, good morning to you, too," Stephanie said. "I hope your day only goes up from here."

Hollis glared at the receiver. "You sound awfully cheerful. What's going on?"

"I called to see if you could go to lunch."

"I guess," she said, "but it needs to be close by. I've got a ton of work."

"It can be. I've got some news."

They agreed to meet at a café located between their two locations.

Hollis picked up the phone again and punched in a number. "Tony? This is Hollis Morgan. I need to ask you a critical question."

Grueber cleared his throat. "This is not a good time, Hollis. Can we talk later, maybe tomorrow?"

"Tony, we don't have to talk long at all. I just need to know, if there is any reason why Zoe Allen's will could be considered invalid? George Ravel can't think what the Allens might be up to."

He was silent for a long moment.

"Tony?"

"Oh, I am sorry Hollis, I got distracted. Of course we can talk later. How about I call you this evening, say four o'clock? No, make that five."

Hollis hung up the phone with a puzzled look. Tony sounded strange. Something was wrong, but she didn't know him well enough to sense what it was.

When Hollis arrived at the café, Stephanie was already there. The room was full and the servers were moving swiftly from table to table. The smell of good food and the sound of clinking dishes had a calming effect and pushed back her as-yet unidentified source of anxiety.

She and Stephanie exchanged air kisses and hugs.

"Thanks for getting me out of the office." Hollis scanned the menu. "I'd be there still, only hungry."

"Well, we haven't done this for a little while and …." Stephanie paused dramatically. "And … I have news."

Hollis looked with curiosity at her friend. "What?"

"I had a date with Detective Dreamy."

Hollis squinted and looked blank. "Who?"

"Detective Daniel Silva and I went out for drinks and dinner yesterday evening." Stephanie grinned.

"You are kidding me." Hollis regarded her with amazement. "How was the date?"

Stephanie teased her by waiting until after the server who came to the table to take their order had left. Finally she said, "Hollis, you know I don't have the greatest dating record. And it's been a while since I've been in a long-term relationship, but Daniel … Daniel could be the one."

Hollis kept a smile on her face but she was trying hard to reconcile the cool demeanor of Detective Silva with *Daniel*.

Stephanie had a track record of instant love, followed quickly by instant boredom, and ending with instant irritation and flight.

"That's wonderful. So what made the date so special?"

Stephanie went into a gushing description of a delicious dinner at a San Francisco restaurant and later drinks on the wharf. She emphasized how their conversation uncovered their compatibility and similar sense of humor.

She paused when the server brought their lunches, then said, "It was like we'd known each other forever. We are so much alike."

"Gee, I don't know if I could handle two of you," Hollis said, half-serious.

"Very funny." Stephanie bit into her sandwich. "I just hope you're going to be happy for me, Hollis."

"Of course I'm happy for you." She hesitated. "But maybe you should take things a little slow. Like you said, you've had some relationship ups and downs."

Hollis saw a frown crease her friend's brow, and she reached across the table to pat Stephanie's hand. "But you only live once, so go for it. I'm very happy for you."

"Thanks, Hollis." Stephanie beamed, but then her face turned solemn. "I know he's the investigator on your killer text. We didn't talk about it last night, and I don't think you and I should talk about it anymore either."

Hollis tilted her head in agreement. "I think that's best." What she didn't say was she would miss having Stephanie's access to inside intelligence at the police department, as well as her friend to bounce things off.

However, Stephanie couldn't stop herself from reciting the praises of her newfound beau, and for the next twenty minutes, Hollis held her tongue and made appropriate comments in the right places, praying for the moment she could escape.

LATER, FACING DETECTIVE SILVA IN his office, Hollis could

hardly put out of her mind Stephanie's burgeoning infatuation. His stern face showed little of the "awesome sense of humor" she had touted. In fact, the detective looked anything but jolly as he finished up a conversation on the phone.

"Sorry for the interruption. I was waiting to get some test results." He brushed a quick hand through his hair. "Now, do you want to tell me if you've had enough time to remember Olivia Shur?"

Hollis bristled. "I didn't need time. I repeat, I don't know the lady."

"But she knew you. She called you and you talked."

"Look, I know what you're getting at, but I never heard her name until our receptionist set her up for an appointment to see me."

"What about?"

"I don't know. Typically when someone asks directly for me, it's because they know I do probate law. That's probably why she had my contact information with her ... someone referred her. My staff thought that a probate issue was the reason for the meeting."

He just looked at her, flipping his pencil from point to eraser and back. Then he leaned across the table.

"We have a problem. You know that question you asked me yesterday?"

Hollis looked blank. "No, I ... I don't ...."

"You asked me: who was Olivia Shur? The funny thing is, we don't know. Other than your name and contact information, there's nothing else we can find out about her. We're running her prints, but the car was wiped clean."

She stiffened. "I don't understand. Her car?"

"The car is a rental. It was rented under a phony name, phony address, and phony driver's license. She paid cash and her credit card information is basically a fake. So you see our problem?"

She looked thoughtful, her mind racing with the

implications. "Why would a woman with a false identity need a probate attorney?"

Silva slapped the table. "There you go, you see my point." He peered at her. "Let's go over what we do know to be true." He pulled out a pad of notes. "Two weeks ago you received two calls from an unknown Private Caller. For purposes of getting through this conversation, let's say unknown private callers are those we can't trace. Then last week you received a call from an unknown Private Caller and held a conversation for more than two minutes—"

"That's not—" she protested.

He held his hand up. "Let's say your *phone* was in service with Private Caller for three minutes. Then last Monday, you intercepted a text from Private Caller implying a murder was being planned, and on Friday Olivia Shur is murdered."

Hollis stared at him. "Can you still triangulate where she was when she placed the calls?"

"We're working on it."

She sighed. "This whole thing is … is unbelievable." Hollis rubbed her forehead. "Can I see the paper she had with my name on it?"

He looked puzzled. "Why?"

"I don't know, maybe I could recognize the handwriting."

She could tell he was thinking about her request. Then he nodded. "It's in the evidence room. I'll be right back."

Hollis leaned back in her chair. She felt a roiling in her gut she only got when things were not going well. She hadn't realized she'd closed her eyes until she opened them and Silva was entering the room. He passed the evidence bag to her.

Inside was a three by five piece of stationary with an edge that indicated it had been torn from a pad. Its only contents were her name and the time of the appointment. She flipped it over, but there was nothing on the reverse side. Her business card was in the same bag.

Hollis inhaled sharply.

"What is it?" Silva asked, taking back the bag and raising it to see what had caught her attention.

"That's not my current business card; the phone number on that card is the one I used when I first worked at Triple D as a paralegal."

After a deep silence, Silva excused himself, ostensibly to get a bottle of water. But Hollis was under no illusions. It was more likely he had gone to get an officer to listen in behind the mirrored wall she faced.

She was wrong. He brought the officer and the water back to the room with him.

"This is Detective Lee. He's going to be working with me on the Shur murder. Feel free to contact him if I'm not available."

Hollis felt her gut ease. Something had shifted in the past few minutes and Silva's voice now implied they were all on the same side, versus her in the defendant's seat. Maybe Silva believed her. She shook hands and Lee sat next to her.

Lee pointed to the business card in the bag. "Silva tells me this is an old card. How would Olivia Shur be able to get a hold of one?"

"Good question," Hollis said. "See this logo? This was Dodson Dodson & Doyle's logo when I first started work there. About a year later, it was changed to our current logo. They wanted something more modern looking. See?" She reached into her purse and pulled out a recent business card.

Silva exchanged looks with Lee. "How long ago are we talking about?"

"Almost eight years."

Silva shook his head. "Nothin' is ever easy."

JOHN WAS HOME WHEN SHE arrived. She could hear the shower upstairs and she tiptoed into the bathroom, still carrying her purse and coat.

"I can see you, Hollis. Don't even try to sneak up on me," he called out over the torrent of water.

She laughed. "One day, Sherlock, one day."

She went back into the bedroom and flopped onto the bed like a snow angel. She lay there, her mind going over the day's events, until the water stopped and John emerged wearing nothing but a towel. She lifted her head for a peek.

He bent and gave her a long kiss. "Don't you think you'd be more comfortable with your purse off your shoulder and your clothes off?"

"I don't have the strength. I just want to lie here and vegetate."

"Tough day?" He lifted off her purse and jacket and put them on the large upholstered chair in the corner of the room. He took off her shoes and started to massage her feet.

"Ooohhh, that feels fantastic. Please don't stop."

He grinned. "Where have I heard that before?"

"Later," she chuckled. "Just don't stop working the feet." She moaned with pleasure.

He rubbed them for a few minutes. "When are you going to tell me what's going on?"

She stiffened. "I've told you everything I know for sure." She added the last words so it wouldn't be a complete lie. She hated lying to John.

"Rather than listening to you fumble and stumble over a story you won't remember ..." John began, "I talked with Roland Lee today. He plays handball with a friend of mine. He told me his new assignment was to discover the identity of an Olivia Shur. She had your contact information on her when she was murdered."

Hollis sat up. "John, I—"

He shook his head. "So, I'll go back to my first question. When are you going to tell me what's going on?"

"Now." She averted his eyes and sighed. "Other than making an appointment to see me and having my name in her car, the lady has nothing to do with me. I don't know her. There was nothing to tell." She leaned against him. "It all started with that text I told you about."

For the next few minutes Hollis recounted the events of the past two weeks and her conversations with Detective Silva. He didn't interrupt, and when she finished, she noticed he'd stopped rubbing her feet.

"Now that wasn't so bad," John said. "Don't start keeping things from me, Hollis. When you do it starts piling up as garbage that separates us."

"I'm learning, it's just hard for me to … to share sometimes." She squeezed his shoulder.

He tapped his mouth with his fist. "Why would Shur have your business card from eight years ago? Maybe you knew her under another name."

"Maybe." Hollis gave him a small smile. "Because eight years ago I was getting out of prison and starting parole."

CHAPTER EIGHT

⁓

THE LAW OFFICE WAS BUSTLING when Hollis arrived. It had been hard to leave home early with John there. Still, she flashed back to her wake-up call from him and a smile played on her lips.

"You've had two messages already this morning," Tiffany said, holding out the phone slips. "And George wants to see you as soon as you're available." She turned to assist another caller.

Hollis read the messages as she walked hurriedly back to her office. There were no surprises—Detective Silva and Tony Grueber. Both said urgent.

It's going to be a great day.

Hollis walked down the hallway and tapped on the door jamb. "George, you wanted to see me?"

"I've been served." He held out a thick packet of paper. "The suit claims Zoe Allen's will is fraudulent. There's also another injunction, this one drawn up by their law firm, to cease all processing of the will until which time the plaintiffs can prove their case."

Hollis quickly scanned the particulars and sat down.

"This must be why Anthony Grueber is trying to get in touch with me." She glanced up at his drawn face. "The suit alleges that the witnesses to the will, a Phyllis Mason and a Chris Tappen, were contrived and don't exist. That's easy to defend; Grueber was probably there when they all signed."

George pursed his lips. "I don't like it. That's too easy to push back. All we'd have to do is present the witnesses. There has to be something else."

She took a hard look at George. He did not look his best. His hair had been finger-combed and his eyes darted back and forth as if he were air-reading. There was a small ketchup-like stain on his tie and his shirt appeared limp. No, he did not look good.

"Let me go and contact Grueber to get his take. Your response isn't due for thirty days, but we can have this issue resolved and dismissed way before then. I definitely got the feeling from the Allen clan that they had no interest in the wheels of justice turning slowly."

He frowned. "Let me know what Grueber says. Then maybe we should all get on a conference call."

"I'm your attorney. Why don't you let me handle things? I'll make you a copy of the complaint." She stood. "Don't worry, I'll be talking to you."

When Hollis got back to her desk, it was Silva she called first. Life and death matters trumped paperwork.

A female officer responded. "Detective Silva is not available, but he left a message that he would contact you later today."

She punched in Grueber's number.

"Hollis, I assume you know that Ravel has been served. Virgie Allen called me in the middle of the night to tell me." He cleared his throat. "What does he want to do?"

"Do?" she asked. "He wants me to defend the suit by producing the witnesses. Who are they?"

There was silence.

"One I know," Grueber said slowly. "Tappen I'm not familiar with."

Hollis frowned. "Do you mean you don't know the name? Or, you don't know who Tappen is?"

"Both, I'm afraid," he said. "I wasn't there when the witnesses signed. I was with Zoe at the end, but she had already signed the will. She was fading fast, and all she wanted to talk about was her son, George, and why she'd given him up."

"She said nothing about the will?"

"Only that she wanted me to assure her that she had done everything correctly," he said. "Remember, she had handwritten her own will, and since everything looked in order, I saw no problem. At the time I wasn't aware of the revised trust being developed in San Diego. Frankly, as she never executed it, I don't think it needs to be considered."

"But the will ... you never questioned her about the witnesses? She never gave the slightest indication who they were?"

He cleared his throat again. "I ... I ... actually know one of them, er ... Phyllis Mason. She and Zoe have been friends for years. She and I became ... estranged ... and I don't know where she is now." He paused. "Ah, did you notice that the signature dates are different? That means—"

"That the witnesses weren't together when they signed and they won't be able to verify each other." Hollis scribbled a note. "Tony, was there someone taking care of Zoe when you came to visit? Was there anyone else in the room when she died?"

"Well, certainly none of the Allens were there. I don't think they visited her, even once. She did have a caretaker, a nurse." He rustled some papers. "I have her name somewhere. She's the one who called me to come and see Zoe. I can't locate it now, but I know I have her name somewhere. I'll have to call you back."

"All right, Tony, call me as soon as you can." Hollis clicked off.

She debated going to see George with the latest update, but she opted to wait until she heard back from Tony. She picked up Zoe's will and glanced at the names of the witnesses: Phyllis Mason and Chris Tappen. There was no phone number or address for either of them. Hollis tried to refrain from judgment. *Save me from homemade wills.* Still it could have been worse; at least there was a will.

Her phone buzzed as she was making notations in George's file.

"Detective Silva, I got your earlier message. What is so urgent? Have you found out about Olivia Shur?"

"That's why I'm calling. I want you to see her picture. Maybe you can identify her."

Hollis felt chilled. Something told her it would be a morgue photo.

"Er … sure, that makes sense. When would you want to meet?"

"Detective Lee and I are about ten minutes away."

She sighed. "All right, I'll see you then."

They arrived promptly in ten minutes. Tiffany seated them in a small conference room off the lobby. Hollis noticed that both men looked stern and spoke little other than to take one black and white photo and one in color out of a manila envelope. Lee pushed the first over to her.

"Do you recognize this person?"

Hollis exhaled the breath she had been holding and peered at the picture. She knew immediately that she didn't recognize the dark-haired young woman who stared straight ahead, but there was something about her that was familiar. She looked at it a long moment. Whatever it was that caught her attention was gone. She passed the photo back.

"Is this her driver's license photo?" she asked.

"Passport," responded Silva. "Do you know her?"

Hollis shook her head. "No, I don't. Is this the woman who was killed?"

"Take a look at this one. Do you know this woman?" Lee passed her the second picture without responding.

It was a Department of Corrections and Rehabilitation photo and Hollis stared at a face she knew only too well. The woman had aged since she last saw her. She actually looked much better. She must have had her teeth fixed to fill the obvious gap in the upper front that used to make her self-conscious. Her eyes still had a hard glint, and she was unsmiling. But then she'd never smiled much.

"Ms. Morgan, do you recognize this woman?" Silva urged.

"Yes," said Hollis. "Only I didn't know her as Olivia Shur. When I knew her years ago, she was Melanie Jones." She looked up at the men. "She was my cellmate in prison."

Lee and Silva exchanged looks.

"Were you in contact with her after your parole?" Silva asked.

"No, I don't remember any contact with her. We were only cellmates for a short while, less than three months. My parole came through and we said goodbye."

They exchanged looks again.

Lee said, "Ms. Morgan, we discovered Melanie Jones, aka Olivia Shur, through her fingerprints. Can you think of any reason why she would want to get in touch with you after all these years?"

Hollis shrugged. "No, I can't. We weren't close in … in prison. We weren't hostile either—we were just doing our time. I didn't know her that well. And why she would need the assistance of a probate attorney … well I can't even guess."

"Do you know anyone who was hostile to her? Did she ever mention she was fearful of someone or something going on the outside?" Lee asked.

"Detectives, really, it has been eight years. No, I can't remember any conversations at all with Melanie, other than simple cordial ones. Nothing stands out."

Silva folded his hands and leaned in. "Work with us, Ms. Morgan. You get a text which sounds a lot like a murder plot, and a few days later your former cellmate is killed." He raised his hands. "You're a bright woman. What would you make of it?"

Hollis sighed. "That I'm the common denominator."

As soon as the elevator doors closed behind Lee and Silva, Hollis went to the first aid cabinet and picked up the aspirin. They seemed to believe her, but it was their job to distrust. They left her with cautions to contact them immediately if anything came to mind. But it was their request that she not leave the area without notifying them that gave her a chill.

"Hollis," Tiffany said in an almost whisper. "Are you okay?"

She looked up from holding her head in her hands at Tiffany standing in the doorway. "I'm fine, just a little headache. What's up?"

"Mr. Grueber called again, and he insisted I get this message to you right away." Tiffany handed her the slip of paper.

It was the name of Zoe Allen's nurse, Leticia Lund. He'd also provided her phone number and asked Hollis to call him after she contacted Lund.

"Some of us are going to lunch at the new deli up the street," Tiffany said. "Can I bring you back a sandwich?"

Hollis gave her a weak smile and nodded, yes. She gave her some cash and told her to use the rest on her own meal. She was behind on the routine work that was rising in her in-basket. A lunch at her desk would help her make strides into the backlog. But first she had a call to make.

"This is Leticia Lund," a warm voice answered after Hollis introduced herself.

"Ms. Lund, I was referred to you by Anthony Grueber. He thought you might be able to help me contact the witnesses to Mrs. Zoe Allen's will."

"Oh …." She hesitated. "Yes, I remember Mr. Grueber. He would visit Mrs. Allen. She was a charming patient, even though she'd been ill for some time. I was definitely sad to see her go. She hadn't been a resident long, and we weren't confidantes like it can be with some patients but we were friendly. What are the names of the witnesses?"

Hollis picked up a copy of the will. "Phyllis Mason and Chris Tappen."

Lund cleared her throat. "Yes, of course. Well, I know one of them. Phyllis Mason was Mrs. Allen's friend who lives in a senior residence home in Castro Valley—I'm not sure which one. A lovely woman. A caretaker would bring her to see Mrs. Allen from time to time. They would sit in the garden and talk about the flowers."

Hollis wanted to cheer. Maybe she would have a good day after all.

"Ms. Lund, what about Chris Tappen, does that name ring a bell?"

"No, I don't know her at all."

Strike one.

Hollis asked, "You said 'her.' If you didn't know Chris Tappen, what made you think she was female?"

"Oh, you're right. I guess I said 'her' because my niece is named Chris."

"So, you're only familiar with Phyllis Mason," Hollis went on. "Do you know which facility in Castro Valley she resided in?"

"Er ... no, I never thought to ask, and Mrs. Mason's caretaker was not very talkative."

Strike two.

Hollis licked her lips. "Ms. Lund, I have just one more question. Why do you think Mrs. Allen didn't ask you to be a witness?"

"Oh, she told me," Lund said breathlessly. "She left me some of her jewelry, and she said it was best that a person who was a beneficiary to a will not be a witness to that will."

"She was right. Her will could have been contested on that point."

At least she hadn't struck out.

HOLLIS WENT TO PENNY'S OFFICE and gave her the assignment of calling every senior residence home in Castro Valley to locate Phyllis Mason. Some people would have groaned at the task, but Penny took it on gladly.

A few minutes later Hollis was on the phone with Grueber. "If Zoe was smart enough to know that Leticia Lund shouldn't be a witness," he insisted, "wouldn't it stand to reason she would have selected only qualified persons to be a witness?"

"I would think so, but I could also argue she was running short of time and she was desperate to leave a will acknowledging her son," Hollis persisted. "And perhaps she signed it herself."

He fell silent.

"Tony, we're only getting started looking for Mason and Tappen. Let's see if we can come up with them in the next few days." Hollis paused. "I'm hoping that Phyllis Mason might know Chris Tappen. You said you knew her … do you know how to contact her?"

"It's been a few years since we've spoken. I would have used Zoe to get in touch with her. Let me see if I can find her."

Before they clicked off, she and Grueber agreed to keep each other informed of any discoveries.

And then she was free to muse.

Hollis stared at her desk. As much as she tried, she couldn't keep her mind off Melanie Jones. Her brain churned on overdrive and she couldn't get the woman out of her head. The circumstances surrounding her own prison internment had formed memories that refused to stay away. At times they loomed before her like a relentless, ever-deepening hole that always threatened to swallow her up.

Melanie Jones had been sent up for embezzlement. Hollis had no sense of whether she was innocent or guilty. They never spoke of it, or of Hollis's insurance fraud charge. Jones was a pleasant enough thirty-five-year-old who had lived in Los Angeles. Neither were interested in "bonding," since they were both aloof loners. Still, Hollis racked her brain for some thread of rationale as to why Melanie would be contacting her now.

More critical was, who among her acquaintances had

Hollis's number for a text message *and* knew Melanie? That was the relationship triangle that was making Hollis hit her head against the wall. She could think of no one. Then there was the final question: why would anyone want Melanie dead?

Tiffany put a brown bag on her desk. "Here's your sandwich, and I brought you a drink."

Hollis thanked her. "Tiffany, when you spoke with Olivia Shur, did she say anything about knowing me already, or anything at all about her needing to see me?"

Tiffany scrunched up her face in thought. "She sounded really anxious to see you. When I suggested next week, she said that wouldn't work, the paperwork had to be in by the end of the week." She frowned. "I just assumed she had some kind of probate claim deadline."

"But nothing about me? She didn't say she knew me?"

"Yes, in a way. She said you were referred to her and that she had been trying to reach you and had finally spoken to you a few days before, and it was you who suggested she make an appointment. That's why I didn't insist on her phone number."

"What?" Hollis blurted out. "I don't remember talking to her at all."

Tiffany shrugged. "I've got to get back to the front desk." She moved to leave. "But that's what I told the police."

HOLLIS GOT HOME EARLY ENOUGH to start dinner. Her mind was still whirling from the conversation with Tiffany, until at last, she did remember talking to a woman who did not give her name as Olivia Shur, or Melanie Jones, and in fact had not given her name at all.

She went through her mental contacts list trying to remember the call. Penny had been out of the office and would have ordinarily screened the call, but Tiffany had put her through to Hollis.

"Hey, I'm home." John leaned over and kissed her. "You were so deep in thought you didn't hear me come in."

Hollis smiled. "It's been one of those days."

"You've had a lot of those lately. Want to share?"

"Not really. I'd like to talk about something completely different. How was your day?" She began to set the table.

"Ah, no. I don't want to talk about my day either. Working for Homeland Security is a great job, but I've learned to close the door on it when it's time to go home. By the way, I have to go out of town next week." He opened the refrigerator and took out a bottle of water. "I leave on Monday and I'll be back on Friday. I'm actually being called in as an advisor on a crisis team. It's an interesting assignment."

Hollis was getting used to his travel schedule; she suspected the last-minute assignments were due to the eruption of a high profile case. His absences didn't bother her at all; in fact, they made her feel less guilty about the time she needed to get her own job done. The aspect of his work being possibly dangerous crossed her mind, but she wouldn't let herself dwell on something she could do nothing about. John had to be John. She reached over and nuzzled him on his cheek, which was already starting to feel rough with stubble.

"I can tell. You should see your face; it's all lit up. The team sounds challenging."

John took the plates from her hand and finished setting the table.

"Yeah, I'm looking forward to it. But getting back to you, what's going on?"

"After dinner," she said. "I brought you rum raisin ice cream for dessert."

They ate companionably. They both hated small talk, so they talked about mutual friends and a potential vacation. Hollis could sense John was giving her space to confide in him on her own without the pressure of questions. She also suspected, due to the intra-agency involvement, that he knew more about the Shur/Jones investigation than she did.

The dishes were put away and the kitchen light turned off.

John took two wine glasses down from the cabinet and grabbed a bottle of wine with one hand and Hollis's arm with the other. He poured them both a glass of wine.

"Okay, let's hear it," he said.

Sitting next to him on the sofa, Hollis sighed. Opening up was not her usual mode of operation, but she was attempting to change. She recounted the findings of her day and the meeting at the San Lucian Police Department.

"I'm so frustrated. I don't think Lee and Silva believe me. Heck, when I listened to how I must have sounded, *I* wouldn't believe me."

"So you didn't recognize Melanie Jones's voice when you talked on the phone?" John prodded.

Hollis furrowed her brow, trying to remember. "It had been years, and I didn't know her that long when I did know her."

"Well you're half right, I think," he said. "I had a chance to speak with Detective Lee. They'd been watching Jones for the past several months as a part of a sting operation, but she dropped off their radar. Her re-appearance as Olivia Shur answered that question, but where had she been and why was she trying to contact you are the answers they need now."

"I've gone over and over the events of that week. There are only two calls I remember taking that could have been Melanie Jones. They were both pretty typical." Hollis took a sip of wine. "As always, I took notes. I take notes of all my calls, just in case I need background."

"Even if they don't leave a name?"

Hollis scrambled off the sofa and ran upstairs. She was back shortly with her briefcase, and in a moment she retrieved a thick legal pad. She flipped through the pages.

"You see, each call is dated with a name and contact number. When the caller doesn't leave a name I just put down the date and question marks." She read and flipped the pages. "Here's the first one."

John leaned over to read alongside her.

"This one was pretty straightforward," Hollis said, pointing to the note. "She just wanted to know the difference between a will and a trust and how much they cost. Ordinarily Penny would have handled this call, but she was out."

She flipped through a few more pages.

"Here's the other. This is the one they're probably looking for. The call corresponds to the date on the printout." Hollis scanned her notes and frowned. "She avoided giving me her name and asked about name changing in a will. She had legally changed her name, but all of her assets were in her birth name. She wanted to know, could she have a will that didn't disclose her earlier name."

Hollis stared at John.

"Did she say how long ago the name change was?"

She shook her head. "No, I told her to make an appointment and bring a list of the type of assets and an estimated value with her. I was pretty sure she was going to need a trust, but I don't do interviews over the phone."

"Did she say why she wanted to keep her birth name secret?"

Hollis looked down at her notes. "She was anxious to get this settled because she was getting married …." She paused. "Now that this has blown up, I remember thinking she was lying—that she wasn't telling me everything. Take a look at this notation." She pointed to a series of circles. "This means that I felt there was a bigger story, or a problem she didn't want to share over the phone. It's not unusual. This happens sometimes when families are arguing and they don't want it known they're seeking legal help, or the ownership isn't clear, and the client wants a bargain quote."

"So, if this is Shur, she could have had another reason for contacting you besides what she owned up to." He pointed to the phone number. "Did you check out the number? Does this match up with your 'Private Caller'?"

"You told me to leave it up to the police. I didn't want to get in the middle of things. Besides, I didn't know about Melanie

Jones, or now, Olivia Shur." She dug in her tote for another piece of paper. She glanced down and did a double-take. "Yes, this number matches one of the Private Callers on my cellphone. My gosh, John, this might be the first link."

CHAPTER NINE

HOLLIS PROMISED JOHN TO GET in touch with Silva or Lee as soon as she got into the office. As she waited for one of them to come to the phone, she was tempted to tap in the number herself, but John had warned her off. It would do no good to have her number show up on a cellphone record.

"Ms. Morgan," Silva said, "I understand you have some information for us. Detective Lee and I will meet you in the park across the street from your building and we can talk there."

"Are you kidding me?" Hollis protested. "It's cold outside. Can't we just meet in our offices here, or the library, or any other warm public place?"

He covered the phone and spoke to someone. "All right, we'll come there. We thought you might be tired of having detectives show up at your office. See you in thirty minutes."

They made it in twenty-eight minutes. Tiffany directed them to a conference room without lobby windows. They both accepted Hollis's offer of coffee and she had brought in her own cup of green tea.

She waited until they had fixed their coffee to their liking.

"Detectives, I made a discovery last night that surprised me and we … I wanted to pass it on to you as soon as possible." She went through how she'd reviewed her notes and the phone number that had no match.

Lee took notes but Silva just looked at her until she finished. He said, "Can I see your notepad?"

"I took just the page out that related to Olivia Shur … I mean, Melanie Jones." She pushed it across the table between them where it could be seen by both.

They read the page for the next few minutes.

"We'd like to keep this," Lee said and put it in a file folder without waiting for her response.

"And the phone number?" Silva asked. "It's not familiar?"

"No," she said, "but it did correspond to the dates of one of the private callers on the cellphone printout. A friend of mine advised me not to try calling it."

Lee nodded his approval.

"How do you think Melanie Jones got your business card?" Silva asked.

She frowned. "Like I said before, it's an old card. Back then she could have gotten it from anywhere, maybe from my parole officer? I really have no idea, except I know I didn't personally give it to her."

Lee made another note. Hollis knew he would be checking to see if they shared the same parole officer.

He took out a phone and handed it to her. "This is a disposable phone. We want you to place a call to see who answers."

Hollis couldn't suppress her surprised look. "You want *me* to call? Why can't you make the call?"

"Ms. Morgan," Silva said with condescension, "there's a chance the person at that number knows you, or is expecting a woman to call for Olivia Shur." He edged the phone closer. "Please, make the call."

"But this is a throw-away phone. Whoever it is won't know it's me."

"We'll take the chance. Go ahead and make the call," Silva said.

Her lips set in a grim line, Hollis picked up the phone and punched in the number.

There was a recording, female, asking to please leave a message. Silva made a motion with his hands for her to leave her name and number from the disposable phone. Hollis did as directed then clicked off.

Lee and Silva exchanged looks and stood. Silva slipped the phone into his pocket.

"Ms. Morgan, we'll take it from here," Silva said, moving out into the lobby. "We'll let you know if there is any news."

Hollis returned to her office and was greeted by Tiffany before she could sit behind her desk.

"Hollis, please return the Allens' calls." She handed over six messages. "These are all from them: two from Charles, two from Virgie, Paul, Mazie, and finally their attorney, Tim Hallinan. Each time, I told them you were unavailable until this afternoon, and that you would call them. But they kept calling. Are they nuts?"

Hollis chuckled and reached for the messages.

"Thank you, Tiffany, I'll get right on it."

She was glad to have something else to occupy her mind other than Melanie Jones. Hollis went to see Penny.

"Any luck finding Phyllis Mason?" she asked from the doorway.

Putting down the phone she had in her hand, Penny grinned sheepishly. "I never knew there were so many senior homes in Castro Valley. I'm down to the last three. What do you want to bet that Mason will be at the last one?"

Hollis laughed. "I think the odds would be in your favor."

Penny chuckled and then looked serious. "I'll be done by the end of the day. I've got those other filings you gave me to process, and one has a deadline. Will that be okay?"

"No problem."

She returned to her desk and picked up the phone to call Hallinan first. Hollis hoped the attorney would be the most rational.

"Ms. Morgan, good afternoon, thank you for returning my call." He sounded a bit distracted, as if he were working on something else while carrying on the conversation. "I told the family it was obvious you'd received their lawsuit, but as you've probably already figured out, they are a hands-on group."

"Yes, I've been contacted by various members, some twice already. What do they want?"

"They want to know your client's response."

"The law requires I respond in thirty days, and since we're in the 'law' business, that's what I intend to do." Hollis didn't try to keep the curtness out of her voice.

Hallinan let out a breath of acceptance. "I told them that, but I wanted to talk to you. There's a lot of money involved for them."

"Mr. Hallinan, these are your clients and you are bound to represent them. I must represent George Ravel; he is my client. I'm not going to manage your clients' curiosity by providing regular updates on how I'm going pursue my client's interests."

"Of course not."

"And you should get back to … hold on," she picked up the slips, "Charles, Virgie, Paul, and Mazie and tell them I'm not going to return their calls, and that from now on, until there is a formal legal substitute, I will only communicate with you."

He took a breath of resignation. "I will do that. Actually, it makes my life easier. The Coronado Legal Group has represented the Allens for many years," Hallinan gave a small laugh, "and they're all irritatingly alike."

Hollis smiled. "Irritating, but wealthy."

"Well, I won't take up any more of your day."

She shook her head with an amused smile, grateful she did not have Hallinan' job. She looked up to see Penny in her doorway.

"Hollis, I found her." Penny didn't even try to disguise the triumph in her voice. "Phyllis Mason is at the Rose Trellis Home on Leland Boulevard, next to the shopping center."

Hollis beamed. "That's great news. Let me have the number and I'll call to make an appointment to see her."

Penny shook her head. "I've already taken care of it. You can see her at three o'clock."

It was not Hollis's first visit to the Rose Trellis Senior Home and Care. As a paralegal, she'd handled two previous client matters that involved the residents there. It was a pleasant two-story structure. A tall white trellis covered in white cabbage roses trailed along a low picket fence encircling the grounds and separating it from the parking lot next door. The path to the front door was concrete with tinted pink swirls Hollis assumed were meant to resemble roses. Double glass doors swung inward from a slight pressure on the handle.

Nothing had changed since her last visit, she thought as she walked on the thick green carpet bordered with a rose and leaf pattern. The reception desk, which looked like that of a hotel concierge, had two upholstered chairs in front. Seated behind, a middle-aged woman sat talking intently on the phone, evidently to a family member who was insisting his father needed a bigger screen TV.

Hollis stood quietly, waiting for the call to end. The woman looked up at her with a silent   plea for understanding. After a couple more minutes she said her goodbye, narrowed her eyes, and put the phone in its cradle. She took a breath before looking up at Hollis.

"I apologize for the delay. Some people … well, how can I help you?"

"I'm here to see Mrs. Phyllis Mason."

Reclaiming her efficient manner, the woman patted her perfectly coiffed hair. She gave off an air of competency and control. Hollis squinted to see the name on the badge she wore but it was in such a tiny font she only felt safe in saying it had eight letters. The woman gave a quick glance at the monitor that occupied the right side of her desk.

"You must be Hollis Morgan. Mrs. Mason is expecting you. I'll take you to her room." She got up and put a "Will Be Right Back" placard on the desk.

They went through another set of double-glass doors covered from top to bottom with a sheer drapery. During her past visits she'd never gone into the actual residences. The clients met with her in a small office behind the reception desk, or she just dropped off papers. The high-traffic carpet in the lobby transitioned to a noise-absorbing thick floor covering, and soothing instrumental music imbued the residence hallway with an atmosphere of quiet waiting.

A long hallway turn later, they stopped in front of a door with the name MASON in bold black script on a white nameplate.

The woman—Hollis still hadn't deciphered her name badge—knocked on the door and entered. "Mrs. Mason, your visitor is here."

She peeked in, then opened the door wide so Hollis could follow. The room was designed as a studio apartment. The double bed was made up with a rust-colored duvet and a couple of plump toss pillows. The moderate-sized sitting area had a brown herringbone loveseat and a tan overstuffed chair with a walnut coffee table in the center. A tiny alcove served as the kitchen, with a microwave, a two burner stove top, and a small sink. The cabinets underneath probably contained a refrigerator and storage. Everything was neat and orderly.

An elderly woman sitting tall in a straight-back chair smiled at Hollis. "Hello, come in." She motioned to the nurse. "Linda, before you leave us, please open that far window so we can have some fresh air." She turned back to Hollis. "I think these rooms can smell like old people, don't you?"

Hollis stuttered, "Well ... I ... I do like fresh air."

Phyllis Mason had aged beautifully. She had thick, snow-white hair that appeared to have been recently styled. Her nose was still pert and her smile was generous over still white teeth. She wore no glasses, showing off large green eyes that seemed to see through Hollis, as if to say she understood her.

Linda with the eight-letter last name went to the corner of the room and opened the window. Hollis noticed the thin line of her lips and assumed Mrs. Mason's comment did not sit well.

"I'll leave you two to visit," she said. "Don't forget, Phyllis, we have early supper today." And she was gone.

"She's a pill, isn't she?" Phyllis chuckled. "And yet she means to do right."

Hollis perched on the loveseat across from Phyllis. "Mrs. Mason, I want to thank you for seeing me on such short notice. I'm an attorney with the law firm of Dodson Dodson & Doyle in Oakland and we are representing George Ravel, in a matter concerning … Zoe Allen." Hollis hesitated a moment because she didn't know how much Phyllis Mason knew about Zoe's acknowledgment of a son.

Phyllis Mason stiffened in her seat and her eyes shone with tears.

"Please call me Phyllis," she said. "Zoe was my dearest friend. I knew her for over fifty years. We went through everything together. My divorce, and her … her pregnancy and then marriage with Howard." She reached for a tissue in a box on a side table. "She waited to marry but by then … she was very cautious."

Phyllis opened her mouth to go on, but instead her lips formed a firm line.

"Mrs. Mason … Phyllis, call me Hollis. It's my understanding you were a witness to Zoe Allen's will. Can you tell me anything about that transaction? How did she seem to you?"

Phyllis pointed to the kitchen area. "Would you like some cookies or a glass of water?"

Noticing the cane leaning against a lounger, Hollis said, "No, thank you, can I get you something?"

Phyllis ignored her question. "Toward the end she was sickly, but her mind never faltered." Glancing past Hollis, she may have been remembering another time with her friend. "Not once did she lose her faculties. She called me one day and told me she had written a will and wanted me to witness it on my next visit." She dabbed her eyes again. "I tried to visit her every other week or so, if I could."

Hollis leaned in. "Did she tell you anything about the contents of her will?"

Phyllis nodded and blew her nose. "I knew about George almost from the beginning. I used to work for the county and I helped her with the paperwork. She didn't like talking about the birth and she asked me not to bring up the adoption unless she did first. However, about a year ago when Howard started getting ill, she mentioned him a little more."

"Did you read the will?"

"No, she said I just had to sign the last page, and that's all I did," Phyllis said. "It was none of my business. Zoe knew what she was doing. However, she was really agitated that day. I think she knew the end was almost here." She dabbed at her eyes and took a deep breath.

"Mrs. Mason—I'm sorry, I mean Phyllis—the Allens have filed a lawsuit against George Ravel alleging that the witnesses to Zoe Allen's will are fraudulent, and ... and don't exist."

"Why that's just silly. Of course I exist and I will swear that Zoe was of clear mind."

Hollis smiled. "That's good. Hopefully it won't come to that. What I would like to do is prepare an affidavit of your statement for you to attest and you shouldn't be inconvenienced any further."

Phyllis shifted and straightened in her chair. "I'd be happy to. Just show me where to sign."

"I'll prepare your statement and I can bring it back with me." Hollis wrote a note on her pad. "Phyllis, do you know a Chris Tappen? Or, do you remember if Zoe Allen ever mentioned the name?"

"Tappen, Chris Tappen ...." Phyllis tapped a finger against her chin and cocked her head. "No, I don't believe so. Who is Chris Tappen supposed to be?"

"He, or she, is Zoe Allen's other witness," Hollis said. "Do you remember if there was a signature already present when you signed her will?"

Phyllis frowned, trying to remember. "I ... I don't think so." She shook her head. "No ... no, there wasn't, because I remember thinking that I needed to write my name small so the next person would have space for their name."

"And you don't remember Zoe ever mentioning the name 'Chris'?"

She spoke with certainty. "No, I don't know a Chris, and I don't know if Zoe did either." Phyllis paused and looked into Hollis's eyes. "Does this jeopardize her son securing his inheritance? Oh, don't look at me like that. I didn't read her will but I know something of the Allens, and Zoe told me that Howard would never accept him."

Hollis kept her expression blank. "I'm relieved that you knew of her intent to leave her estate to George Ravel." She paused. "However, in order for a will to be valid it must have two signatures. Fortunately we have some time to figure it out. If you do remember anything, here's my card."

She handed her a card from her purse and stood. "Is there anything I can get you before I leave?"

"No, Hollis, I'm fine." Phyllis smiled. "Hollis is an unusual name, but it fits you."

"Hollis is my middle name. It was my grandmother's family name. My first name is actually Rebecca. I changed it when ... when I was able to."

Hollis didn't think it necessary to go into how a name change was not uncommon for ex-felons wanting to wipe the slate clean as they started their new lives.

"I understand," Phyllis said, as if she really did.

CHAPTER TEN

———⚹———

HOLLIS DEBATED TELLING GEORGE ABOUT the missing Chris Tappen, but she didn't want to worry him unnecessarily before she had a chance to seek Tappen out. That morning she asked Penny to meet with her and bring her ideas along with a pad of paper.

"We need to locate a Chris Tappen. Could be Christopher or Christine," Hollis said as she paced around her office. "Do a Google search, and if nothing shows, see if you can get access to Zoe Allen's belongings. I wouldn't think the family would be focused enough to clear out her things, yet. Maybe she had a phone book or journal or something that could give us a clue. Let me know if you get access and I'll make time to go."

Penny wrote quickly. "Do you think the nurse, Leticia Lund, might remember something?"

"She seemed certain she didn't know anything, but you could try again. Maybe ask her about Zoe's visitors in her last months."

"She also might have keys to the house," Penny said. "Should I just go ahead on my own?"

Hollis hesitated. Lately, visiting empty houses had not been lucky for her and had in fact exposed her to life-altering danger. She didn't want Penny to take unnecessary risks.

"Let me check with Hallinan." She scribbled a note. "Oh, and of course, time is of the essence. We need to locate Tappen as soon as possible."

"Of course." Penny smiled ruefully.

Somewhat to her surprise, Hallinan didn't have a problem with Hollis having access to Zoe Allen's residence.

"Don't bother Nurse Lund. We have an affiliate in the Bay Area. I'll have them deliver the key this afternoon." He paused. "Is there anything else?"

"No."

"You haven't had any more calls from the Allens, have you?"

Hollis flipped through the messages Tiffany left on her desk. "No, all is quiet."

They finished their conversation with the standard pleasantries. Hollis went back to her messages, found one from Stephanie, and called her.

"What's so urgent?" Hollis asked.

Stephanie rushed her reply. "Can you go out for drinks after work?"

"No, I can't. John and I are invited over to friends' for dinner. What about tomorrow? Are you going to the flea market?"

San Lucian's Saturday flea market was a regional favorite. Rain or shine, it convened under a huge canopy in an abandoned industrial parking lot.

"Okay, let's meet for coffee at Cleo's first. I've got something to tell you."

"Why do you do that?" Hollis protested. "You know I'll go crazy trying to guess. Does this have to do with Detective Silva?"

"I don't call him Detective Silva," Stephanie responded. "I call him Dan. And yes, in a way it does."

"In a way?"

Stephanie chuckled. "Okay, in a big way. But this time, Hollis, you're not going to squeeze it out of me. I'll see you tomorrow at eight thirty."

Hollis smiled. She hadn't seen Stephanie this happy in a long time. Then she sighed. She just hoped it lasted.

HOLLIS AND JOHN WERE QUIET on the drive to Mark and Rena's for dinner. She guessed he was preoccupied with a mental checklist for his trip on Monday. She recognized the signs in herself. She put her hand lightly on his arm.

"A quarter for your thoughts," she said.

He gave a small laugh without taking his eyes off the road. "To be honest, I was thinking about you and this Melanie Jones. Something doesn't feel right."

Hollis shrugged. "She's dead. We'll never know what she wanted."

"Yeah, but her killer knew you."

Hollis thought to protest that it could be just a coincidence, but remained silent. John parked the car in the driveway.

He picked up her hand, and they faced each other.

"I'll take that quarter you gave me to ask for your thoughts," he said.

"I'll give them to you for free," Hollis said. "I don't know why Melanie Jones would look me up at all, let alone after such a long period of time. But I don't see how I will ever find out, so this time I will leave things up to the police."

John grasped his chest. "Get a recorder. I can't believe I actually heard you say that."

"Very funny." Hollis opened her door.

"We were wondering how long you two were going to sit in the car." Rena laughed, giving John and Hollis hugs. This evening Rena had pulled her long brown curly hair into a bushy ponytail that trailed down her back. Her café au lait complexion emphasized her hazel eyes. She was stunning as usual in black slacks with a simple off-the-shoulder white silk blouse, and large silver hoops.

Hollis sighed as she smoothed her own turtleneck over her jeans and fingered her gold button earrings.

Mark bent down to give Hollis a hug then reached his hand out to shake John's. He led them into the dining room, where the table was set elegantly for dinner with a brocade runner over a dark-green table cloth, white china trimmed in gold dinner plates, topped with gold salad dishes, and in the center a wrought-iron candelabra centerpiece. As always, Rena's taste was impeccable. Hollis followed Rena into the kitchen.

"Is everything okay?" Rena asked. "You guys weren't arguing out there, were you?"

Hollis shook her head. "Not at all. In fact he was paying me a backhanded compliment."

Rena peeked out the doorway. The men had moved into the living room and were positioned in front of the television. Returning, she poured two glasses of red wine, handing one to Hollis.

"So, what's going on?" Rena took a sip from her glass.

"An ex-con I knew when I was inside tried to get in touch with me. I hadn't talked with her since I was paroled. Anyway, a few days before they found her dead body, I received a blind text indicating a murder was in the works." Hollis took a taste of the wine.

Rena practically knocked her glass over. "You are kidding me. What's her name?"

"Melanie Jones. You don't know her, do you?" Hollis peered at Rena. "She changed her name to Olivia Shur."

"No, I don't ... wait, maybe," Rena murmured. She took a swallow of wine and immediately started choking.

Hollis patted her back. "What is it?"

She frowned. "Hollis, do you remember when I first came to the Fallen Angels Book Club? Well, Jeffrey sent two of us. The other was Olivia Shur, who you knew as Melanie Jones, but she never showed up."

Hollis stiffened. "Did you meet her?"

"Only that once, in Jeffrey's office. He was signing my papers and she was his next appointment." Rena twisted the stem of her glass. "He wanted me to meet her. You remember Jeffrey … he wanted all his clients to return to society without carrying the baggage of their past."

Hollis winced. Jeffrey Wallace was the parole officer who founded the Fallen Angels Book Club. It was his support and guidance that put the members back on track to lead lives that made a real contribution. His recommendation gave her a second chance and she owed him everything. She still hadn't gotten over his death.

"Did she—"

"What are you guys doing in here? We're hungry." Mark looked into one of the pots on the stove. "Is this what I can expect from married life? To be relegated to second place."

Rena slapped his hand. "Dinner will be ready in five minutes. You and John go ahead and sit at the table."

He took a hasty look inside another pot and left. As Hollis put the trivets out on the table to receive the hot dishes, she said over her shoulder, "We'll talk after dinner."

It pleased Hollis that John fit in with her friends as if he had always been there. He was both thoughtful and witty. Onlookers might wonder if anyone in the group was listening, since everyone was talking at the same time, but it worked for them. The focus of dinner conversation was the upcoming wedding and how the planning was gradually becoming overwhelming for Rena.

"I keep offering to help," Hollis said. "You don't have to do everything by yourself." She swallowed her last crumb of cheese cake.

"This from a woman who put the 'c' in control," Mark laughed.

Rena smiled. "Thanks, Hollis, but I've got lists for everything and I keep them with me in a tote that I don't let out of my sight."

John rose from the table and picked up his plate. "Well, can I at least help with the dishes?"

Rena waved him away. "Go. Hollis and I know how to put things back together in half the time it would take you."

Mark held up his hand. "John, they want to talk. Let 'em have at it. We will sacrifice ourselves by checking out my new sound system."

John chuckled. "They are so lucky to have us."

Rena and Hollis exchanged looks of exasperation and quickly went about clearing the dishes.

"Did she stand out in your mind in any way?" Hollis asked, returning to their earlier conversation as they hand-washed and dried the china.

"I don't remember her that well." Rena opened the dishwasher and put in the less fragile items. "But I do remember thinking she didn't seem that interested in books."

"WHEN ARE YOU GOING TO tell Silva about your conversation with Rena?" John was going back and forth from the closet, filling his suitcase.

Hollis had spent the last few minutes relaying Rena's revelations about her connection to Olivia Shur.

Hollis gave him a mock salute. "Sir, first thing in the morning, sir."

She sat cross-legged on the bed folding his socks and watching him get ready to leave on assignment. Her cellphone buzzed, but after checking the caller ID, she put it on the floor.

"It's Stephanie. I'll call her later."

"You had breakfast together yesterday," he teased. "More news?"

"I doubt it," she murmured.

The meeting with Stephanie the day before had left her curious and somewhat uneasy. She had to cut short their breakfast because "Daniel" needed her to go into the department and do a little lab work.

"But what did you want to tell me that was so urgent?" Hollis insisted.

Stephanie shook her head. "It wasn't exactly urgent; besides, I'd rather talk about it when we can really spend the time, and I can't right now."

Hollis was taken aback. "Stephanie, he wants you to go into work on your own time?"

Stephanie had shrugged it off, saying it was no big deal and for Hollis not to tell anyone, particularly John.

Now, with John readying to leave, Hollis had no qualms about discovering what was going on with her friend.

She placed her hand against his cheek. "I'll miss you."

He gave her a sidelong glance. "What's the matter?"

"Nothing's the matter," she said indignantly. "But you're going to be late if you don't hurry."

John searched her eyes for the truth and kissed her. He returned to his packing until he was ready to close the bag.

Not long after, she was standing in the doorway, watching him drive away. He insisted she never accompany him to the airport. He tried to make light of it, but she knew there was a deeper reason. He never wanted them to say goodbye.

After he had turned the corner, she ran upstairs and picked up her cellphone. She'd lied to John. If he knew that she was still getting mysterious calls, he would be worried about leaving her alone. She'd felt a twinge about lying, but she didn't want to send him off unable to concentrate on his job.

It hadn't been Stephanie who called; it was a voicemail from a Private Caller.

CHAPTER ELEVEN

HOLLIS PULLED A NOTE OFF the top of her monitor. The key to the Allen house had been delivered over the weekend and Penny had left the office to locate information about the Tappen witness.

Hollis scanned the files in her in-basket waiting for her action. Good, nothing too pressing right now. She needed to stay on top of all her work.

That morning she ignored her shaking hands as she went through her cases. Even a cup of tea only provided a minor calm. Silva said he would meet her in her office before noon. In anticipation of his visit, she debated running out to get a third phone, while she had time. But she wanted to listen to the voicemail once more. It was a robotic voice: "Sorry for involving you, but you're involved, now. The police can't help you. Just do what the letter says."

What letter?

A shiver went up her arms. She put her phone in a large manila envelope.

"Hollis, Detective Silva is in the small conference room," Tiffany's voice announced over the intercom.

*

SHE WATCHED SILVA'S EXPRESSION AS he listened to the voicemail for the second time. She wondered what he was trying to discern. He pushed the play button again. He'd come without Detective Lee. His brow was furrowed and his lips were set in a thin line.

Hollis sighed. She just wanted him to be done with it.

"What letter?" he asked, slipping the phone into the envelope.

"I don't know."

Silva glanced at her as if he expected her answer. He took out his pad.

"We haven't gotten any leads from that call you left on your phone." He rubbed his chin. "Whoever it is knows, at least now, how to get in touch with you. If they've sent you a letter, it's more likely it will come here. While there's a chance they know where you live, I think it's more likely they will make contact through your firm."

Hollis pressed her lips together in a slight grimace.

"Of course, I'll let you know as soon as I receive the letter," she said. "Now, Detective, can you let me know one thing? Melanie Jones had to have started calling herself Olivia Shur about four years ago; that's how she was introduced to one of my book club members, Rena Gabriel. So, what was she involved in? What is this about?"

He put his pen down and avoided her eyes. Then his shoulders slumped and he took a deep breath.

"Money laundering. We don't know the source—if it's floated using drugs or foreign currency. But Shur was well funded. Olivia Shur wasn't her only name. She'd taken on two others; at least we found the papers for two more."

He peered at her as if trying to read her reaction.

Hollis's brow wrinkled. "I keep trying to come up with a connection to me. Why did I get a text at all? Now, this voicemail has to be someone who has me on their call list." She licked her lips. "I thought her crime must have something to do with probate law, but money laundering …. I'm stumped."

"Have you ever assisted on a case with questionable clients? Ones where you just turned a blind eye to how they built up their estate?"

Now Hollis knew why he had been so willing to confide in her about Melanie's—or Olivia's—crime. He needed her to think through her client list. She bristled.

"First, I don't turn a blind eye when I'm working with a client, nor have I ever. Second, I've gone through my client list, and as I've already told you, none of them had the numbers listed on your printout."

"You said your friend recognized Olivia Shur's name. So, she never knew her as Melanie Jones?"

Hollis nodded. "She only met Olivia that once, and she never had contact with her as Jones."

He flipped back pages in his notes. "Rena Gabriel did time for felony bad check writing. Wallace, your parole officer, introduced her to Shur thinking they would both be welcome in the book club." He flipped to the top sheet of his pad. "Shur never shows up. Did your friend let Wallace know?"

"I don't know, I think she would have told me. I …."

She stopped. A crazy thought entered her mind.

"What did you just think of, Ms. Morgan?"

Hollis tried not to let the excitement show on her face. She took out her own pad of paper and scribbled a notation.

"Ms. Morgan?"

She looked up at him. "I'm sorry. I have a meeting with a client in a few minutes and I just remembered where I put some information I need."

Half lies are more believable.

She could tell Silva was trying to read her note upside down, which was why she had written it in code.

"We'll be contacting Rena Gabriel in case she remembers anything else." He paused as if waiting for her to protest. When she didn't, he continued, "I would appreciate it if you didn't let her know in advance of our contact."

Hollis smiled. "Of course."

She watched Silva get into the elevator. She waited ten minutes then told Tiffany she had to run an errand and would be back before her next appointment.

Hollis half ran to the hotel on the next block. Her ability to spot a lie was matched by her ability to tell one. Still, lately she'd discovered that lying could be more trouble than it was worth and of limited use— if it just meant putting off the truth for a bit. It remained her fallback when time was of the essence, as it was now.

Ignoring the curious glance from the hotel concierge, she dashed to the bank of phones along an empty corridor and called Rena.

HOLLIS SAT AT HER DESK, intent on the names scrolling down her computer monitor. If memory served, the records should identify a client she worked with, or rather didn't work with, when she was a paralegal. Her old boss, Avery Mitchell, usually let her handle the client's paperwork while he did the face to face. Only for this client, he handled the entire matter. Unfortunately, Avery was doing time in Chino and wasn't available to answer her questions.

Going through the old Triple D records, she wanted to make sure that Olivia Shur hadn't been a client of Avery Mitchell's. But after almost an hour of going through billing records, she found no reference to Olivia Shur or Melanie Jones. She was tempted to go downstairs and rummage through the mail room to see if the letter had been delivered, but Vince was diligent and would deliver the mail as soon as he had it sorted, usually before noon.

At eleven o'clock, she rose from her desk and went down the hall to the attorney mailboxes. Vince had been there and the secretary was deftly putting mail in the slots.

"Hey, Hollis, looking for your mail? I already put it in your box."

"Thanks, there's something important I'm waiting for."

She laughed, "You and every other attorney in the office."

Hollis had to chuckle at the truth of her words. Attorneys were notorious worrywarts and always waiting for the mail to be delivered. She grabbed the small stack of envelopes and returned to her office.

It was there, postmarked the week before Olivia Shur's murder. It was an ordinary business size envelope, her name and address typed. Using a letter opener, she reached for a tissue to pull out the single page of typed white paper.

> Dear Hollis,
>
> I hope you'll remember me. Those months at Chowchilla almost seem like they never happened, only they did.
>
> I'm going to make an appointment to see you, but I'm writing, first, because I didn't want to scare you by showing up at your job. I'm in a bit of a bind and you're the only law person I know who might be able to help me. Sorry, I had to tell some people you were my contact. You can call this number: 925.555.3453 and say you want to speak to Jule. You'll find out about the list and get some background for our meeting. I know all of this sounds weird but I don't want to put anything in writing. I'll answer all your questions when I see you. Whatever you do, don't tell the police.
>
> Regards,
> Melanie Jones (I changed my name to Olivia Shur)

What list?

She turned the paper over but there was nothing on the other side. She picked up her phone and punched in Silva's number. He didn't answer so she left him a message. She looked at the number and took a deep breath and punched it in.

"Capital Consulting."

Hollis swallowed. "Is ... is Julie there?"

"Hold on," a man responded.

Hollis's heart was beating out of her chest. She deliberately hadn't waited to ask Silva for approval to call, since there was a good chance he'd say no. Finally, the same voice returned to the line.

"This is Jule Berman."

Her first thought was that Olivia had not misspelled his name and after a short hesitation, she spoke. "Olivia Shur asked me to call you."

This time the silence originated with him, but she could hear the typical sounds of a busy office in the background.

"Is this Hollis Morgan?"

It was her turn to pause; then she answered with a tentative, "Yes."

"I can't talk now. Can you meet me for a late lunch, say one thirty, at the Red Door in Chinatown?"

"All right, I hope you'll be able to tell me what all of this is about. How will I ... I don't know what you look like."

"Doesn't matter. I know what you look like."

FOR THE NEXT HOUR, HOLLIS left messages for Silva and Lee to contact her as soon as they could. She even tried to reach Stephanie to ask her to come along, but Stephanie was attending a training course. Besides, their last meeting on Saturday was a bit strained after Stephanie left to conduct her special assignment from Silva. Hollis didn't want to think Stephanie's relationship with Silva might be coming between them. She would go it alone. If nothing else, this should be the loose end that would allow Silva to do his job. She was more curious than fearful about meeting Berman.

The Red Door was a fifteen minute walk from her building. She'd eaten there often, usually earlier in the day when fellow workers crowded the large room of circular tables and metal chairs squeezed into every possible space. If nothing else, she'd have a good lunch and maybe leftovers for dinner.

The smell of homemade Chinese food greeted and in some way centered her as she pushed open the glass door covered with a bright red curtain. The restaurant was practically empty. Her eyes rested on the table where a man who looked to be in his thirties—wearing a shirt and tie but no jacket—waved her over.

Berman smiled and held out his hand. "Thanks for meeting me on such short notice. I know you must have a lot of questions." He held up a menu. "I'm starving. Did you want some lunch?"

His appearance was ordinary, other than his dark brown eyes—almost black. They peered at her as though studying and evaluating her worthiness.

"Yes, I'm hungry too." Hollis didn't need the menu; she would order her favorite wonton soup.

The server came over to their table with water glasses and tea, quickly took their order and left.

"Okay, let's get to it," Berman said. "Olivia has something—rather *had* something—that didn't belong to her. It's dangerous information. She said she was going to give … give it to you. "

Hollis stared at him. The words with their implied threat were coming from a cheerful face with a genial smile. She inadvertently tilted her head as if to confirm that she was hearing what she thought she was hearing. From the outside, no one would guess his covert hostility.

"I don't understand," was all she could get out.

"What part?" Berman smiled, and this time she noted the menace in his eyes.

She could feel the anger building, creating a tightness in her chest. She hated being threatened as much as she hated being afraid. Two could play at this game.

"I must tell you that you've picked the wrong lady to mess with." She smiled and nodded at the server who placed their steaming dishes of food on the table. She kept the smile even as her eyes narrowed. "I don't know what you're talking about. Olivia Shur never met with me, and I don't think I'd recognize her if she walked in here now. She left nothing with me, for you or anybody else."

Berman's smile vanished.

"If that's true, how did you know to call me?"

She took out her wallet and put down bills for her lunch. "Look, I don't know you and I don't know what you want. All I do know is that you have the wrong person."

She rose to leave but he put a light hand on her sleeve.

"Wait, you could be in danger," he said in a low voice. "We know Olivia contacted you. Give me that. Unfortunately other people know about you too and may have jumped to the wrong conclusion. Olivia is dead, but you're not. "

Hollis thought she could hear the *yet* on the end of his sentence. He took a deep breath, but she didn't feel inclined to speak without hearing more.

"I think I may have started us off on the wrong foot." He ran his hand over his close-cropped hair. "Olivia trusted you, and I guess I will have to as well."

She didn't think twice about concealing that she didn't have a clue what he was talking about.

He swallowed his whole cup of tea and poured another. The server came with another pot and he waved him away.

"The story isn't that long." Berman hesitated. "Olivia is … *was* a good friend. She tried to go straight after prison, but … but she didn't have it in her. Her parole officer—she said he was yours too—well, he went over and above board to get her into jobs that could use her talents. Did you know she was an artist?"

"I really didn't know her well … or long."

"Yeah, well, she just wasn't interested in an eight to five. I think something died inside of her when she was convicted."

Hollis grimaced. She could relate. It was all she could do to not let resentment and bitterness take over her life and keep her eye on attaining a new life after prison. However, she wasn't swayed by Berman's caring observations.

He was looking down at his cup as if reading tea leaves. "She met a guy who romanced her; he could see she was bright, beautiful, and charming. He used her to gain access to some powerful men, and she did what he asked because she loved him. Eventually, he realized he really was in love with her and if they were to have a life together, he would have to disentangle them both from the path they were on." He looked Hollis in the eyes. "And that would be no easy task."

Berman had Hollis's attention.

"What happened?" she asked.

"They decided to trade information for their freedom. The … the men were into criminal activity that crossed state lines. Olivia knew the key players. She knew how they linked together. She'd kept a list of names and their contact information. We were going to work with a go-between because what we had would hurt a lot of people and we didn't want our faces known." He turned his head to look over his shoulder.

Chills ran down Hollis's arms.. She didn't know if Berman realized he had said, *we.*

"She said she knew someone who she'd met when she was inside but now worked for a law firm, who was honest and had shown her kindness. She meant you." He licked his lips. "So, the idea was she would contact you, get you to take the list to the police and work a deal so we would get off."

Hollis managed a deadpan expression. The pieces were coming together.

She frowned. "But weren't you … but wasn't she taking a big risk? I mean she … we hadn't spoken in years. Where's the list now?"

"We were desperate. Like I said, she didn't see another way." He shrugged. "I don't know where the list is. Olivia told me the day she … she died that she made three copies. One for you, one she hid in a safe place, and one she mailed to herself."

Hollis frowned again. Something wasn't making sense.

"And what is your part in all this? Did you ever see the list?"

"No, she said that to protect me, it was best I never knew the names." He gave her a small smile. "Yeah, I thought you'd figured out I was the guy."

"So now the bad guys are after the list?"

He shrugged. "Olivia had the list with her when she was coming to see you. Whoever killed her has it now." He looked her in the eyes. "I'm not saying this to scare you, but they know Olivia contacted you and they want all the copies."

"The police said she had nothing with her except some odds and ends."

And my business card.

"Right," he said pointedly.

Her eyes grew wide. "Are you … are you saying that the police are involved?"

"I'm saying someone with the San Lucian Police Department could have that list and knows its worth."

It was almost three o'clock when Hollis returned to Triple D. Her head was whirling with the implications of her lunch with Jule Berman. It must have been clear from the look of shock on her face that he'd struck a chord. But then he also realized Hollis had been telling the truth; she had no knowledge of Shur's trade list. Berman said he'd get back in touch with her. His story shook her, and something nagged at her not to completely trust him, but she couldn't deny that it made sense.

The truth she didn't want to face—and the one that wouldn't go away—was that Detective Silva had said they had bagged the evidence found in Olivia's car, so he must have seen the list, unless Berman was right and the killer had it. She thought back to Olivia's warning in her letter. She picked up the phone.

Silva had left three voicemails returning her frantic call that morning. She needed to buy more time to think.

Silva answered before the second ring.

"Ms. Morgan, I got your messages. What's going on?"

"Detective Silva, I … I heard from a friend of Olivia Shur's. He wanted to meet with me. I … I … put him off until you and I could talk. I knew you'd want to be in on it."

"You're right about that. What's his name?"

"I … I don't know. He wouldn't give it to me. He called in on the main line, so I don't have his number either."

The lies slipped off her lips. She knew as well as he did that it would be highly unlikely that he could get a warrant to search the law firm's confidential phone records.

Silva was silent for a moment.

"When you called I was interviewing Rena Gabriel. She pretty much recounted what you told us." He shuffled a paper. "Did you know that Shur tried to contact her, too? They initially met some time past, then as recently as two weeks ago she reached out to Gabriel."

Hollis froze. "No, I didn't know."

"The call you got must have really shaken you up," he said. "You're usually pretty cool under pressure. When he calls again, reach me immediately. I'll let the desk know that they are to find me wherever I am."

"I will."

She knew she didn't sound convincing but too much was happening too fast. She needed to talk to Rena.

HER MESSAGE LIGHT WAS BLINKING. As she suspected, there were two calls from Rena. But when she called back, the message machine picked up.

"Rena, this is Hollis. It appears we're playing phone tag. I thought I'd drop by your apartment after work. If it's not convenient, just send me on my way, but I really need to speak with you."

Hollis went to George's office, but he hadn't returned from court. She needed to talk to someone, to hear how her thoughts sounded to someone else. She missed John. Stephanie would usually be her backup confidante, but she had already put up a barrier because of her involvement with Silva.

She sighed. She'd had to think things through on her own before; she would do it again. Exasperated, she sat down heavily at her desk. Her message light was blinking.

It was Rena, saying she wouldn't be at home until late and if Hollis wanted to speak with her, it would have to be at her job.

"I'M SORRY WE HAD TO meet here, but I have a buyer's meeting coming up, and I wanted to give you the most time possible." Rena pointed Hollis to what appeared to be a storage room for racks and racks of dresses. A small table stood in the middle, surrounded by three chairs.

Hollis looked at shelving along the walls holding pair after pair of shoes. "I've never seen where you work; this is amazing. No wonder you always look so great."

Rena gave a small laugh. "You've seen that cabinet I have for a closet at home—that's the real me."

Somehow Hollis didn't think so; the truth was probably somewhere in the middle.

"Rena, I don't do small talk and I don't want to waste your time. But I need you to trust me enough that you can be upfront with me about Olivia Shur. You've talked with her since you met her in Jeffrey's office, haven't you?"

Rena frowned and started picking at her cuticles. "I don't know what you're talking about. Olivia Shur and I barely knew each other."

"And yet you didn't answer my question," Hollis said. "This is serious. The police think I know more than I do, and then there's this guy who also thinks Olivia wanted me to help her turn herself in."

Rena pulled back. "Why you? You're not in criminal law."

"I thought about that. I don't think she knew what area of law I practiced, or she didn't care. She just knew I worked for a law firm." Hollis put her chin in her hand. "She trusted me because she knew I would understand her."

"Well, I can't add to what you already know."

Hollis looked away. The wall Rena had thrown up between them surprised and disappointed her, and she didn't understand it. Rena's whole demeanor had cooled.

"Well, I won't keep you from your … your clothes." Hollis rose and headed for the door.

Rena seemed truly surprised. She clearly didn't expect Hollis to give up so easily. As she walked out the door, Rena called out to her.

"I'm … I'm sorry, but I've told you all I can." Her voice shook.

"No, you've told me what you wanted to tell me," Hollis called back over her shoulder. She turned to face a pale Rena holding her arms on the front steps. "Remember, the basic rule: don't try to con a con."

Driving home, Hollis realized how angry she was with Rena. She felt betrayed, more than a little annoyed, and at a loss for the first time. Ordinarily she would have gone after Rena for the truth, but she knew her friend well enough to realize that if she was lying, the reason was not straightforward. Rena was clearly conflicted.

She kicked off her shoes as she flopped down on her bed, used the remote to turn on soft jazz, and closed her eyes. Her phone vibrated.

"Hey, how's my lady?" John's voice sounded warm and close.

She debated telling him about her fears regarding Silva and her conversation with Rena; instead she opted to skirt around the situation. He would only pester her for answers she didn't have. "Things are evolving, but nothing new."

"Would Silva say the same thing?"

Hollis gave a short, self-conscious laugh. Fortunately, John couldn't talk long, and after hearing about his travel adventures and the first day on the team, she could tell he was enjoying himself. He signed off, promising to call her the next night.

She snapped up her phone when it rang.

"Hollis, it's me." Rena said. "I'm on my way over. I need to talk to you about this afternoon."

"Wha—"

Rena had clicked off.

Barefoot, Hollis got up, put a pot of water on the stove and searched the pantry for boxes of tea. She glanced at the clock on the wall: eight thirty. At the sound of the doorbell, she peeked through the view port then opened the door.

"Rena, what do you want?" Hollis asked, smoothing out her clothes and not bothering to hide her irritation.

"You're still in your work clothes? I'm sorry, but we need to talk." She edged into the entry.

Hollis stepped aside and let her in. She followed Rena into the kitchen, where she went to the cabinet and got a cup.

"No tea for me. I need a glass of wine."

Hollis raised her eyebrows, but took down two stemmed glasses and handed one to Rena, who proceeded to fill her glass halfway from an open bottle of Malbec on the counter. "I can't stay long. I asked my mother to watch Christopher, but it's bingo night at her senior center."

Hollis sat and watched her. "Okay, what is it that you want to say?"

"I know you think I … I misled you, but don't be so quick to judge."

"What should I be? You didn't 'mislead' me; you lied to me. You knew Olivia Shur. You'd seen her recently."

"I didn't *know* her. I told you the truth. Jeffrey wanted us to try out the book club together, which I thought was kind of strange, since she had no interest in books. But I think he wanted her to be around ex-cons who were on their way back." Rena paused at the sight of Hollis raising her eyes to the ceiling. "Do you want to hear my side, or would you prefer to remain judgmental?"

Hollis shrugged and looked at her.

Rena took a sip of wine and said, "I hadn't seen her since Jeffrey's office, and then out of nowhere, about two weeks ago, she called. She wanted to meet for a drink 'for old times' sake,' which I thought was curious since she and I never had any 'times' together, old or new. But when I was about to decline, she pleaded for my help." Rena sighed. "So I picked a place not far from work. I just planned to hear her out and make a quick getaway after a half-hour."

"Why didn't you tell me?"

"She made me swear not to mention her call to anyone." Rena twisted a long curl around her fingers. "Oh, I don't know why I didn't tell you. It was like the last eight years had been erased and I was back inside prison. Every fear I ever had rose up to meet me. You are my dear friend, but Olivia sounded like a desperate person trying to sound normal." Rena licked her lips and closed her eyes. "I knew that feeling. I'd been there."

Hollis leaned back in her seat. A few more of the puzzle pieces were falling into place. She waited for Rena to continue.

"I know what you're thinking, but I'm almost finished." She straightened. "She was already sitting in the bar when I arrived and I vaguely recognized her. It had been a few years. Anyway, she goes on about how she's met this guy, but before she can plan for the future she's got to deal with her past."

"Why was she telling you this?"

"That was my question." Rena chewed her bottom lip. "She would only say that she didn't get along well with women, but that she remembered meeting me through Jeffrey, and she trusted him completely." She held up her hand when Hollis pretended to gag. "She remembered what Jeffrey said about me, and she felt she could trust me. She didn't have anyone else she could depend on."

Hollis motioned for her to continue.

"Anyway, by this time I was fidgeting, trying to make her get to the point. You must be rubbing off on me. For some reason I didn't trust her. I told her I had to leave. Well, she went ballistic and told me that she needed help and if I wasn't going to help then I had to swear not to mention to anyone that we had ever met. No matter what happened to her." Rena swallowed.

Hollis knew Rena was telling the truth—gullibility was one of her major faults. "She didn't say anything more?"

"She said she'd gotten involved in some bad business and the only way out was to trade her way out."

Hollis said, "And what did she have to trade?"

"I don't know." Rena finished the wine. "That was it. She kept looking out the window the whole time, then all of a sudden she stood up, knocked over my tote, and gave me this big squeeze hug as if we were long lost buddies. After we shoved everything back in my bag, she sat down again and spent the next five minutes saying how much better she felt. Then she reminded me about my oath and dashed out."

"What was the secret?"

"That's what I asked her. She just said that she didn't want anyone to know what she was planning, and she thanked me for just letting her get it off her chest. But now I don't think that was it at all."

Hollis's ran her fingers through her hair. "No, I don't think so either. What plans? Did she ever give you any specifics?"

"No, and she never contacted me again." Rena air-crossed her heart.

"She must have said something. How did you two end the conversation?"

Rena frowned. "I didn't pay her much attention, because I could see she was super hyped up. But as I followed her out the door she turned around and added: 'don't trust the police.'"

Hollis took a sip of wine and let Rena talk the experience

out of her system. She didn't remember much about Melanie/
Olivia from prison, but she did remember that the woman
never did or said anything without having a good reason.

CHAPTER TWELVE

—◆◆◆—

THE NEXT MORNING HOLLIS WOKE after a restless night, and when she got to the firm could only mutter, "Morning."

"You're late, for you," Tiffany teased. "It's been so long since I beat you to the office, I had to think about where the light switch is located."

Hollis gave her a smirk and headed for her office.

She leaned back in her chair and closed her eyes. The same thoughts that ran through her head the night before were still there this morning. Could Silva be a crook? Did he take the list? How would Stephanie feel? At their lunch on Saturday, her friend was practically glowing over her new boyfriend. Why would Olivia contact Rena? Unlike Rena, she only half believed Olivia's story.

Hollis groaned.

"What's the matter? You okay?" Penny came in and plopped in a chair.

Hollis's smile was grim. "Not really, but I'll get it together. What did you find at Zoe Allen's house?"

"Nothing that shed any light on the identity of Chris Tappen, but I can tell you who she or he isn't. I spent almost an hour going through her desk and cabinets, even her bills, but no success."

"Penny, I'm impressed," Hollis said. "That sounds pretty thorough, even if it didn't reap any results."

The paralegal beamed at the praise, then her expression grew serious. "Hollis you're going to think I'm crazy, but I think someone is either living in that house or removing the old lady's possessions." She pushed her glasses up on her nose and lowered her voice. "There's an outline of dust where some items and furniture used to be."

The muscles in Hollis's face tightened. "It must be the Allens. I'll let Grueber know. Someone has to talk to Hallinan to call off that clan of piranhas."

She pressed the heel of her hand to her forehead.

"You look tired. Are you sure you can get it together?" Penny's voice didn't hide her concern.

"Yes. I need to speak with George about what's going on with our witness hunt, and there's a ton of paperwork to focus on. Will you be here tomorrow?"

"I'll be here."

HOLLIS TAPPED LIGHTLY ON GEORGE'S door.

"I need to talk with my client."

George looked up and smiled. "You've got both my ears. What's up?"

Hollis brought him up to date with the search for the second witness and her conversations with Leticia Lund and Phyllis Mason. "Neither knew of this Chris Tappen. I don't suppose you recognize the name."

George shook his head. "Sorry, I didn't know my … Zoe Allen, let alone anyone she might know."

Hollis frowned. "Penny thinks someone is sneaking things out of the house. We can request that new locks be put on the doors. The Allens could file an injunction, but then they'd be showing their hand."

"Do it." George stood and went over to his office window with the expansive view of the bay. "I've been thinking. I want to be fair, and I understand the Allen family outrage ... maybe not the greed, but I think I would be upset, too. I'd like you to draw up an agreement that gives them ten million before taxes in exchange for dropping their suit and any future claims."

Hollis looked at him. "George, that's half of your inheritance. Are you still sure?"

"I've given it more thought," he said. "Seven million after taxes is plenty for me. Unlike my step-relatives, I wasn't expecting anything at all." He paused. "I would have given it all to have known my mother, but—"

"But the millions will help to make up for it." Hollis smiled broadly.

"Yeah." He grinned.

ON THE WAY BACK TO her desk, she met Tiffany holding out a message slip. "You got a call from a Phyllis Mason. She is such a nice lady. She said she thinks she may have remembered the man you were looking for."

Hollis arm pumped the air. *Finally.*

She dashed down the hall to her office and dialed the number on the slip.

"This is Leticia Lund."

Hollis's rush came to a halt. "Oh, Ms. Lund, hello, I wasn't expecting you to pick up the phone." She stiffened without realizing why. "Is Mrs. Mason available? She was trying to reach me."

Lund hesitated.

"She's not here. She had an episode and they took her to the hospital."

"Hospital." Hollis frowned. "She just called me a few minutes ago. What kind of episode? When did it happen?"

Leticia Lund's voice was cool. "Just now, her heart started to ... to fibrillate and ... and they took her away."

She's lying.

Hollis responded. "She called me. She remembered Chris Tappen. Were you there when she called? Did she tell you about Tappen?"

"No, she didn't. I just came by to visit with her. I didn't listen to what she was saying. She was already growing pale and I could tell she was having some sort of physical event."

Hollis said nothing for a moment. Thoughts of frustration and disbelief, mingled with genuine concern, weighed heavily on her mind. Finally she sighed.

"Can you call me later and let me know how she's doing? I've visited with her, and we really hit it off."

"I'll call you if I hear anything." She clicked off.

For no reason she could justify, Hollis knew she would have to contact the hospital directly if she wanted to hear about Phyllis.

SHE PUNCHED A NUMBER INTO her phone.

"Hollis, what's the matter?" Grueber's voice was strained. "Are the Allens up to no good again?"

She resisted telling him about the injunction and the search for Chris Tappen.

"And more," she said. She recounted what she had heard from Penny. "Tony, I'm recommending that we change the locks on Zoe Allen's house."

"Yes, I suppose that would be best. Go ahead and contact Hallinan."

"Tony, there's one more thing." Hollis took a breath. "Phyllis Mason called me, but I wasn't available so she left a message saying that she thought she might know Chris Tappen."

He hesitated before answering, "That's great news. Now we can put an end to all this foolishness."

"You don't sound so enthusiastic. Besides, it appears as if she was almost immediately taken ill and rushed to the hospital."

"What!"

Hollis kept her voice even. "It was her heart. Leticia Lund just happened to be visiting her and saw the whole thing."

He was silent.

"Hollis, can you drive me to the hospital? I'd like to see Phyllis tonight ... before ... well I'd like to see her as soon as possible. Can you pick me up at the BART station in San Leandro?"

"Sure, but I need to find out which hospital and if she can have visitors."

"Check with Puritan in Hayward. That's where Zoe was being treated."

Of course, Tony was correct. When Hollis called, a nurse verified that Phyllis had been admitted. She was resting and could have visitors. When Hollis got back to Tony with the news, he said he would be on the one o'clock BART train and she could pick him up. She purposely didn't tell him about George's proposal to share his inheritance, just in case George had second thoughts about his generosity.

Hollis was grateful that she'd have a couple of hours to do some of the routine work on her desk. She also needed to get back to Penny about the locks and the possible good news about Tappen.

She finished writing instructions for Penny and would have briefed George, if he had been in his office. She'd update him tomorrow. At least then she would have some real news.

Tony was waiting for her when she pulled into BART's passenger loading zone. He looked as dapper as he had at their first meeting, except his expression was haggard and his manner subdued. He put his cane in the backseat and said a muted, "Hello."

"Did you know Phyllis, too?" she asked, pulling out of the lot.

"A long time ago I was married to her."

Hollis's eyes widened and her mouth dropped open. "It's nice you remained friends after all these years." She moved into traffic and onto the freeway entrance.

Tony didn't say anything more. He seemed nothing like the devil-may-care man she'd lunched with the week before. His concern was tangible and they drove in silence. As she pulled into the parking lot, he began to gather his jacket around him and clicked loose the seatbelt.

She found herself running after him.

They found Phyllis Mason's floor and stopped at the nurse's station. A young, efficient looking nurse peered up from her computer monitor.

"I just took away her dinner tray, but she's not allowed visitors until tomorrow."

"I don't understand, this isn't ICU." Tony's voice was raised. "Why can't she have visitors?"

The young woman scrolled through the screen. "Evidently, her doctor is taking added precautions after talking with her caregiver. If nothing happens overnight, she can have visitors in the morning and may even go home."

Grueber's face turned a deep red.

Hollis put a hand on Tony's arm. "Calm down. I don't want to be visiting you in ICU."

He shrugged off her hand and tapped the nurse's monitor. "I'd like to speak with her doctor."

Hollis saw him flinch and rub his leg. It was clear the dash from the car had been more than his limb was used to.

The nurse shook her head. "I'm sorry. He's already seen her today and he's in surgery the rest of the day. But her nurse is with her. Actually, Miss Lund hasn't left her side since Mrs. Mason checked in. I'll go get her."

Hollis and Tony exchanged looks.

He frowned. "What is she doing here?"

Before Hollis could respond a tall woman with graying blond hair strode commandingly in front of the smaller day nurse.

"Hello, Leticia," Tony said. "What's going on?"

"Hello, Mr. Grueber, I was with Mrs. Mason when she … when she had her attack." Lund licked her lips and spoke in a low voice as the nurse passed her to return to her station. "I felt obligated to stay with her until she ... she recovered."

Hollis leaned in. "Recovered from what?"

"I'm sorry," Lund said. "Who are you?"

Hollis put out her hand. "I'm Hollis Morgan. We've talked on the phone. Mrs. Mason was trying to reach me when she was taken ill. You said you were with her?"

Lund turned pale and she began to blink rapidly. Hollis noticed that Tony caught the change in her, too.

"She wanted to tell me about Chris Tappen. Remember, he or she signed as the second witness to Zoe Allen's will." Hollis put on a broad smile.

"She was agitated and disturbed." Lund licked her lips "I think that's what caused her episode."

"Leticia, what *is* wrong with Phyllis?"

"It's her heart. She couldn't catch her breath," Lund said. "I didn't want to take any chances because of her age. So I brought her in. I really can't discuss her medical condition with you."

"What does the doctor say?"

"Well, he didn't see her like I did, and since I'm a registered nurse, he deferred to my experience."

Lund seemed to have pulled herself together. Her voice no longer quavered.

"Yet, you told him you were her caregiver." Tony searched her face. "I didn't know you knew her that well to be so ... committed." He stepped to the side. "I'd like to just pop in and see her."

Lund blocked him. "She's resting."

Hollis's internal radar was beeping off the charts.

Tony squinted. "I'm her attorney."

"I don't think so," Lund said. "Mrs. Mason's attorney is a woman; she brought her to visit Mrs. Allen. Mrs. Allen was going to use her to draw up her new trust, and then she remembered you." Lund looked down at him. "I was the one who looked up your number for Mrs. Allen."

Hollis sensed rather than saw Tony's anger and she stepped between them. "Mr. Grueber is very concerned about Mrs. Mason; maybe he could just wave at her from the door."

"No. I can't chance her health."

It was all Hollis could do to hold in her irritation. She wasn't sure she was ready to go all the way to accusing Lund of deliberate stalling, but she wasn't ready to let go of the idea either.

Another flush of red had crept onto Tony's face and without responding, he limped back to the nurses' station. He leaned over the counter. Hollis followed rapidly behind him and when she looked back, Lund had gone inside Phyllis's room.

His voice was steel. "What time are visiting hours in the morning?"

CHAPTER THIRTEEN

SETTLING INTO HER OFFICE THE next morning, Hollis felt the impact of two days' lack of sleep. She hadn't been able to get Rena's conversation with Olivia Shur out of her head.

Trade her way out—with the list.

Tiffany buzzed her on the intercom. "Hollis, your phone is still forwarded to me. Give Tony Grueber a call."

The phone only rang once before Tony picked up, and without any greeting, said, "I'm on BART now. Can you pick me up at the San Leandro Station in fifteen minutes?"

"Ah, sure. I may be a couple of minutes late, but I'll be there."

Hollis grabbed her purse and jacket, waving at Tiffany as she signed out.

THEY DROVE IN SILENCE, AGAIN. And again, Tony jumped out before Hollis could take the key out of the ignition. She half ran to keep up with his galloping limp.

"Tony, you're going to have a heart attack. I know you're worried, but—"

Ignoring her, he passed through the automatic double doors. He tapped his finger on the now familiar nurse's station counter. "We're here to see Phyllis Mason."

This was a different nurse from the one the day before. She was short and stocky, her humorless expression seemingly set in stone. She looked them up and down and then pointedly glanced up at the clock.

"She already has visitors, we don't like too many—"

Tony limped determinedly down the hall.

Hollis gave the nurse a small apologetic smile. "He's a little anxious. They're in love."

The nurse blinked in surprise and said nothing. Hollis scampered behind Tony. She almost bumped into his back as he came to an abrupt halt in the doorway. She looked around his shoulder, and she could see the room was full—full of Allen family members.

"What's going on here?" Tony demanded.

Everyone turned around. From their almost unified frowns, they were not pleased.

"Tony?" Phyllis called from the bed. Her voice revealed her astonishment.

"Hello, Phyl," he said, edging into the room. "It's been a while, but you were always one for the dramatic. Are you all right?"

Like a flash from the corner out of sight from the door, Leticia Lund appeared. "I'm sorry, only three guests at a time." She attempted to herd them back.

Tony didn't budge. "Do you make these rules up as you go along?"

"We were here first," Ned Allen said with a whine.

Virgie Allen sat back in the chair, pushing a small travel bag underneath, as if staking her ownership claim. "We're not leaving. We have some business to discuss with Mrs. Mason. Isn't that right ... er ... Phyllis?"

Phyllis turned a bright red, her hands clenching. "Well ... I ... I ...."

Charles pulled a pair of glasses from his inside jacket pocket.

"Mrs. Lund, I think we can count on you to take care of these people. Please make sure we have privacy." He moved to Phyllis's side, blocking Tony from coming any closer.

That turned out to be a wrong move.

With a little force, Tony pushed him aside, knocking him off balance into the service tray, the items on which rocked precariously before settling back down. Hollis raised her eyebrows and stepped in front of Lund.

"Really, this is uncalled for," Virgie Allen blustered.

"Tony, stop," Phyllis cried out. "I'm fine, really. This won't take long. Please, will you wait?"

Hollis could almost read Tony's mind, then deciding to give it voice, she turned to Charles Allen. "You are aware Mrs. Mason is a witness in a pending lawsuit. What business do you have with her?"

"None of yours," Ned wheezed.

"For once, he's right." Charles glared. "Please leave." He smiled at Phyllis. "This shouldn't take much longer."

Virgie Allen rose from her chair and took a step toward Tony, clearly ignoring Hollis. She halted about a foot away from his rigid stance.

"Mr. Grueber," she said in a muted, conciliatory tone. "I can tell you are worried about your friend. I assure you we will only be a few minutes more. We only need to finalize our discussion, and we will be gone from here. Please?"

Everyone seemed to be holding their breath except Tony, who was at Phyllis' side.

He reached down and picked up her hand. "For you, I'll wait outside."

Phyllis blushed and nodded. She looked around at the Allen visitors without much assurance, but she gave Tony her old smile and everyone breathed easier.

Hollis and Tony found visitor chairs a few doors down the hallway. They sat without speaking. She smiled weakly at him and he smiled back. She didn't want to worry him more, but she didn't trust the Allens, and she could only imagine what business they had with Phyllis.

As if reading her thoughts, he finally said, "What do you think they want with her?"

Hollis stared straight ahead. "I think Lund told them Phyllis remembered the name, or knew Zoe Allen's second witness, and that she was getting ready to tell me. Then the buzzards circled and decided to pay her a visit."

Tony replied grudgingly. "I'm afraid you're right."

It wasn't fifteen minutes before the Allens poured out into the corridor, murmuring with their heads together. Charles pointed to Hollis and Tony, and the murmuring went lower. Grinning, Ned Allen sent them a wave and toddled toward the elevators.

Hollis and Tony entered Phyllis's room. They found Leticia Lund straightening the chairs and smoothing Phyllis's bedcovers. She gave them a furtive but indignant look.

She picked up the small green plastic pitcher. "Mrs. Mason, I'll get you some water and then I'll leave you to your ... guests."

Phyllis and Tony exchanged glances.

"Leticia, why don't you leave, now?" Phyllis snapped. "I think you've done enough and I'm not sure I can take much more of your thoughtfulness."

Lund drew herself up, outrage radiating across her reddened face. She stuttered, "You're ... you're going to need help getting home. I ... the Allens ... I ... you'll need me."

Hollis picked up the black purse and dark jacket hanging on the coat rack and handed them out to Lund. "I think you've already done your best. We'll take care of Phyllis from here on."

"Yes, Miss Lund," Phyllis said, her voice gaining strength. "I think my ... friends can take care of me."

Leticia Lund took her belongings from Hollis and just missed bumping into Tony as she dashed out. Hollis shut the door behind her. Tony took a seat near Phyllis' side, and Hollis stood at the foot of the bed.

"Hello, Phyl," Tony said.

"Tony." Tears filled Phyllis' eyes, but she deftly wiped them away with the side of her hand. "It's been a lifetime."

"What's happened, Phyl?" Tony asked.

"You look well. What's it been, thirty years?" she said.

"Thirty-two."

Two pink dots of color appeared on her cheeks. "That's a long time." Her voice drifted. She took a deep breath and sat up. "But I don't want to talk about it now. Will you just get me out of here?"

"I'll go see what it takes to check you out of this hotel and be right back," said Hollis.

She left them to talk. The head nurse informed her that the doctor had already seen Phyllis that morning and approved her release. He hadn't seen the need for any medications in addition to what she was already taking, so a trip to the pharmacy wasn't necessary. She could leave at any time, and it would free up a bed if it were sooner rather than later.

When Hollis returned, Tony was standing looking out the window. He motioned with his head that Phyllis was in the bathroom.

"You stay and help her get ready, Hollis. She can be stubborn. I didn't want to leave her alone. I'll sit just outside." Head down, he moved with his cane and limped dejectedly to the door.

"Did she say—?"

"We'll talk after we get her home."

But they didn't talk after they got Phyllis home. In the car, she said she was exhausted after her adventure and would appreciate it if they would leave her to rest and visit her the next day.

"Tony, Hollis, I know we need to talk but if I could just get back to my own things in my own surroundings, I would feel so much better." Her eyes pleaded with them to understand.

Hollis could see Tony wanted to stay behind, but she also knew Phyllis was right. "Of course, we can come back tomorrow. Can't we, Tony?"

He mumbled, "I suppose so."

After taking Tony to the BART station and confirming with Ritz that he would leave the café early and pick him up, Hollis hurried back to Triple D. George was passing through the lobby when she got off the elevator. He waited for her to pick up her messages and head back to her office.

"You ready to tell me what's going on?" He settled in the chair in front of her desk, stretching out his long legs.

Hollis told him of Lund's hijacking Phyllis into the hospital until the Allens could converge on her there, and how she and Tony had reinstalled her back in her home.

"You think she knows the name of the other witness?" he asked.

"If not the name, then maybe who he is and where we can find him."

George shook his head slowly. "This is causing a lot more trauma than I thought it would. I've given it some more thought, and I'm sticking to my idea of giving the Allens half of the inheritance." He ran his fingers through his hair. "This thing is escalating. Something could have happened to Phyllis Mason while Lund was playing bouncer for the Allens. Mrs. Mason could have been hurt. Have you drawn up the papers?"

"Yes." Hollis said. "George, what did you expect? We're talking millions of dollars and a family's survival. People have been murdered for a lot less." She took some papers out of a file and handed them to him. "Here's the draft agreement."

"I'll read it and get it back to you before I leave the office."

After he left, Hollis leaned her elbows on the desk and put her head in hands. The Allens were at best a major annoyance. She would meet with Tony then arrange a meeting with Tim Hallinan. This was one annoyance she didn't want to last one more day than necessary.

Then, as much as she tried to put it out of her mind, the shadow of Olivia Shur's list of names to be traded for her freedom crept forward from the corners of her mind.

Could Detective Daniel Silva be a dirty cop? After their breakfast last weekend, Hollis was sure Stephanie was falling for the guy. She didn't think it right to bring up the fact he was becoming one of her biggest nightmares. But the withholding of feelings and information was forming a wedge in their friendship—a friendship Hollis cherished more than she'd realized.

On the other hand, she felt no allegiance to Olivia Shur. They had not been close in prison. But evidently Hollis had made more of an impression on her than she thought, especially if Olivia felt she could count on Hollis to help her change her life. Ironically, all Hollis remembered about her was a quiet, nice-looking lady who kept to herself. It was hard to imagine that this quiet personality had a list of the names of bad people—people who were willing to kill to protect their identities. Still, everyone deserved a second chance.

Hollis picked up the phone.

Jule Berman answered immediately. "You've had a couple of days. Have you thought things over?"

"You said there were three copies. There's the one that was with her in the car—we don't have a clue where it is, probably with her killer. One might be with the police—though it may still be in the 'safe place' she described—and then there's the copy Olivia mailed to herself. Can you get into her house?" Hollis scrunched the phone against her shoulder while she changed from her heels to jogging shoes.

He hesitated. "She lived in a condo; the mailboxes are in the lobby."

"That doesn't answer my question. What's her address? Can you get into her condo lobby?" She wrote down the location as he rattled off the address.

"Yeah," he said. "I can get into the lobby and her unit, but I don't have a mailbox key. Besides it's been almost two weeks since … since she was killed. I'm sure the management is collecting her mail so it can be forwarded to her next of kin or maybe her attorney."

"Exactly. There's a good chance her mail is being held by her landlord. They could have taken it to the post office, but they could also be holding it for family." Hollis stood and looped her tote over her shoulder. "At any rate, we won't know for sure until we check things out. Meet me there in a half-hour."

Hollis knew of Olivia's neighborhood, but not enough to hold back on a low whistle at its opulence. How could Olivia Shur afford the community of Tudor-style townhomes fronted with recently groomed box hedges and bordering large expanses of green lawn. She parked behind Berman's car and he got out to meet her.

"From all this, I assume you've changed your attitude about getting involved," he said.

Hollis shrugged. "It seems I may have no choice. If I want to get out of the sights of a murderer, I need to find that list and turn it over to the police."

"But, I thought … Olivia told you that the police are in on this, too."

"Maybe, but I refuse to believe the entire force is dirty."

Berman stared at the ground. "Did you ever think about selling the list to the people who want it most?"

"No, I never did." Hollis looked at him with speculation. "Besides, I thought you didn't know who they were."

"I don't, but once you get the list, we should contact them." He looked around. "We need to move this conversation inside."

"I agree. Come on, *Julie*, let's hope this drama will be over soon." She walked up the path to the security panel next to the double glass doors. "The manager is in two-oh-four. I think we should contact him now, instead of showing up at his door."

She pushed the button. A shrill woman's voice greeted them.

"Hello, I'm an attorney for Olivia Shur and I'm here with her … her fiancé." Hollis put her fingers to her lips when Berman started to protest. "We're here for her mail."

"Who did you say you were?"

Hollis repeated her statement and ended with her name.

"Well, Miss Morgan, the police already collected Miss Shur's mail yesterday. Her unit had been burgled. I'm surprised they didn't tell you." She paused, and then added, "They told me to let them know if anyone comes around asking about her unit."

Hollis wanted to kick herself. Now Silva and maybe even John would know that she was conducting her own search. She and Berman walked back to their cars. He didn't seem surprised at the outcome.

"You know," Hollis said. "If the second copy of the list was in the mail, there's a good chance the police have it, too." Hollis glanced around the street trying to spot an unmarked car.

Berman, one eyebrow arched, said, "So what are you going to do now?"

"What am *I* going to do? Why should I do anything?"

"They know Olivia was in contact with you. They'll think you have a copy of the list or possibly know the names on the list."

"Let me think about this," Hollis said. "It's getting late. I've got this other case I have to follow up on that means a lot to me." Hollis could feel a headache coming on and pressed a palm against her forehead. "I'll call you tomorrow. In the meantime, can you think of anyone else or anyplace else where the third list could be?"

Berman looked past her. "Yeah, but I don't think we have much time."

Chapter Fourteen

———

Tony had left a message for Hollis to meet him for breakfast at Maud's. First she had to get a filing in the mail; that should leave her just enough time to get there.

She still felt guilty after talking with John the night before, or rather not talking to him about her conversation with Rena and the wasted trip to Olivia's condo with Berman. She decided to wait until confronted, ask for his forgiveness, and limit the amount of time he had to reprimand her.

As on her previous trip, by the time she pulled into Maud's parking lot, it was already nearly full. A dozen people stood in line. Hollis mumbled "excuse me" several times until she was inside and could wave to Tony, sitting in his corner.

"How did you get here? I could have picked you up." She gave him a quick hug before sitting down.

"Ritz came and got me on his way in. I had some paperwork to do and I can use the quiet time to get it done here."

At that moment Ritz came to their table to take their order. He shook Hollis's hand in recognition.

"We've got to watch out for him, Hollis. He's got high blood pressure, and while he's lookin' pretty good right now, this morning his skin was gray and he looked real tired. You must have cheered him up." He moved away from Tony.

"You know, Ritz, it's against the law to give out my private medical information," Tony said, only half kidding. "Now, can you go and do your job? Hollis and I have business to take care of."

Ritz moved away from the table but not without first motioning over Tony's head so that only Hollis could see that he was concerned. She gave a gesture of acknowledgment.

"Tony," she said, "I spoke with Phyllis. She had a good night's sleep and is doing fine now that she's back home. I'm going by there today for a visit. I'll talk with the director at the home to let her know what happened, so that Lund won't be able to bother her again."

If he heard her, he didn't say anything. A server brought her tea and Tony's oatmeal.

She squeezed lemon into her cup. "Tony, there's something I haven't told you because it wasn't definite until yesterday."

He looked up. "Phyllis isn't—"

"No, I'm sorry I shouldn't have said it that way. It's about George."

She couldn't miss his deep exhale of relief.

"I held back telling you before because it wasn't final, but he's willing to sign what we're calling a letter of understanding so the injunction gets lifted. That's just a name I came up with—it can be called anything the Allens want it called—but George will give half of his half of his interest in Zoe Allen's estate to the Allens—that is, if they drop the lawsuit. He's willing to reflect it in a formal binding agreement."

Tony took out a pad of paper and scribbled a note. "This is good news. The Allens will drop their suit and we can close the case." He dug into his oatmeal.

"In fact, with Phyllis remembering the name of the second witness, there shouldn't be a thing to worry about."

She smiled broadly, but Tony started to fidget with his

napkin. "I'm coming with you to see Phyllis," he said. "I won't be able to rest until I can see her for myself."

Hollis was prepared for his reaction. "All right, we'll go straight from here. I need to get back to work. I've got the letter for George to sign, but I want to finish the agreement and get it to the Allens' attorney as soon as possible."

Less than an hour later Hollis and Tony were on the road. This time the drive with Tony was entertaining. He was talkative, and he had her laughing over anecdotes about his past clients.

"I'll be eighty-two on my next birthday, and I can tell you that in all my years as a lawyer, I haven't made a lot of money, but I love my career choice. Not every minute of it, mind you, but overall it was a good match for me." He lowered his voice and rubbed his eyes. "Did I tell you Phyllis worked to put me through law school?"

Hollis looked over at him, but he was staring straight ahead. "No, you just told me that you and she were divorced."

"She remarried, but she's been a widow now for many years." His expression was wistful. "I was a fool. She loved me, and I cheated on her and left her for another woman." He began to choke up as he went on, "A woman who couldn't hold a candle to Phyl, but I couldn't see that then. I … I couldn't see."

Tears filled his eyes.

"She seems to have gotten through it all right. Now she needs you to be strong for her." Hollis exited the freeway. "You know, I think she still cares for you."

"Then she's a fool, too."

HOLLIS WAS GLAD SHE'D CALLED ahead, but as soon as they settled in Phyllis's room, she could tell there was something wrong. Phyllis was dressed in a sky-blue velour running suit that complemented her green eyes, and her white hair was attractively done in a soft chignon. The television was on a morning game show, but she was restless and kept jumping up to ask them if they wanted "coffee, or water, or orange juice, or tea."

"Phyl, sit down, will you?" Tony said. "We didn't come here to get you to wait on us." He patted the seat of her lounger chair. "We want to find out if you're doing okay."

She took the seat. "Oh, my, of course I'm doing okay. I don't know where that heart thing came from. I've never had it happen to me before."

"Phyllis, you don't think Leticia Lund had anything to do with it, do you?" Hollis asked quietly.

"Hollis, why would you say a thing like that?" Tony lashed out. "You're scaring her."

But Phyllis and Hollis exchanged glances and Hollis knew she'd had the same thought.

"Tony, stop yelling," Phyllis said. "Hollis has a good heart, and I trust her." She got up and went into the kitchenette. "Can I get anyone some cocoa?"

"Thank you, no, I—" Hollis started.

"Phyllis, will you please sit down? We need to talk to you about something." Tony pointed to her chair and she meekly sat down. "Go ahead, Hollis."

Phyllis's shoulders stiffened and her mouth formed a single straight line.

"Phyllis, when you called me yesterday, it sounded like you recalled Zoe Allen's second witness. Did you? Who is it?"

Phyllis looked out the window then down at her hands. "Did I? My memory is not what it used to be. I … I don't remember what I was going to say."

Tony frowned. "Phyl, this is very important. Your memory was perfectly all right yesterday when we spoke. It is important you try to remember."

She shook her shoulders. "Tony, don't bully me. I said I don't remember."

Hollis stared at her. Something was not right. This was not the Phyllis she had bonded with the other day. Tony, too, stared as if he couldn't recognize her.

"Phyllis, have I told you the story of my background?" Hollis said.

"What? Why, no," Phyllis said, relieved at the change in topic.

Tony gave Hollis a curious look.

Hollis got up and walked to the window, positioning herself at the back of Phyllis' chair. "The short version is that I was married to a man who was a crook, who wanted money so badly, he hurt a lot of innocent people. He didn't care." She paused, then took a deep breath and continued, "I loved him more than I loved myself, and I turned my back on my truth, my integrity, and what I knew to be right."

The room was still until Tony coughed. "Phyl—"

"They ... they said they would ..." Phyllis began. "They said they would pay my nursing home bills for as long as I wanted to live here. They ... they knew my pension wasn't enough to cover the rising rates and that I didn't have enough money to stay here after next year." Phyllis turned to look up at Hollis. "I ... I don't know how they knew." Her voice dropped.

"Leticia Lund," Hollis said with certainty. "She's on their payroll. As her nurse, she was spying on Zoe Allen, and then they asked her to spy on you. When you called me, she interrupted our call, remember? I bet she ran out of the room on some pretext?"

Phyllis frowned in thought. "I think you're right. She said she had to ask the director something. She said I looked as if I was having a heart attack. She told me to lie down on the bed, and then she ran out of the room." Her voice gained strength. "I was so thrown off guard I didn't think on my own and I just did as she said."

"She knew there was nothing wrong with you. She played on your doubts and fears, while she called the Allens, to see how fast they could get to the hospital," Tony said.

Hollis returned to the sofa. "Phyllis, we'll work out some way to pay your bill. I'm sure—"

"You don't have to bribe me. I'll manage. I do know what's

right." She smiled, then held her chin high. "I think Chris Tappen was Zoe's gardener."

HOLLIS LEFT TONY WITH PHYLLIS; he said he would get a ride to the BART Station. She drove a little above the speed limit, eager to get back to work and tell George the news about Chris Tappen. George had appeared strained and tired the last few days. He was in his office on the phone, and he waved Hollis into a chair. After a short time, he hung up.

"You look like you're ready to explode," George said, rubbing his forehead.

"I am, George," she said. "We found Chris Tappen. The Allen suit is over."

"You met him, or her?"

"It's a *him,* and no I haven't met him, but I know right where to look."

Hollis briefly went through the last forty-eight hours of restoring Phyllis, the interchange with Leticia Lund, and the duplicity of the Allens.

George shook his head. "It's hard to believe there are people out there who are that desperate." Then he chuckled. "What am I talking about? I have clients who think like this all the time. It's just feels different when it's happening to you."

"As attorneys we do tend to see the less honorable side of human nature." Hollis glanced at the time on her cellphone. "George, I want to get on this as soon as possible, locate this guy, and get him to sign an affidavit."

He nodded. "Before you go, give me the agreement to sign, and then when you get back, contact Hallinan today and let him know his clients aren't walking away empty-handed."

"You don't have to give away half your estate to these greedy nutcases, now that they have no hold over you." She leaned in. "As your attorney, I need to advise you that if you give the Allens a share in your estate, it will never be enough and don't be surprised if they come back for more."

"And since you're my attorney, I'm sure you've written that agreement to state they will forfeit any rights to make future claims." He sat back in his chair and crossed his arms. "I'm ready to move on."

"You've got it." Hollis picked up her purse, "I'm off to find Mr. Tappen. I'll drop off three copies of the agreement for your original signature before I go." She stopped at the door and turned back to him. "George, do you think you could do something for Phyllis Mason? Without her we wouldn't be in a position to settle with the Allens."

"I'm already ahead of you." He smiled. "She will never have to worry about where she'll be living in the future."

HOLLIS HAD NO TROUBLE LOCATING Chris Tappen. She went back to Zoe's neighborhood and knocked on the door of a neighbor whose yard looked groomed and well cared for. The owner, a woman who was getting ready to run, acknowledged that Chris—she didn't know his last name—was one of the yard workers on a team that came each week. In fact, they would be there the next day.

She'd had thoughts about getting the name of the yard service from Hallinan, but she didn't want to chance placing any more diversion temptations in front of the bickering Allens. However, when she did call Hallinan after she returned to the office, she made it clear the agreement was George's idea and not hers.

"We found Tappen, and I'll be filing for a dismissal day after tomorrow."

Hallinan was silent.

"I told them their tactics weren't going to work," he muttered. "So, Ravel is really going to share the estate? What does the agreement say?"

"If you don't mind, I'd rather answer your questions after you've had a chance to read the agreement. To move things along, I'm overnighting it to you, and you'll have it tomorrow."

Hollis rushed her words; she didn't want to spend any more time on the phone with Hallinan than she had to.

She was ready for home.

That night the call from John was short.

"We're pulling an all-nighter and I've got to get back."

"I'd feel sorry for you, except for the excitement in your voice. It sounds like you're going to Disneyland." She laughed. "You can't fool me."

"Yeah, it's really something," he chuckled. "You okay? How's everything there?"

"Oh, I'm fine. I'm a probate attorney. What could be more uneventful than that?"

CHAPTER FIFTEEN

⚬

HOLLIS ARRIVED AT THE OFFICE early, ready to get on top of her mounting paperwork. Her lengthening "To Do" list was making her crazy. She picked up the phone to call Tony, but out of the corner of her eye she saw movement in her doorway. It was Vince.

He looked handsome in a pair of khakis and a navy long-sleeved polo shirt. She sighed. He'd confided in her that he'd be glad when his needle marks didn't show anymore and he could wear short sleeves. She glanced at his eyes, which were clear.

"Why Mr. Peterson, to what do I owe this visit?" She smiled, hoping her face didn't reflect the worry she saw in his.

"Er ... Hollis, can I come in?"

"Sit. What's the matter?"

He rocked from one foot to the other. "I don't want to scare you, but the couple of days I seen this guy following you."

"What do you mean?"

He scratched his head. "I mean last week I was waiting at the bus stop and you were walking back from the hotel on the corner. This BMW was cruising just a little ways behind you, and I swear this guy had a camera." He started pacing. "When you came into the building the dude double parked, got out of the car, moved this orange cone that was in a parking space and moved into the space."

Hollis motioned to him to take a seat.

He sat and leaned over, elbows on knees with his hands clasped. Hollis remembered she had gone to the hotel lobby to call and warn Rena about Silva's imminent interview.

Vince continued, "Then the next day. I was goin' home and I saw you pull out of the parking garage and this same guy pulled out of the same space across the street and fell in a few cars behind you. Only this time he wasn't in a BMW—he was driving some kind of Toyota—but I still recognized him."

"Wait …. Are you sure he was following *me*?"

He nodded. "Oh, I'm sure all right. He was following you, and I was following him."

"I didn't know you owned a car."

"Ah … no, not yet, but a couple of days ago, my friend let me use his car." He got up and started pacing again. "But, Hollis, I can't keep watchin' 'cause my friend took his car back. That's why I'm here to let you know to be on the lookout."

He looked so distressed Hollis knew it was best she took him seriously. "All right, I've got a lot on my plate right now but—"

There was a tap on her office door and Tiffany walked in. "Hollis, Detectives Silva and Lee are here to see you. I put them in the small conference room." She looked over her shoulder. "They don't look too happy."

Hollis closed her eyes and steeled her resolve. "Okay, I'll be right there."

With a curious glance at Vince, Tiffany left, closing the door behind her.

Vince's foot tapped at rapid speed. "What do you think *they* want?"

She shrugged. "Honestly, this time I have no idea. But you're going to tell them what you just told me."

He frowned and his foot tapping escalated. Hollis frowned.

"What's the matter? They're not here for you."

"Er … Hollis, I borrowed my friend's car … but … er … um … I don't have a driver's license."

She sat back in her chair shaking her head. "The car wasn't stolen, was it?"

"Of course not. I'm not a criminal." He looked down at the floor.

"Cheer up. I'll cover for you." Hollis smiled. "Considering how bad things could be … and compared to everything else that's going on, I think we can deal with that." She caught his eyes. "But no more driving without a license."

Triple D's small conference room held two people comfortably and four people in a crush. Vince's lanky form competed with Silva's long legs for floor space. But Hollis was feeling contrary and didn't seek a larger space.

"Who is this guy?" Lee asked. "He can't stay."

"Vince is an employee and a friend." Hollis looked him in the eye. "I asked him to tell you about some information that you might find interesting."

Silva's eyes narrowed in a one minute assessment of the nervous figure in front of him. "Go ahead, speak."

Vince ran his hand up and down several times on the sleeve of his other arm. His eyes blinked, his lashes falling on increasingly red cheeks. But he said nothing. Hollis saw the transformation in slight alarm.

"Vince, it's okay. Just tell them about what you saw when I went to get my car the other day," she prompted.

He turned to her with his deer in the headlight eyes. "I … I …."

"That's right." Hollis urged him on with a motion of her head. "Remember, you told me you saw a man waiting to follow me and …." She reached out and lightly touched his arm.

He jerked it back, but she could see he was starting to regain his composure.

"A man was following Ms. Morgan?" Silva said soothingly.

"It was good you were there. Can you describe him?"

For the next minutes Vince told his story again. When Silva and Lee had gotten everything they could from him, they thanked him and said he could go. Vince dashed out of the room.

Silva, with a knowing smile, turned to her. "What was he in for?"

"Vince used to have a drug habit," she said. "But he kicked it, went back to school, and is attending college at night. He's one of our best employees."

Lee and Silva exchanged looks.

Lee put his pen down from his note taking. "Sometimes success is harder to deal with than failure."

"Why, Detective, how profound," Hollis retorted, then wished she could take the words back. "I'm sorry; it's just that Vince has come such a long way on his own strength of character. I know him, and you don't."

Silva frowned. "Let's put him aside for a moment. We got a call that you were trying to get into Olivia Shur's condo to retrieve her mail. You're an attorney, Ms. Morgan. You know we could bring a charge of interfering in a murder investigation against you. Yours could be a short legal career. You're on very thin ice."

Hollis sat back in her chair. "Detective, I could sit here and argue with you, but I'm in just plain overload. I've told you the truth. I don't know what Olivia Shur was up to, but I do know that now my life may be in danger, and I don't like feeling like a victim."

For a brief second she thought she detected a sign of empathy in his eyes, but it was so fleeting, she couldn't swear it was there. More probably it was wishful thinking.

"The condo manager said you had someone with you—Shur's fiancé. What's his name?"

Sorry, Julie.

"His name is Jule Berman. There may have been a slight

misunderstanding on my part about the fiancé part, I don't know him well. I do think they were friends."

Lee sneered. "How'd you know to get in touch with him? You said you never had contact with Shur."

"She sent me a note saying she was coming to see me and that she could be reached through Jule Berman." Hollis recovered, but sloppily. It sounded like a lie to her own ears.

"Where's the note?" Silva asked.

"Ah … I'll have to look for it and get it to you. It was only a few lines. It came days after Olivia was killed." She looked him in the eyes. "I didn't think it was important."

Silva took out a pen. "How do we get in touch with Mr. Berman?"

"He's at a company called Capital Consulting." She scrolled on her phone for his number and scribbled it on a slip of paper.

Silva was looking at her phone as if he'd like nothing better than to dump her contacts and run another printout, but he knew she likely wouldn't cooperate this time, and he would be right.

HOLLIS DIDN'T RETURN TO HER office after Silva and Lee left. She had to get some air and clear her head. She was crossing the lobby headed for the double doors when Tiffany stopped her.

"Hollis, please call the Allens' attorney. He wants you to know that they accept the deal as you've laid it out." Tiffany looked up to the ceiling. "He made me promise to tell you so you couldn't change your mind about the compromise."

She smiled, and pumped her arm in a "yes."

"Thank you, Tiffany. I shall return Mr. Hallinan' call when I get back to my office."

"You've really earned your fees with this case. You won't have to deal with them anymore, will you?" Tiffany held up her hand with her fingers crossed.

Hollis laughed. She turned back to her office; she'd wait to get the fresh air. Hallinan answered on the half-ring and said all the family members had signed.

"How soon will you probate the will?"

She looked at the calendar. "An uncontested will should take no time. The trust ends and all beneficiaries are satisfied, so we should be done within thirty-days."

He signed off with a "nice doing business with you."

George was looking out the window at the sailboats in the bay when she went to tell him her news.

"I'm glad this is over," he said. "I'd like to talk to you about a couple of things. Have you got a moment?" He returned to his desk.

"Not right this minute. I need to reach Tony Grueber, and I know he's going to want to go out and see Phyllis Mason." She looked at the clock on his wall. "Can we make it toward the end of the afternoon?"

George said, "Not a problem. I have a settlement agreement that needs drafting. I'll see you later."

Back in her office, Hollis picked up her phone to call Tony and give him the good news.

He was ecstatic. "How soon can we drive out to see Phyl?"

"As soon as you like, I'll pick you up from the BART station," Hollis said. "I could use a happy ending about now."

HOLLIS ARRIVED EARLY OR THE BART train was late. Whatever the reason she knew it wasn't because Tony had any say in it. He was probably yelling at the conductor to hurry. She glanced out the window at the comings and goings in the parking lot. There was another car idling not too far from hers. She took a deep breath. She needed to slow down. Maybe she and John could take a vacation, go someplace quiet.

A few minutes later, she glanced through the crowd of clearly irritated departing passengers and spotted Tony. She couldn't help but smile. He was wearing a dark suit and tie, and in his arms was a bundle of fragrant white Asiatic Lilies.

"Tony, how handsome you look, and how beautiful the flowers."

"I thought I'd look like an attorney, for once," he said sheepishly.

Hollis raised her eyebrows. "Well, frankly, you look like you're courting," she teased.

He turned red. "Oh, the flowers …. No, no, that's all in the past. I messed up and I'm too old." He pulled on his seatbelt. "I called ahead to make sure she knew we were coming."

This time Hollis didn't even try to stop him from rushing out of the car. She hurried behind him. He should consider entering the senior division of a track meet; even with his cane he was a fast runner. He'd already tapped on the door by the time Hollis caught up to him.

This time, Phyllis was wearing a deep maroon velour running suit that added color to her cheeks. She must have a suit for every mood and occasion. With her impish sparkling eyes, she looked quite beautiful. Evidently Tony thought so, too.

"Good evening, you two," Phyllis gasped at the sight of the flowers. "Tony, they're beautiful." She accepted them, inhaling the pervasive fragrance. They gazed at each other.

Phyllis went to the kitchen for a vase. "These are my favorite, Hollis."

Hollis smiled. "I've seen them before but I've never stopped to really appreciate their beauty and smell."

"You've got to stop running through life," Tony said, speaking to Hollis but looking at Phyllis. "You'll leave behind the things you cherish most."

Hollis was settling in on the sofa, but she looked up at Tony's comment and realized she was quickly becoming a third wheel. She reached into her briefcase and pulled out a folder of papers. Phyllis and Tony joined her in the living room. Phyllis sat next to Tony.

"I'm not going to be able to visit long." She cleared her throat. "Tony, I can come back after I see another client, or I can arrange a ride for you if you prefer."

"Oh, I was hoping you would stay for dinner," Phyllis said, touching her arm.

"Hollis, can't you stay?" Tony asked half-heartedly.

She wanted to chuckle but kept a straight face. "No, I really do have to get going, but Phyllis, I have some papers I need to go over with you."

Phyllis stiffened and sighed. "What kind of papers?"

Hollis realized she was expecting the worst. "Nothing bad. Actually, I think you're going to be pleasantly surprised."

She told her about how much George appreciated her willingness to put her future care on the line by telling the truth, and that he had arranged to pay her living expenses at the home for as long as she lived.

"He's spoken with the director here, and they will bill him for your care. You can use whatever services they have without concern." Hollis smiled into Phyllis's eyes, which already brimmed with tears. "And Phyllis, if you ever decide you want to live someplace else, just let me know and I'll arrange for the same stipend to follow you there."

Phyllis started to cry into Tony's shoulder, who held her tight. Hollis picked up her things and was ready to leave when Phyllis dabbed at her eyes with the back of her hand and said, "Thank you, Hollis, and ask George to come see me as soon as he can."

Hollis nodded and gave Phyllis a hug.

Going to her car, she found another vehicle blocking her in. She looked around, but the driver wasn't in sight. She sighed with irritation and headed back into the residence home.

She said to the efficient looking woman covering the information desk, "Excuse me, can you make an announcement that a," she looked out the glass doors at her car, "a black Solara is blocking my car."

"Oh, I hate it when that happens," the woman said. "It's not uncommon here. But sweetie, can you just run out and get the plate number so I can announce it on the system?"

"Sure."

But when she went to her car, the other vehicle was gone. Hollis set her shoulders; she wasn't going to let one jerk bother her. She smiled, recalling the look in Tony's eyes as he took Phyllis's hand.

BACK IN HER OWN OFFICE, Hollis quickly sorted through a tall stack of files that Penny had left for her signature. She smiled with satisfaction. Thank God for Penny. Her work was professional and complete; she deserved a year-end bonus. From the hall, she could hear doors closing and the muffled sound of footsteps and voices heading for the elevator. Triple D workers were ending another day.

Her next order of business was a pile of memos from the office manager requesting her to submit billing statements and past due expense reports. This task was more tedious, but she had gotten halfway through when George poked his head in her office.

"Have you got a minute, now?"

"Absolutely." She looked up with some curiosity. "Let me grab a cup of tea and I'll meet you in your office."

All the vertical blinds in his office had been pulled back to reveal the full expanse of the bay. It was a typical Bay Area summer day, gray with late afternoon fog hovering over the Golden Gate Bridge and the San Francisco skyline. It was Hollis's favorite weather.

George sat behind his desk with his cup of coffee and pad of paper.

Hollis settled in the chair in front of him.

"What's up?" she asked.

"I'm leaving the firm," he said solemnly, his eyes searching hers for a reaction.

While she straightened in her seat, she hoped her dismay didn't show.

"Just give me a chance to let those words sink in," she said. "Can you tell me what you're thinking?"

George seemed to gather energy as he moved to the edge of his chair. "All my life I've been a competitive achiever, but I've played off of a playlist that wasn't my own. In high school I played football so I could get a scholarship to college. I worked hard to be on the starting lineup, and when I made all-star, I was pumped ... but I hated football."

She took a sip of tea and waited for him to go on.

"Then in college, I got hurt in my junior year and I couldn't play. It was one of the best gifts of my life. Fortunately, I had good grades and I earned money for my tuition from tutoring and teaching-assistant assignments. I looked around for what I was going to do when I grew up and I settled on the law, not because I love it like you do, but because it paid well." He took a long swallow of coffee. "Remember, I was adopted I didn't have the ... the assurance of who I was, like most people. I was operating out of survivor mode."

She wrinkled her brow. "Are you saying you've been working in a career that you can't stand?" She raised an eyebrow. "I can't believe that. You're too good at what you do."

He smiled. "I know." He started doodling on the pad. "That's what always made it hard. I'm good at pretty much anything I set my mind to." He gave Hollis another smile and said, "But until recently I've never asked myself the question: what would I do if money wasn't a concern? What is my passion?"

Hollis tried not to appear taken aback by George's internal conflict, but she'd had no idea. She was happy for George, and it made her reflect on her own life. When she asked herself the same question he had, the answer was still the law.

"Ah," Hollis said, and with genuine curiosity inquired, "what did you come up with?"

He laughed. "A woodworker." He waved his hand. "I know, I know, this must sound like it's coming out of left field, but I love working with my hands. I love the smell of wood when it's freshly sanded. I love making something useful and beautiful from a block of potential."

"Wow, woodworking," Hollis said, trying not to show her shock. "Have you ever made anything?"

George grinned. "For the past year or so, I've been giving my Saturdays to kids at our community center. It's a wood shop class. The teacher before me moved out of state, and I agreed to fill in until someone else could be found. But no one else ever stepped up. It was just three kids at first, but this session I have fifteen boys and girls enrolled." He stood and gestured with excitement. "They're great kids. They've made shelves and boxes and even small furniture pieces. I've had to offer another session."

"Wow, woodworking ..." Hollis said again, thinking it was time to come up with another word. "So, you're going to take up woodworking full time?"

He walked over and took the chair next to her. She could feel the intensity of his feeling. "But first, I plan to recommend the management committee consider you for a senior attorney position when I leave. You don't need a supervising attorney anymore."

Hollis blushed. "Thank you, George. That almost makes up for you leaving."

A broad smile appeared on his face. "I'm going to miss you, too, but I'll be learning my craft by apprenticing myself under this great woodworker in Marin County. Then I'm set to teach full time at the community center for a whopping eighteen dollars an hour."

"Wow ..." she started, then cut herself off and said, "I imagine your mother's estate will give you the ability to make your dream a reality."

"It sure will." He stood and picked up a sheet of paper from the top of his desk. "Here's my letter of resignation, effective in thirty days."

THAT EVENING IN HER KITCHEN, Hollis smiled over her dinner salad. The day had turned out pretty well, her blocked car aside. It was worth putting up with all the Allens in the world to see Phyllis's tearful smile and Tony's grin of gratitude. And then there was George's decision to leave Triple D to fulfill a life's dream. It had been a good day, but she was exhausted.

She reached for her phone at the ringtone.

"Hey, miss me yet?" John said.

She grinned. "Boy, do I ever. What time do you get in tomorrow?"

"Ah … would you mind if I took the first flight out Sunday morning? The team is wrapping up tomorrow and we thought we'd go out to dinner to celebrate."

"Say, who's on this team anyway? Are there any gorgeous girls?" she teased.

"I wouldn't know. I only have eyes for you."

Her breath caught. He had the uncanny knack of choosing words that made her fall in love with him all over again.

"Well, then in that case, I guess I'll see you Sunday morning," she murmured.

"Don't bother getting out of bed."

She clicked off her phone and leaned back in the chair. Anyone coming into the kitchen would wonder what kind of dinner salad could make her beam with such joy.

The ringtone went off again.

She grinned. "Let me guess, you don't want me to bother with pajamas."

"Er … Hollis, it's me, Stephanie."

She blinked. "Oh, Stephanie, I was just talking to John and … just forget it. Gee, this is a surprise." She glanced up at the clock.

"Can I come over? I need to talk to you."

"Of course you can. John is still out of town and we can have the house to ourselves."

"I'll be there in fifteen."

Hollis got out another wine glass. Her earlier feeling of fatigue was slipping away, and she looked forward to gabbing with her friend, even if Stephanie had made it sound urgent. She'd missed their late night talks.

The bell rang in twelve minutes. Hollis let her in and noticed she was wearing her coat over her pajamas. They exchanged hugs and sat on the sofa.

"Ah, is something the matter?" Hollis pointed to her pajamas as Stephanie took off her coat and draped it over a chair. She handed her a glass of wine.

Stephanie swallowed and sat back in her seat. "I cannot do this any longer. We need to talk about Dan." She gave Hollis a pleading look. "I miss you, you're my friend, and now, during the most important time in my life, I don't have you to share it with."

Hollis pressed her lips together, suddenly glum. "I avoided you because it seemed like you wanted distance, and I didn't want to put you in the awkward position of dating a guy who could have me arrested."

"And I didn't want you to treat me like a stranger and cut me off from what was really going on with you."

They looked at each other and broke into smiles.

"So, how are you and the handsome Detective Silva getting along?" Hollis tucked her legs underneath her.

"I'm afraid to tell you how good it is for fear of messing it up." Stephanie reached for the sofa throw and placed it around her shoulders. "He's wonderful and considerate and bright. He mentions work sometimes but we have an unspoken agreement not to talk about you."

"So, how are we going to handle this?" Hollis asked. "It's hard for me not to talk about what's going on."

Stephanie tapped her chin. "I miss our adventures, too. Say, wasn't there that time when somebody got shot … well, it's only a vague memory."

They both laughed, but Hollis remembered the terror and the guilt at seeing her friend in a hospital bed when the bullet was meant for her.

Hollis said, "Let's start with a happy ending." She spent the next half hour recounting the tale of the Allens and the likely reuniting of Tony and Phyllis. "I feel partly responsible for their rekindled relationship."

"What about George … do you think he will stay at Triple D?"

"No, I know he won't." Hollis frowned. "He told me he was resigning to pursue a life dream."

Stephanie yawned. "Can't fault him there. All I know is, if someone left me millions of dollars I don't think I'd come to work at the sheriff's lab the next morning. George is a nice guy and he has a great family. I'd say it was his turn for good luck."

Hollis agreed. The thought of losing another mentor who was also a friend made her sad, but she liked him too much to not wish him well.

"You're right."

Stephanie took a sip of wine. "So, tell me about this list."

"Silva told you about the Shur case?"

"Well, I don't think I would use the word, 'told.' I overheard a conversation he had with his partner day before yesterday, and by his muffled tone, I knew it had to be about you."

"Overheard?"

"Perhaps some might say eavesdropped, but I think that's such a value-laden word, don't you?"

"Absolutely." Hollis made a sympathetic face. "So, what did you hear?"

Stephanie put her glass down and her expression grew serious. "Hollis, that list is a big deal. Evidently your jail cell buddy was stupid enough to threaten a lot of people in high places with its exposure, trying to get her prison time reduced. Then I guess she realized her mistake and tried to get you to lobby for her, but it was too late. Somebody didn't want to risk that list getting in the hands of the police, and without any official protection, it was all over for her."

She nodded. "Yeah, that's what I figure, too."

"Wait, there's more. Olivia Shur and her list were pawns in a much bigger money-laundering sting. I don't know if it's the feds or local, but that list contains the names of undercover agents who can't let their names get out there."

Hollis groaned with realization. That explained the intensity of Silva and Lee's interviews. This was no ordinary criminal gang activity.

"It's starting to make more sense; I thought there might be more to the picture." Hollis let her voice drift. She was reluctant to bring up Olivia's warning not to go to the police at the risk of losing her friend's confidence and maybe even friendship. "I wonder if there's someone on the inside trying to get the list?"

As she raised her glass, Stephanie's hand froze in midair. "What are you getting at?"

"Olivia Shur left me a note telling me not to trust the police."

Spots of color appeared on Stephanie's cheeks. "That's no surprise. The woman was an ex-con; you can't trust her. She's hardly a judge of a cop doing his job."

Hollis was silent and took a taste from her glass.

Realizing her implication, Stephanie said, "Oh, I'm sorry; I didn't mean you, Hollis. It's just my mouth operating before my brain kicks in." She leaned over and patted her hand. "Forgive me?"

Hollis waved her hand in dismissal. "I assure you, I'm not that sensitive. But maybe you're closed to hearing what you don't want to."

Stephanie ran her fingers through her hair. "I have to admit, Dan's caught my attention ... and maybe my heart." She smiled. "He is so considerate and ... and affectionate. The other night I knew he was tired, but he saw I was too, and he offered to give me a foot massage. Can you imagine?"

No, I can't.

"Well, then I can see why he's a keeper," Hollis said.

Her friend smiled weakly and then grimaced. "You're serious, aren't you? You think Dan could be involved in ... in this thing?"

She shrugged. "With what you told me, I honestly don't know what to think. I feel like I'm a player in a game where I don't even know the other players, let alone the rules." She reached over and patted Stephanie's arm. "But I'm happy if you're happy."

Stephanie couldn't hide her Cheshire cat smile. "I am *so* happy." She put her glass on the table. "But it's time for me to go. I've got to get some sleep. I have a busy day tomorrow." She clasped Hollis's shoulders. "I didn't want another day to pass without us having a real conversation."

"Me, too," Hollis said, relieved.

They gathered her things and walked to the front door. Hollis opened it and Stephanie paused, looking up at the night sky and walked out.

Her brow wrinkled. "That's strange. That Solara was parked down the street when I pulled into your driveway. There was a man in it then, and there's a man in it now."

A tremor went through Hollis. "A black Solara?"

"That's the one," Stephanie said.

Hollis returned to the foyer. "I think he's been following me." She leaned against the wall, trying to make sense of it.

Stephanie stepped back into the house. "I'm not leaving you here alone. I'll stay the night."

"Oh, come on. I'm not afraid," Hollis protested.

Stephanie shut the door and put on the deadbolt. "Well, I am."

CHAPTER SIXTEEN

ORNING WAS A LONG TIME coming, and Hollis slept little. Every so often she'd look out the window to see if the car and the man were still there—and they were. She must have fallen asleep at some point, because when she woke, the sun was breaking light in the sky. Stephanie was folding her blankets from her night on the sofa, and the car was gone.

"He's gone." She smiled wanly. "I think I scared him away."

"He probably realized we spotted him," Hollis said. "Thanks for staying over. Want some coffee or tea?"

Stephanie shook her head. "Nah, I'll grab some when I get to the lab. I'm only going in for a short time."

Hollis wanted to ask if she were doing side work for Silva, but she didn't want to sully their reconciliation. "Yeah, I'm heading to the office for a couple of hours, too. When John's home, my time isn't always my own."

Stephanie chewed her bottom lip. "You've got to tell Dan about your buddy out there." She held up her hand. "Whatever you think he may or may not be, you could be in a lot of trouble if you don't let someone on the case know." She looked with concern at her friend. "I trust him, Hollis. I trust him with my life. He's not your dirty cop."

Hollis looked at her, then down at her hands. She sighed. "All right, all right, I'll give him a call."

"Good, now one last thing …. You can't stay here tonight. Stay with me."

She protested. "Absolutely not. John will be home in the morning and I want to be here when he arrives. I need to straighten the house and … and," she smiled, "do a lot of other stuff. So, no, I'm staying home." She patted Stephanie's arm. "I'll be fine."

Exasperated, Stephanie said, "One day you'll have to tell me about the other stuff. Okay, if you're going to stay here tonight then call me every couple of hours."

"No, I'm not going to keep calling you," Hollis insisted. "I'll call you once, when I'm heading to bed; that's it."

Stephanie heaved a deep sigh, and they exchanged heartfelt hugs.

EVEN ON SATURDAY, HOLLIS WASN'T alone at Triple D. At least two other attorneys were busily working at their desks. She paused, as she always tried to do, in front of the expanse of bay windows to breathe in the glory of San Francisco Bay and the three bridges strung like necklaces around its rim.

She had just sat down when her phone vibrated.

"Rena, what's wrong? You never call me this early, and on the weekend."

"Oh, Hollis," Rena said, "I need your help. My sister was coming with me to the cake tasting, but my niece was rushed to the hospital with appendicitis, and she can't make it."

She rolled her eyes. "You want me to taste wedding cakes?"

"Yes, and I need you to meet me this afternoon at four o'clock," Rena said. "I know I said if you agreed to be my matron of honor, I wouldn't ask anything else, but … but this is an emergency." Her voice rose. "And before you say anything, no there isn't anyone else I can ask."

Hollis sighed. "What's the address?"

SHE HAD JUST OPENED A file marked by Penny's warning note indicating it had a deadline coming up when her cellphone rang again. The view screen said Private Caller. She debated whether to pick up, but her curiosity won out.

"Thanks, Hollis." The noisy background might be a restaurant or bus station.

"Julie? I'm sorry, but I had to give them your name. That land lady spilled her guts to the police. She must have thought there was a reward in it for her." She smothered a laugh and tried to sound remorseful.

He was not amused.

"First, my name is Jule, pronounced like *jewel*. If you can't get your lips to form that word, then call me Berman."

Oops.

"Second, have you given more thought to where the list might be?" he prodded. "You could be in a lot of danger, and we don't have a lot of time to find it."

Hollis wasn't overly determined to keep her sharp tongue in check. "Well, 'Julie,' I don't know how many ways I can say this, but I don't have a clue where that list is. I can tell you this: I'm not sure I would tell you if I did."

She could feel the heat of his anger through the phone.

"So, you plan on making your own deal?"

She cast her glance heavenward. But before she could make a parting retort, another call showed on the office phone. She recognized the number.

"Sorry, I'd love to chat further, but I've got another call and I've got to run."

Ignoring his protests, she hung up.

"Hello, Detective, I see you work Saturdays, too. But how did you know to call me here?" She shook her head, trying to put Berman's call out of her mind.

"Ms. Morgan, I'm here with Detective Lee. The information you gave us regarding Jule Berman was incorrect. There is no Capital Consulting, and the number didn't work."

Silva had her on speaker phone. She could hear Lee click his pen off and on.

"We called in hopes that your memory had improved," he said.

"My memory is fine. Capital Consulting is the response I got when I called." She rubbed her eyebrows. "And this is a Saturday? Look, this day is already nuts, I was just on the phone with Berman," she said shaking her head. "And before you ask, he called me."

There was silence on the other end.

"What did he want?" Silva asked.

Hollis knew she was walking a thin line. Charges of withholding information didn't stack up when the information was the only leverage you had to stay alive. On the other hand, she realized she trusted Silva and Lee only slightly more than she did Jule Berman.

She licked her lips. "There's this list."

Silva said grimly. "I was wondering how long it would take you to bring up the list. Do you know where it is?"

She snapped. "You mean do I know where a copy is? The answer is no. Don't you already have a copy?"

Silva and Lee murmured, and Hollis started to feel uneasy.

"I'll meet you back at the station," Lee said to Silva, then, "Ms. Morgan, I have to leave but we'll talk again."

Silva could be heard giving instructions, and then he came back on the phone. "Ms. Morgan, it would be great if I could come to your office. I can be there in ten minutes. I won't be long, and then you can get on with your weekend."

"I don't see how I can say no," Hollis responded.

She went downstairs and waited in the lobby to let him into

the building. After courtesy hellos, they took the elevator up to the Triple D offices in silence.

Silva took out his phone and laid it on top of the conference table. "Any chance I could get a cup of coffee?"

"Sure, someone here must have started a pot." Hollis went down the hall to the lunch room and came back to set a steaming cup in front of him.

"Ms. Morgan, I know this is a tricky situation because we both share Stephanie Ross's friendship, but I sense for some reason you aren't telling me the complete truth. Stephanie told me she spent the other night with you because your place was being watched." His eyes narrowed. "I can't help you if you don't trust me with what's going on."

"That's not—"

He held up his hand. "Please, let's not play games. Time is running out. There are lives at stake, maybe even your own." He took a gulp of coffee. "We need to know who's on that list."

She frowned. "How do you know lives are at stake if you don't already know who's on the list? Besides, don't you already have at least one copy?"

She wished she could take back her words; it would do her little good if he thought she knew too much.

His eyes held hers. "Unfortunately we don't have a copy of the list. If we did, I assure you I wouldn't be wasting my time speaking with a civilian."

"That's not true. Didn't you take the list from Olivia Shur's car? She had it with her." As the words left her lips, she closed her eyes in disgust … *nerves.*

He put his phone and pen in his pocket and picked up his writing pad. "I think we need to finish our talk at the station."

THERE WAS ONLY ONE OTHER time that Hollis had entered a police station from the rear entrance. That was when she was arrested for insurance fraud, and her life had never been the same again. She felt herself retreating to survivor mode and she shuddered at the same time she straightened her back.

"There's a room over on the left," Silva said, pointing. "We'll talk in there."

She looked around the almost bare, windowless room and noticed the two cameras at the corners of the ceiling and the large opaque window that almost filled one wall. She took one of the four seats at the faux wood table.

"Coffee?"

"Could I have some tea?"

He shook his head. "I don't think we have any, but I'll go check."

"If you don't have tea, I'll take water."

At first she was surprised he'd left her on her own, but then realized it had been a smart move on his part. He wanted her to know she wasn't under arrest *yet,* and therefore they could have a friendly chat. But she also knew that Lee or someone like him was watching her through the glass. She wasn't going anywhere.

In a few minutes, Silva returned with cup in hand.

"Evidently there are several officers who drink tea here." He handed her the cup. "I'm sorry, I forgot to get sugar."

"No worries, I drink it plain. Thank you." She gave him a small smile.

He took the chair facing the door and placed his pad and pen in front. "Ms. Morgan, I know you don't want to spend any more time here than necessary, so if you answer my questions as straightforward and complete as you can, we can all get on with our day."

"What do you want to know?"

He folded his hands. "I want to know the first time you heard of the list, and if you've ever set eyes on it. I want to know about your relationship with Shur since she's been out of prison, and I want to know about this Jule Berman."

Hollis cast her eyes down. She knew her answers would not make Silva happy. Truth and lies tended to take on shades of gray in her life. Both served a purpose but in this instance her choices were narrowing.

"I first heard of the list from Olivia Shur. I told you I had received a note *mailed* to me from her. It specified a phone number, the one I gave you for Jule Berman, and said for me to contact him, so I did. Berman later told me Olivia wanted me to pave the way for her to … to essentially turn herself in with the list."

Keeping an eye on Silva, Hollis took a sip of her tea.

She continued, "They both said not to trust the police." Hollis wasn't ready to mention the warning of a police leak.

Silva tilted his head as if trying to hear her better, but didn't say anything.

"Berman went on to say that Olivia had made three copies of the list: one was with her when she was killed, one she mailed to herself, and one she had hidden." Hollis took a deep breath. "As I have repeatedly told you, after I walked out of prison I did not have any direct contact with Olivia Shur, who I knew only as Melanie Jones."

"Tell me about Berman."

"Look, I don't know him, really. He said he and Olivia were a couple and wanted to start a new life together with a clean slate."

"Had he seen the list?"

Hollis paused with a question in her eyes. "He said he hadn't, but he could have been lying. I got the feeling he's a good liar." She finished her tea. "There's one last question of yours I want to answer. I have never seen the list, I do not know who is on the list, and finally, I don't have a clue about what the list is about." She sat on the edge of her seat. "That's it, I'm done."

He pursed his lips in thought, gazing her way but seeing past her.

"Okay, Ms. Morgan, you're free to go. I'll have an officer drop you off at your office."

*

IT WAS ALL HOLLIS COULD do to sit upright behind the wheel of her car. She wanted nothing more than to go home and pull the bed covers over her head, but she had promised Rena to taste cake. She started to laugh at the craziness of life. Here she was off to taste cake and there was likely someone out there who wanted to kill her for what they thought she knew.

Patty Cake Bakery did business on a busy corner in Leimert Park on Park Boulevard in Oakland. Hollis couldn't believe her luck in finding metered parking only five blocks away. She scurried up the sidewalk crowded with people sitting at café tables and relaxing on benches.

"Oh, Hollis, you came." Rena waved from a small table situated near the front of the store and off to the side.

"Of course I came, I said I would." She weaved in and out of the few tables to give her friend a hug. She dumped her purse and jacket in a nearby chair. She tried to move Rena's bag from blocking the aisle. "Your wedding tote is overflowing. Is Mark in there, too?"

"Maybe." Rena laughed. "If I lost this purse, there would be no wedding. I'd have no idea where to show up. I put everything in here. It just keeps getting bigger. I can't throw anything away until we're on our honeymoon." She adjusted the bag to go under the table at her feet.

Hollis gave a sigh of resignation. "All right, so how does somebody taste wedding cakes?"

"It's so easy ... they're going to bring samples out on a tray, then we'll decide the best flavor. Mark doesn't care what I choose. He says he'll be too nervous to eat dessert." From the tote, Rena pulled out a notebook with two sheets of pink paper and handed one to Hollis. "I'm not a big cake fan either. That's why you're here. You are going to represent the guests."

"Okay, bring it on. We the people must be served." She picked up the fork and tapped it against the table.

Over the next hour they tasted four cakes, washed down with tea or coffee. After re-sampling twice more the final two,

Rena pointed to the sample with alternating layers of chocolate mousse and raspberry filling.

"Thank you so much, Hollis," Rena said. "I … I know this kind of thing isn't your … your specialty, but you came through and …."

Suddenly Hollis stopped listening. Rena's voice sounded like it was in a tunnel. A black Solara was parked right outside of the bakery, and a man inside was staring back at her. Her breathing grew more rapid.

"Is there a back exit out to the street?" Not waiting for Rena to answer, Hollis started to grab her things. "Listen to me, Rena. Don't look out the window, just listen. I'm being followed by … by I don't know who, but I've got to get out of here."

Rena wrinkled her brow but nodded, continuing to face Hollis. "Yes, I noticed an exit door next to the ladies' room. I'll cover you if he comes in." Rena squeezed Hollis's shoulders. "Please, be careful and don't go home. Meet me at our house in an hour, and stay with us tonight. John will be home in the morning."

Hollis smiled and half ran down the narrow corridor and out into what appeared to be the employee parking lot. She stopped and then frowned. What was wrong with this picture? She turned around and went back into the bakery. Rena, who had not left her chair, looked at her in astonishment and then worriedly.

"I thought you'd gone. What's the matter now? What did you see?" she called out.

Hollis held up her hand to silence her and put all her things on the table next to Rena. She walked out the front door, ignoring Rena's call to come back. Walking up to the car, she tapped the passenger side window. It rolled down.

"Why are you following me?"

The driver was older than she had thought. His salt and pepper hair was full and thick, framing a paunchy face that had disappearing lips. She couldn't tell the color of his eyes because he stared straight ahead.

Hollis wondered if he was going to answer. He sighed, pushing the latch to release the door lock. By this time Rena was standing in the doorway with the store owner a few feet behind her. She had her cellphone in her hand, waiting for a sign from Hollis.

"Get in. Tell your friend you're not going anywhere." He took another deep sigh. "I'm a cop." He reached in his shirt pocket and flipped up the small leather billfold holding his badge.

She could feel the adrenaline slowly receding from her veins. She took a deep breath and gave an okay signal to Rena, holding up three fingers. Rena gave her a reproving look but went back into the bakery and took a window seat to keep an eye on her.

Hollis sat in the passenger seat but left the door open over the curb. "This must be a new type of unmarked car. Silva must be pretty distrusting of me."

He snorted. "Dan Silva didn't send me to follow you. You have Faber to thank for that."

John.

By the time Hollis got the full story from off-duty Officer Weir, she was balancing extreme anger with extreme relief and extreme irritation. All these extremes left her drained.

"John!" Rena exclaimed. "Are you kidding me?"

They'd left the bakery and driven to a wine bar not far away, with Officer Weir following. He wouldn't give up his assignment until released by John Faber.

"No, I'm not kidding." Hollis sipped her Malbec. "Looking back over our conversations this past week, I wondered why John didn't press me for what I was doing while he was gone. He was far too relaxed. I should have known he'd come up with his own surveillance solution."

Rena grinned. "I know you don't want to hear this, but it was a very loving thing to do." She twisted the stem of her glass. "Although I'll have to rap him upside the head with my knuckles when I see him. I was scared out of my wits when you went out the back way. What made you turn around?"

"I was looking for a way out to the street, and then it hit me: Weir wasn't trying to hide the fact he was following me. He didn't mind if I knew. If it was the bad guys, they would be trying to intimidate me or hassle me, and they certainly wouldn't allow me access to their license plates or the ability to identify them. Once I ruled out the bad guys, that left the good guys. I thought Silva might be tracking my movements and wanting to shake off the bad guys at the same time."

"Why would …" Rena began, then raised her head. "Oh, I get it; they'd see you were being followed."

Hollis ran her hands through her hair. "But I only had that thought for a minute, because no police or sheriff's department has the budget for a twenty-four hour protection tail." She smiled. "And, that's when I thought of John."

CHAPTER SEVENTEEN

HOLLIS HEARD THE KEY IN the lock. She had positioned herself on the sofa reading a novel from the Fallen Angels' monthly book selection. John, looking handsome and a bit windblown, put his luggage at the foot of the stairs and bent down to give Hollis a long, warm kiss. They looked each other in the eye, and he sat in the chair across from her. She put the book down.

He ran his hand through his hair. "Go ahead, let's hear it. Weir left a message for me last night."

She took a breath and closed her eyes then opened them with a wry smile. "I want you to know I've given this some thought." She tucked her legs underneath her. "While I admit at first I couldn't see straight I was so angry with you, when I calmed down I realized you had good, if misguided intentions."

"Sweetheart, I—"

She held fingers to her lips. "I hate being afraid. I can't take living with fear and be prepared for me to push back. My mind was doing circles trying to figure out why I was being followed. Stephanie stayed over one night because we didn't know about

Weir." She crossed her arms over her chest. "I'm really irritated with you."

He came over to sit next to her. "Be irritated. I knew you'd eventually find out, but I needed peace of mind and I didn't like leaving you here with some crazed person out there. I found out Weir wanted to earn extra cash while he was off on forced vacation. He was going to start losing hours. He doesn't have any family, and he was happy to do it." He took her chin in his hand. "I'd do it again. I love you too much."

They reached a truce. Hollis was the first to admit absence does make the heart grow fonder, or at least forgive more easily. They made love, read the Sunday paper, and John talked about his team week and training.

He played with one of her thick curls. "I'll be home for a while. Hopefully this whole Olivia Shur thing will be over soon."

Hollis swallowed and decided it was her turn to disclose her activities of the past week. As she anticipated, John was not happy. He pulled back and got up to slip on a pair of workout pants. He sat on the edge of the bed.

"Okay, start over and tell me again."

Hollis pulled on a sweatshirt, and for a second time, went through her visit to Olivia's condo, her contact with Jule Berman, and Silva's "friendly" interrogation. She took a deep breath and concluded, "The police are acting as if they don't have a copy of the list."

He reached over and held her hand. "Tell me the truth: do you know anything about this list?"

"No, John, I—"

"Look, I believe you. Now tell me what you *think* might be going on."

"Tell you what, I'm hungry. Let's fix breakfast and I'll give you my opinion."

They worked well together in the kitchen and in only a few minutes were sitting down to eggs, bacon, sliced strawberries, and toast. Hollis waited until they were both sitting back in their chairs with full stomachs, and she hoped a sympathetic ear.

"Let's suppose Berman is telling the truth, and that's a big suppose," she said. "There is a list that includes money laundering's 'most-wanteds,' who are desperate to keep their identities hidden. And suppose that on this list there are law enforcement officers whose lives would be worth nothing if it gets out."

John tapped the table with his finger. "You said there are three copies?"

"Yeah, if Berman isn't lying, but about this I'm inclined to believe him. However, here is where my thinking breaks down. I believed the killer or Silva retrieved the copy Olivia was bringing to me when she was killed, or the copy that she had mailed to herself and the police must have picked up when they entered her residence, but today, after talking with him I … don't know. Maybe the police don't have two copies of the list, unless Silva—"

"And the third copy?"

"Olivia supposedly hid it. I think Berman believes I have it," she said. "But I don't have a clue about the list or where it is. Not a clue," she repeated when John opened his mouth to speak.

"All right, so, what's your next step?"

She sighed. "I don't know. According to Silva, Berman has disappeared. He was my only link to Olivia. Now, I guess I'll just have to wait and see. If I'm lucky it will all just go away."

CHAPTER EIGHTEEN

IN THE OFFICE, HOLLIS GOT off to a good start. The stack of files on her desk decreased appreciably even though George had put a couple of new cases in her work tray. He was clearly cleaning out his office. The conference room was full of senior partners and the management committee, and she knew they were discussing George's imminent departure.

Penny dropped off several court files for signature but seemed too preoccupied to engage in anything but the briefest responses. When noon came, she passed by to see if Hollis wanted her to bring back a sandwich, and Hollis ordered tuna on wheat.

She added, "If they don't have tuna, give me a call" and turned back to work.

A few minutes later her cellphone rang and Hollis smiled in acknowledgement. It was getting harder and harder to find tuna sandwiches better than Maud's.

"Hi, Hollis."

She froze. Her heart tap-danced.

"Jule," she whispered.

"Yes, it is I." His voice was low, as if he didn't want anyone else to hear.

"The police are looking for you. What do you want?"

"Why, Hollis, I think you know what I want. I want the list." His voice seemed to gather menace as he spoke.

"I … I … told you, I don't know where it is." She got up and with the phone in her ear, raced down the hallway to George's office, but he was out. She came back to her office and riffled through her top drawer.

Where had she put the recorder?

She slammed the drawer shut, took out a pad of paper, and started writing.

"I know you are talking to the police, and by now you realize how I know. I don't think you understand how serious things are." The chair he was sitting in squeaked. "You have twenty-four hours."

He clicked off.

Hollis closed her eyes and leaned back in her chair. What did he mean that she had realized how he knew about her talking with the police? But once the thought came to her mind, so did the answer—he was working with a cop on the inside.

But who?

The rest of the day her nerves were tense as she waited for the other shoe to drop. But nothing happened. George didn't return to the office and when Hollis had cleared her desk of all but work requiring extra time or research, she left for home. Now that she knew Weir had been acting as her bodyguard and not her abductor, she missed seeing the black Solara.

JOHN WAS HOME WHEN SHE got there. Their conversation was superficial; she could tell he was still winding down from his day. It was only after they had put away the dinner dishes that Hollis brought up the call from Jule Berman.

Silently, he led her to the sofa and sat next to her. "First thing in the morning, call Silva." He held up his hand. "Think about it: Silva is from the sheriff's department. It's not likely he has the connections he would need with the San Lucian Police to monitor criminal activities."

"Okay, that does make sense. I'll … I'll call him, but—"

John shook his head. "No buts. Do you have anything Berman touched?"

Hollis's brow furrowed in thought. "No, I don't know if he did it on purpose, but I can't remember him touching anything at all."

John smirked. "You bet he did it on purpose, and another thing you can bet on: Jule Berman is not his real name."

CHAPTER NINETEEN

———❧———

EVEN THOUGH HOLLIS ARRIVED AT the office early, she found Silva and Lee waiting for her in the entrance to Triple D's lobby.

Lee smiled apologetically. "Ms. Morgan, we need you to come down to the station and work with a forensic artist. We need to know just what this guy Berman looks like because he's gone underground. It won't take long since you're familiar with him."

"I was going to call you," she said. "He contacted me again late yesterday—"

"Let me see your phone." Silva demanded, his hand outstretched.

Hollis handed over her phone. "The call came from a phone booth in the Tenderloin district."

"This must be Faber's work," Silva said, and his scrolling stopped. "Is this the number?"

She nodded. John had called in a favor and had the call traced. When he heard back early that morning from his contact that the call had originated from San Francisco's notorious skid row, he doubted there would be any viable prints.

She held out her hand and Silva returned the phone.

"Like I said, I was going to call you as soon as I got to my office." Hollis directed them into a conference room, where they appeared to have no interest in sitting. "Before you start with the not so subtle threats about my interference with police business, I tried to record Berman's call but I didn't have the technology handy. Fortunately he didn't talk long and I was able to copy what he said."

Lee peered at her. "Can you give us the highlights?"

"Other than the 'twenty-four hour or else' deadline, he hinted he was getting information about my movements from someone on the San Lucian Police Force and that I wouldn't be able to hide from him."

Silva and Lee exchanged looks. Neither seemed surprised by her revelation.

Silva sighed. "Ms. Morgan, I'm not going to address the possibility of an internal mole at the department, but I can understand why you might hesitate to come to the station. How about we get our artist to come here to take your description?" he said. "Now, tell us about Berman's threat."

"I have twenty-four hours to come up with the list or tell him where it is."

"Or what?"

Hollis shrugged. "I don't know. He hung up after that, and that was around four o'clock." The implications of her own words had sunk in. She frowned.

Silva noticed her expression. "I think it's time we went on the offensive. We don't have enough to put a tap on your work phone. I'll have the artist contact you directly, but we'd appreciate it you could schedule him sooner rather than later. This morning would be best." As they headed for the elevator, he glanced at the time on his phone. "I'll ask for a patrol car to see you home, but it may be a good idea for you to avoid being alone until this thing is over."

She accepted his pronouncement. Jule Berman didn't

frighten her personally; he was a bully. But she had a bad feeling about him. He was a desperate man, and for that reason unpredictable and therefore, dangerous.

SHE HAD ONLY BEEN BACK at her office a few minutes when she took a call from Kevin Nelson, the forensic artist, to arrange for his arrival within the hour. She went to brief George.

After he heard her story, he squinted in concern. "I've been so preoccupied with my own problem, I didn't realize what you might be going through."

"I'm good. I just wanted to let you know a police artist will be here soon."

George looked skeptical. "You don't fool me; I can tell you're anxious. What does John say about this?"

She told him about the bodyguard. "He's wary. He'd like nothing more than for me to completely back off."

"And you can't because …."

Tiffany poked her head in the door. "Hollis, your visitor is here."

Hollis gave George a sheepish look and walked into the lobby.

Jule Berman's face came easily to her and Kevin was good at his job, capturing not only his physical features but the character of the man as well. After an hour, the grim face in pen and ink looked back at her, and she motioned to Kevin it was done.

The rest of the day moved slowly. Hollis was going to take a walk to Chinatown but she remembered Silva's cautionary words. She called Rena instead.

"I'm so glad you called," Rena gushed.

"Please don't ask me to taste any more cake."

She laughed. "Very funny. Seriously, we're starting to receive gifts in the mail and I could use your organizational skills to set up a chart or a spreadsheet to track who is giving us what."

Hollis smiled with relief. "Okay, I can do that."

"Just imagine," Rena giggled, "in three weeks Mark and I will be married and on our way to the Bahamas." She took a breath. "There's no rush right now. You can wait until I get more gifts; I'll let you know. Say, why did you call?"

"Just checking in," she said.

Rena paused. "Are you okay? It's not like you to call and just check in."

"Yeah, I guess it's rare," she admitted. "I just had a little breathing space and wanted to make sure you didn't need anything."

Rena couldn't disguise the concern in her voice but said, "Gee, if you just take care of logging in the gifts,that will be great."

Four o'clock came and went. About five thirty her desk phone rang. She jumped.

"Hollis, do you have the list?" Berman demanded.

She scrambled to find the words that would buy her time. Time against what, she didn't know.

"Jule, I keep trying to tell you, I don't have the list. I don't—"

He clicked off.

Her heart thudded loudly, reflecting her growing dread. She called Silva, who said the call had been too quick to trace. There was nothing left for her to do so she nervously left her office for home. She caught a black and white in her rearview and it calmed her. It pulled off as she unlocked her front door.

JOHN WAS LATE, WHICH WAS fine with her. The possibilities of what Berman might do circulated through her head. She ordered pizza and kept it warm in the oven until dinner. When John arrived she was on the deck, thinking and staring out into the darkness.

He caught her eye. "What's wrong?" he asked.

"What's wrong? No kiss, no hello darling, no I'm glad to be home," she chided.

John came over, kissed her lips, and sat down next to her.

"It's in your face, you look … troubled. Now, what's wrong?"

"It's Berman. I have this feeling in my gut—he's planning something." She sat up in her chair. "He called like he said he would, and I told him I didn't have the list and he hung up on me."

"Did you tell Silva?"

"Yes, but they weren't able to trace it. He was too quick."

John held her shoulders. "There is nothing you can do now; the ball is in Berman's court and the police have him in their sights."

"How can you say that? They don't even have his real name. I sat down with the artist today, and he said none of the other witnesses who knew Olivia recognized the name. That's why they needed a picture from me."

The implications of what she had just said out loud hit her like a brick.

She was the only one who could identify Berman as Berman.

She could see in John's face he realized it too.

That evening he was very attentive to her. She knew it was because he didn't want to verbalize his concern and his own deepening worry.

CHAPTER TWENTY

———

JOHN, HIS HAND ON THE door knob, leaned over to kiss her.
"Listen, I want you to promise, if you hear anything from
this nut, you'll contact me immediately. I'll keep my phone on."

He looked across the street. "I see your shadow is here as
promised. Now remember what we talked about."

The unmarked car stood out on a street with no other cars.
Hollis smiled. She didn't mind. At least Silva had kept his
commitment.

"Don't worry, I will," she said, urging him out the door.
"Now, go. I've got to get to work. George is briefing me on all
his cases over the next couple of weeks, and we start today."

She hurried out the door a few minutes behind him and
waved to the young officer who had pulled babysitting duty.
He gave her a tentative wave back.

In the office, she halted in her doorway. There was a cane
lying across her chair—a maroon cane.

Tony's cane.

Hollis caught her breath and looked down the empty
hallway. How did he get in her office? She picked up the cane,
stood it in the corner, and put her things on the desk. Then she

picked up the cane and walked out to the lobby.

"Tiffany, did you see anyone bring this cane in?"

Tiffany finished swallowing a bite of bagel. "Um-hm, a messenger was here early this morning and left it with the guard downstairs. He said your client left it at the police station yesterday, and you would know what to do to find the owner."

Feeling the blood leave her face, Hollis murmured, "Yes, I think I know how to get in touch with the owner."

She half ran back to her office, kicking the door shut with her foot while she punched in a number. She waited impatiently until she reached the person she wanted.

"Ritz, this is Hollis, Hollis Morgan. Remember me? We met through Tony."

"Sure, sure, I remember. How can I help you?" he said. "If you're looking for Tony, he's late. He said he would be here to go over my taxes an hour ago, but he must have gotten caught up with something else. You know he's been with his new *friend* almost every day." He chuckled.

"When was the last time you spoke with him?"

Ritz hesitated. "Why, what's the matter?"

"When, Ritz?" she persisted.

"Last night around eight," he said. "I drove him home from the BART station and made sure he got in okay." His voice turned stern. "Now you talk to me. What's going on with Tony?"

Hollis's mind ran through a number of scenarios. None were good. "This morning I came in my office and his cane was on my chair."

Ritz was silent. Hollis pictured him running his hand through his dark hair.

"He wouldn't go anywhere without his cane," He mused. "He can't walk right without it." His voice lowered. "Are you sure he's not there? Of course he's not. It's a threat, isn't it?"

Hollis was surprised at his quick grasp of the situation. "Can you go home and see if Tony is at his condo? I'll meet you there." She swallowed. "Before I do anything else I need to know if he's at home. I realize it's a long shot, and if you can't leave the café, I can go by myself."

"No, you can't. I've got the key to the building and I'll meet you there." He gave her the address.

Hollis made the trip to Berkeley in almost half the time it would have taken a person who was paying attention to traffic rules. When she got there, Ritz was walking down the steps leading from the building. When he saw her standing next to her car, he shook his head.

"He's not here."

She was silent. Dismay had tied her stomach in knots.

"You know where he is, don't you?" Ritz's tone was almost accusatory.

Hollis rubbed her forehead with her fingers. "No, I don't know where he is, but I think I know who he's with."

She didn't want to give Ritz any more information than he could handle, nor did she want to explain. She got back in her car.

"Where are you going now?" he asked through her open car window, surprised at her abrupt departure. "Hollis, Tony isn't well, and … and he's all I've got. He's my family."

"I know." She saw the concern in his eyes. "Go back to the café and I promise you I'll call and let you know what's going on … soon. Trust me, I'm sure Tony is all right." She tried to sound positive. "I've got to make a couple of calls."

"Who are you calling?"

"The police."

HOLLIS SAT IN HER CAR and watched Ritz leave. She punched in John's number and explained what had happened. John was unnerved. He concurred with her decision and urged her to go straight to the station and meet with Silva and Lee.

"I know you're worried sick about the old guy, but the best people to track him down are the police. They deal with threats like this all the time. Call me when you get back to your office. Or, do you want me to call?"

"No, I can do it."

Hollis closed her eyes and leaned back in the driver's seat. Tony was no pushover even without his cane, so for him to be … Here she stumbled on the thought, because just thinking of Tony being kidnapped sent a simultaneous chill of fear and rush of rage into her chest.

Her phone vibrated. She didn't recognize the number but her throat constricted. She hit answer.

"I want that list," Berman hissed.

"I *swear* to you I don't have it," she insisted.

"You're lying. Olivia said she had hidden it where you could find it."

Hollis was startled. "You never told me that before, but I still have no idea where it is." She paused. "Is … is Tony Grueber there with you?"

"As a matter of fact he is. He's not very happy but he's comfortable," Berman said.

"Can I talk to him?"

There were shuffling sounds.

"Hollis," Tony blurted out, "don't worry about me, this bastard—"

Berman snatched the phone. "Can't talk long. You go to the police, he's dead, and I'll know if you do." His voice turned harsher. "I'll give you another twenty-four hours to give me the list, or you'll force my hand to hurt your friend."

He clicked off.

Tears slowly trickled down her cheeks. She debated calling John again then decided against it. He would still want her to go on to the station, and she wasn't ready to do that. She wasn't ready to risk Tony's life.

She punched in the number for Silva, then disconnected. She didn't know if his calls were monitored, or for that matter, her own. Glancing at the time she punched another number.

"It's me, talk." Stephanie's voice was muffled.

Hollis could picture her dissecting tissue with the phone propped up against her ear and shoulder. "Stephanie, I need a favor. I need to speak with Dan Silva, but not at the station."

"Hollis, what's the matter? You sound terrible."

"I really can't tell you now. But please call Dan and have him meet me at … at the Oakland Museum at the city's historical exhibit in an hour. Tell him not to tell anyone, not even Detective Lee."

One of the reasons Hollis truly appreciated her friendship with Stephanie was that she took her at face value. Clearly she wanted to know what was going on, but she read correctly the urgency in her friend's request.

"I'm hanging up now to give him the call."

She sighed with relief. "Thank you."

Pulling out from Tony's condo, Hollis took a deep breath and drove with a lot more caution than she had on the way there. She did not want to be held up with a traffic ticket. She got to the museum early, parked three blocks away, near Lake Merritt Park, and then rushed through two side streets before approaching the museum's rear entrance. At midday there was no one in line and she flashed her museum pass to the clerk.

The city's history exhibit was a permanent display at the rear of the museum. It was one of Hollis's favorites. She liked looking at the old photographs and memorabilia. Glass cases displayed Indian artifacts as well as remnants from the 1906 San Francisco quake. She took the bench situated in the middle of the moderate-sized room. She looked around; she was alone.

She wanted time to think. Berman's kidnapping of Tony told her several things: he was desperate, he really thought Hollis had the list, and he'd been following her.

And he would have to incapacitate Tony.

She couldn't bring herself to imagine anything more specific. She had to find that list, and to do that she needed Silva. But more importantly, she needed to trust him. She was betting on her intuition that Silva was who he said he was. She heard a faint footfall and turned to the source.

Dan came straight to her and sat down.

"What's happened, Ms. Morgan?"

"Berman has kidnapped an elderly friend of mine, Tony Grueber. He's the attorney for one of my clients whose estate I'm processing." She swallowed. "Berman gave me another twenty-four hours to get him the list or else he would start hurting Tony."

Silva frowned. "How did he contact you?"

"By cellphone, but I don't think we were on the phone long enough for a trace." She moistened her lips. "Detective, Tony isn't well. He's got high blood pressure and a heart condition, and he walks with a cane." She fought to keep her voice steady. "Berman left Tony's cane on my work chair, to show he could get access to me. Tony can't walk without his cane."

Silva held her gaze and squeezed her shoulder. "We're going to find him … alive. Let's focus on what we can do. Worrying is just a waste of energy."

Hollis took a quick swipe at her eyes with the back of her hand. "He implied he's getting regular reports on what's going on with the Shur case from inside the department. That's why I asked you to meet here; he threatened to kill Tony if I went to the police." She looked at Silva for a reaction.

"I thought that was it." Silva stared straight ahead in thought. "You put your trust in the right place. Let me check into it." He turned to Hollis. "I won't put you or your friend at risk. I'll be working on this solo." He took out his notepad. "Give me Grueber's address—Berman, or whatever his real name is, may have left behind some clues."

After he left, Hollis sat for a few minutes more. She hated being on the defensive, and she was slowly coming up with her own plan. She was going to do something about either finding the list or finding Berman.

*

Hollis returned to Triple D to find George cleaning out his files. She gave him a slight smile when she took a seat in his office.

"Don't try to look despondent, George Ravel," she teased. "We all know you're happy as hell and can't wait to get on with your new chapter."

He laughed. "Not true. It's a double-edged sword. I will miss Triple D and … I will miss you. With you around, the job was never boring."

She looked down at her hands for a long moment. "Well, you're not gone yet, and I could use your advice."

He stopped and placed the file he was holding on top of the cabinet. "I'm listening."

Hollis told him about the circumstances leading up to Tony's disappearance. George frowned and didn't take his eyes off her.

"You know Detective Silva will have to bring in the FBI."

She closed her eyes and nodded. "It can't be helped. I wouldn't play with Tony's life, so believe me, I hope I did the right thing by going to the police." She stood and walked over to look out his window at the bay.

"You said you could use my advice. What about?"

"I want to hire a private detective." She ignored his look of stunned surprise. "I can't move around. I'm likely being followed by Berman's spy and pretty quickly the FBI will be all over the place. I need someone who will tell me what's going on."

George walked over to stand next to her. "Are you crazy? You can't start your own investigation. I know you like to think you are smarter than the rest of us, but this would be stupid." He put his hand on her shoulder. "Hollis, I don't know Tony Grueber like you do, but this is no time to play cowgirl."

She sighed. "I can't, and I won't just sit back. Tony is there because of me." She moved around the room. "Okay, maybe a PI is a bad idea. Maybe I'm too close to all this and can't see the forest for the trees, but George … Berman has dumped the onus of finding the list on me."

The last came out just shy of a wail.

George turned his mouth down and sat back at his desk. "I understand what you must be thinking, but dump the PI idea. Give the authorities at least a couple of days to figure things out." His brow furrowed. "How is Phyllis handling the news?"

Phyllis.

Hollis moved to the door. "George, I've got to tell Phyllis."

HOLLIS SAT PATIENTLY, WAITING FOR the elderly woman to turn and continue their conversation. Over the phone, Phyllis had insisted on seeing her, but now, clearly frustrated at not hearing from Tony, she was distracted and had paid her visitor little attention since her arrival. Phyllis, dressed in a cobalt-blue velour jogging suit that highlighted her sky-blue eyes, looked quite beautiful. Then Hollis realized with sadness that Phyllis had dressed to be courted.

She cleared her throat and gave a little cough. It caught Phyllis's attention.

"I don't understand. He's usually diligent about appointments and things like that," Phyllis mused.

"Like I said, I did hear from Tony. He's … he sounded fine," Hollis said. "Now, how are *you*? I wanted to come by and see how's it going since you've been back home."

It appeared as if Phyllis was only half listening, but she seemed to accept her words without comment.

Hollis had started to ask about the financial arrangements at the home when Phyllis held up her hand.

"I've been sitting here for almost fifteen minutes, waiting to see how long it would take you to tell me the truth. I'm really too old to waste time being lied to."

Hollis felt blood rush to her face. "I didn't mean …." She couldn't finish.

Phyllis smiled sadly. "Of course you didn't, but I'm not a

child. I'm seventy-eight years old. Tell me what's going on."

Hollis took a breath. "We think Tony's been ... been kidnapped."

Phyllis closed her eyes and leaned back in the lounger. When she opened them again, they were clear and focused. "Go ahead, I'm listening."

Hollis described the circumstances leading to Tony's disappearance, and what little she knew of Olivia Shur's list. Phyllis reached into the side pocket of the lounger, pulled out a pad and pen and began taking notes. Periodically she would interject a question, or ask Hollis to clarify a point.

When she finished, Phyllis was silent. She rocked slowly in her lounger, wearing a brave smile that didn't come close to hiding the worry and pain in her eyes. Then she tilted her chair forward and went into the kitchen, where she reached into the back of a drawer and pulled out a notebook, which she tossed into the chair.

She stood by the stove top. "I'm making myself a cup of jasmine tea. Can I interest you in a cup?"

Without waiting for Hollis's response, she proceeded to put out two mugs.

"Did Tony tell you about us?" she asked.

Hollis cleared her throat and replied, "He said you two were once married." She didn't think it necessary to mention she also knew of his infidelity that led to their divorce.

"Once married ... yes, we were once married." Phyllis looked past her and then suddenly turned her blue eyes unflinchingly on Hollis. "Do you think he's dead?"

"Dead?" Hollis, caught off guard with the blunt question, jerked up and spilt drops of tea on her lap. "No, of course not. When I spoke with him, he sounded fine. I mean ...." She dabbed at the dampness with a napkin.

"Berman will have to kill him, won't he?" Phyllis looked out the window. "Tony can recognize him; he could put him in prison."

Again, Hollis did a mental tap dance. Phyllis was a lot like Tony; she could not be fooled or fooled with. "No ... no, I won't let that happen. After I leave here, I'm working on an idea that will get Tony back safely." She leaned over and took Phyllis's hand.

"Then go now." Phyllis's erect posture reflected her renewed determination. "But first, I want to help. Give me something to do. I know you think I'm just an old lady with a revolving door memory, but I still know a lot. Did Tony tell you I used to be a prosecutor? I retired as a deputy DA for Russell County."

"No, he didn't." Hollis sat back on the sofa, not even trying to hide the surprise on her face. "I can see why you and Tony are so close—he for the defense and you for the prosecution."

Phyllis smiled generously. "Yes, we were good together." Then a cloud came over her face. "Young people don't realize the advantage of forgiving and forgetting."

Then she fell silent again, perhaps remembering.

Hollis started to gather her things, but Phyllis held up her hand.

"Not so fast, young lady, I need an assignment. If I sit here brooding I *will* have a heart attack, and I'm sure you don't want me on your conscience as well. Besides, I think I can help."

Hollis gave her a tentative smile. "Oh, you are good. Nice touch of guilt. You must have been a great prosecutor."

"I was the best," Phyllis said grimly.

She lifted the notebook and pulled up the lining; it held a thin black booklet.

"I can help you." She lifted the pages for Hollis to see. "You're going to need to get everything you can on Jule Berman. Additionally, we need to know how Melanie Jones became Olivia Shur. By now, the police will have her public records, and the FBI will have that and more. But," she patted the booklet, "but what they don't have is my black book."

"What's in your black book?"

"Names of people who know how to solve problems," Phyllis

replied with pride. "I loved my profession dearly, but so many times our hands were tied by procedure, and we lost too much time. This book is a short cut; it will save us a lot of effort. People still owe me. I plan on finding out everything I can about Mr. Berman and Ms. Shur and that damn list. Once we know where she's been, we'll have a pretty good idea who this Berman really is and where he could be now."

"That's what I was thinking," Hollis said. "Once we know who Berman is, we'll have a good chance of knowing where he may be holding Tony and maybe we can get our hands on the list."

Color had returned to Phyllis's cheeks, and she had started to flip through the pages. "You need to do some homework. Surely you still have prison contacts or someone who can dig up background on Berman? I'll bet you'll discover this isn't the first time he's used this alias. Also, prepare a timeline chart of every step and contact you can recall that Shur made. Don't worry about the gaps."

"I have a friend who—"

"Good. We'll get together at—" she looked at her watch, ."At seven o'clock to compare notes. Now, you need to get going."

Hollis was dumbstruck. Phyllis had transformed herself into a focused dynamo. After they said goodbye, Hollis sat in her car, reflecting on what had just happened. One thing she knew for sure … she would never underestimate seniors again. She glanced at the time.

It was almost three o'clock.

There was only one person she knew who could distill information and uncover secrets about anybody. She hoped Gene was back in town.

ON THE PHONE, HOLLIS HAD to promise John she would disclose everything when she got home. She was secretly gratified to hear he would be later than she.

"It's a case I can't really get into now, but we can exchange our day's events tonight," he said. "You're not getting into trouble, are you?"

Hollis tried to sound contrite. His work involvement took the heat off her, but she could tell he sensed she was up to something.

"John, I promise I'm not interfering in police business." She held back the *not yet*.

He grumbled a skeptical goodbye.

Gene arrived at her office minutes later. They sat in the conference room, where Hollis had set up a laptop, phone, and pads of paper with pens.

"I brought the link and password to connect to the newspaper's archives," he said. Removing his navy cashmere sports coat, he laid it tenderly on the back of a chair. Noting Hollis's smile, he said, "Look, Ms. Morgan, I know your fashion sense is not well-honed—although I do admit it is better than it was—but this coat cost me a few hundred dollars, and … well, one must handle cashmere with care."

Hollis was able to respond with good humor, "I defer to those with the greater sensitivity in the style area." She gave him a little bow.

Gene saw through her false gaiety. "We're going to get your friend back, Hollis. I don't know Tony Grueber, but from what you've told me, I'd like him." Gene took out a pair of glasses and opened up the laptop. "I despise people who hurt the defenseless."

They worked in silence for almost an hour, Hollis preparing the timeline according to Phyllis's specifications. It wasn't very long, but she added her own questions and comments, which referenced a separate note page. After she finished, she looked over her compilation with a frown. There was a parallel contact between her meeting with Berman for the first time and Olivia's encounter with Rena. Had Berman lied about having a copy of the list?

"Hollis, I think I found something on Berman," Gene said.

"The paper has a copy of the police drawing you gave to the artist. I sent that out to a few friends who deal with banking as a hobby—"

"How can banking be a hobby?"

Gene gave her a "please let me finish" look that caused her to run two fingers across her lips in a zipping motion.

"I got two replies," he continued. "One guy is marginally reliable; I knew his brother when I was on the inside. He was up for counterfeiting. The second guy probably knows what he's talking about, but he and I have never trusted each other, and he doesn't know how to spell the word 'integrity.' He only does things for money or information, which in his case is the same thing." He took off his glasses. "And to answer your question, banking is a hobby when you use it for its laundering opportunities."

She listened and took notes.

"What's your friend's name?" she asked.

"Leo Green. I'm pretty sure it's not his real one. He likes the name because it's the color of money."

She rolled her eyes. "Okay, if you think he can help us locate Berman or the list, contact him and find out his price. And Gene, we need to hurry."

Hollis got in her car to head back to her follow-up meeting with Phyllis. She'd put the key in the ignition when she noticed a small folded paper tucked under her windshield wiper. Her heart skipped a beat. She looked around the parking lot, but if someone was watching her, it had to be from a distance. She could see the security guard in his box near the exit, but his back was to her. She reached around and snatched the note.

It was from Silva.

Been to friend's home. I know how he left. Idea about other issue. Contact if need, use mutual. Holding off with other agency.

She leaned back in her seat. So Berman had followed her to Tony's home and snatched him from there. She realized Silva held off with the FBI because it hadn't been forty-eight hours yet. Once they were involved, things would ramp up in complexity, fast. She wished she knew what idea he had about the department leak. At least John couldn't say she wasn't working with the police.

She pulled into traffic.

PHYLLIS OPENED THE DOOR BEFORE Hollis knocked. "Any word?" she asked, her face drawn.

Hollis shook her head. "Nothing yet. But I think we're getting closer." She hoped she sounded more optimistic than she felt.

Someone as sharp as Phyllis would surely see through her. She couldn't miss the ever so slight glistening in the elderly woman's eyes.

"Well, let's get to work." Phyllis put on her glasses and her former persona. "Have you got that timeline?"

Hollis put it in her outstretched hand. "I have other news, too, that you may find even more interesting."

"Yes?"

"A colleague of mine was able to locate an individual who … who may be acquainted with Berman, under the man's real name."

Phyllis took off her glasses and squinted at Hollis. "So, in consideration of our limited time, if I translate what you're saying, one of your ex-con friends probably used his illegal connections to locate another felon who is in cahoots with or knows Berman."

Hollis smiled. "Yes, that would be correct."

"And what does he want?"

Hollis was taken back. "How did you … how—"

"You're a very smart lady, Ms. Morgan, but you don't have a monopoly on intelligence. I may appear feeble now, but I worked thirty years in the DA's office, and I picked up one or two grams of experience. Now, what's his name and what does he want?"

Hollis decided she loved this woman. She was a lady after her own heart.

"Leo Green, and he wants immunity for a felony he's under investigation for."

Phyllis tapped her pen against her cheek and reached for her black book, sitting on the coffee table. She squinted as she ran her fingers down the page, then smiled.

"Hand me the phone, please." Phyllis punched in a number. "Henry, this is Phyllis Mason. Yes, yes, it has been a long time. Sorry to intrude on your evening, but I need a huge favor." She rose, and with her cane hobbled to her bedroom, where she closed the door.

Hollis was nosy enough to press her ear to the door, but she knew Phyllis didn't want her to overhear her conversation, and Phyllis had proven herself to be a wily old lady. Hollis wouldn't be surprised to hear the door was wired. At any rate, the conversation didn't take long.

Phyllis emerged triumphant. "I hate watching sausages being made, don't you?"

Hollis laughed at the reference to behind-the-scenes deal-making. "Yes, I do. Did you have to give up a few chits?"

"No, but I called in a few." Phyllis's expression grew serious. "What I'm about to tell you must be kept between you and me." She waited for Hollis's nod. "Don't worry, Mr. Green will cooperate with the police. It's best if you don't go back and say anything to your ex-con friend. The less he knows, the better. Henry will take it from here. I expect to hear back from him within the hour."

Hollis stiffened; she didn't doubt that "Henry" was the current district attorney and upcoming gubernatorial favorite.

Phyllis sat back in her lounger. "Hollis, do you think you can trust Detective Silva?"

She frowned. Could she trust Silva? Stephanie was sure of him. "I think so; my gut tells me he's legit."

"Think hard. Tony's life depends on it." Phyllis's voice had a small tremor.

Hollis took a deep breath. "Yes, I trust him."

"Good." She scribbled a note on her pad. "Now, talk to me about this timeline."

She took a quiet Phyllis through her timeline and discussed the details.

"On its face, it doesn't tell us much," Phyllis said, "but we may be able to use it to bring him down in the court case."

True to his word, the DA called back in fifty-two minutes. Phyllis again took the call in her bedroom. When she re-entered the living room, she was pensive. She sat on the sofa next to Hollis.

"This 'list' is a very big deal. The word on the street is that some of our more marginally notorious citizens are worried about being identified." Phyllis took a sip of her now-cold tea. "Berman's real name is Edward Wade." She handed Hollis a slip of paper. "Here's his address in the Bay Area and," she pointed with emphasis, "here's the address for the house he has in Truckee, not far from Lake Tahoe."

"You think he's there?"

"Yes," said Phyllis, taking Hollis's hands in hers and looked forlornly into her eyes. "I love him, Hollis. Please bring him home."

SITTING IN HER CAR, HOLLIS called Gene and thanked him for his help. She knew that if he hadn't heard back from her, he'd keep snooping around like a bloodhound.

"You found out something, didn't you?" he probed.

She dodged the question. "Without you, we'd still be wandering in the desert."

"Have it your way. Anytime I can help, let me know," he said. "What are you going to do now?"

Hollis remembered Phyllis's words of caution. "This time I

won't hesitate to do the right thing by turning the follow-up over to the police."

"Humph! If you don't want to tell me, just say so."

"Okay, I don't want to tell you."

"All right, but remember, I've got your exclusive story." He was silent a moment. "And, Hollis, be careful."

SHE DROVE HOME BY ROTE, her brain working overtime, exploring different scenarios but finally settling on one. She circled the block leading up to her house. No one appeared to be following or watching for her, but she knew the keyword was *appeared*.

John was in their dining room with a thick binder and a stack of papers in front of him. He looked up at her with a beaming smile.

"Hey," he said, "how'd it go?"

They kissed. Sitting across the table, she took him through her conversations with Silva, Gene, and Phyllis. At the latter's name his eyebrows rose.

"I know her. Well, I know *of* her. Phyllis Mason is still revered by the sheriff's office for putting away the bad guys, and recently I met a dude with Homeland Security who mentioned she was an iron lady who could not be messed with. She's still missed."

Hollis licked her lips. "John, it was Phyllis who came up with Tony's likely location." She knew she had to tread carefully if she wanted his cooperation. "I don't have the list, and I have no idea where it is, so … so the only way we're going to get Tony back is by grabbing him out of Berman's clutches."

"So, this is how you operate," John said. Unsmiling, he leaned back in his chair. "I'm seeing your rationalization and plotting from the very beginning. Interesting."

She threw up her hands. "John, you don't know Berman. I do. He wouldn't think twice about hurting Tony, especially if he thought he was going to be arrested and could be identified. Besides, if I know Berman, he's not at the lake house." Hollis got up and started walking around the room. "He wouldn't want to be two and a half hours from the city. He could easily leave Tony up there." She paused, imagining the conditions under which Berman would have left Tony alone. "Anyway … anyway, we have to go up there tonight."

"Who's *we*?"

She looked down at her hands. "I'm planning on asking Dan Silva to come with me."

For a moment John was silent. Then he said, "At first I thought you were going to ask Vince, so Silva is an improvement." He twisted the pen in his hand. "At least he has law enforcement jurisdiction. But why didn't you ask me?"

"I need you here, John. I need you to keep an eye on where Berman might crop up. I can't have him tailing me. If he's following me or having me followed, as soon as I get on Highway 80 East, he'll know where I'm headed."

"Wouldn't it make more sense to involve the police, instead of a two-person guerilla unit? Besides, I can't see a professional enforcement officer including you on the raid."

"Technically, he hasn't yet. And it's not a raid. Like I said, I don't think Berman is up there," Hollis said. "And there's a leak in the San Lucian Police Department. Tony knows me, and he's not going to trust Silva, not after what's he's already been through. We'll need to move fast. Tony's life is in danger."

John frowned. "What do you mean there's a leak in the department?"

"Sweetheart, I do not have time to bring you up to date on everything I found out today, but believe me, I will, as soon as I get back home."

John shook his head as he considered her words. She looked over at the clock, and he caught her glance.

John took a deep breath. "Contact Silva."

IT TOOK OVER AN HOUR to get the plan coordinated and agreed to. Hollis snuck out the back door, taking a small path leading to an alley between the condo units. Stephanie waited for her a block away and they went to Stephanie's apartment. Convincing Silva didn't take as long as she thought it would. Stephanie had assured him that under ordinary circumstances, Hollis would have tried to do it alone.

He still wanted it his way.

"There'll be a backup team at the highway intersection and an ambulance waiting with them," he said. "Additionally, the sheriff is giving us a sniper to cover us in."

Worried about the time it was taking, Hollis was still glad to have the officers of the law by her side. To her relief, when the three of them were gathered in Stephanie's living room, Silva held up a piece of paper.

Stephanie squinted. "What's that?"

Hollis smiled. "A search warrant?"

He gave a thumbs up. "I happen to have a friend in Nevada County who has a judge for a friend."

"So that's where you dashed out to," Stephanie said. "It must be a good friend if they can wake up a judge at home."

He grinned. "There's nothing like having the law on your side."

Hollis looked away. Ironically, having law enforcement on her side was not always her first alternative, but she had to admit she breathed easier with his plan and the warrant in hand.

"Detective, I think we need to get on the road," she urged.

John sent Silva a text verifying that a car parked across the street and one house away was still there. They were safe to leave. Another hour later, Hollis and Silva, driving an unmarked car, were able to get on the road. Hollis had left her cellphone behind in case Berman and his police friend had put a GPS tracer on it.

Now they were making good time through the foothills and not long after, they took the exit into the Martis Valley. Huddled along the edge of the valley, Berman's chalet-styled house stood alone in a grove of trees behind a small rise in the land. There were no street lights, there was no street, only a long gravel driveway that led to a wrought-iron gate. They almost missed it in the darkness. The house was completely dark; even the walkway lights were off.

"Keep your fingers crossed," Silva murmured as he eased the car up to the gate, pointing the lights toward what appeared to be a heavy chain and padlock. "Good. When he turned off the electricity, he turned off the gate."

Hollis squinted. "Are we going to have to climb the wall?"

"Nope." Silva jumped out. In the trunk he found a pair of bolt cutters.

The chain was so thick that severing it took Silva several tries. She frowned. Even if Tony could have stumbled out of the house into the night, he never would have gotten through the gate. Silva drove the car on low beams to the end of the driveway near an orderly stack of firewood and parked. No other cars were visible, but Hollis noticed a two-car garage off to the other side of the house.

Silva got out of the car. "Stay behind me until I wave you forward." He turned on a flashlight and pointed it toward the ground. "I've got to make sure Berman isn't here."

"Or doesn't know we're here," Hollis murmured, reaching in the backseat for the blanket she'd brought for Tony.

There was little light from the half-moon, but Hollis tried to walk in the footsteps Silva left behind. They approached the wide steps leading to a broad wrap-around porch and a large wooden front door with beveled glass panels. Silva motioned her to step behind him. Taking a gun in his right hand, he raised the flashlight in his left. He peered through the side panel window and pointed to a large emblem attached to the glass—a security system. His lips formed a firm line, and he gestured for Hollis to come closer.

He whispered, "If that's a real system and it's turned on, Berman will immediately know we're here. If he's not here, it won't matter. I can handle talking to the response security team."

Hollis stepped back and looked up at the house. There wasn't a light to be seen. She lowered her voice as he had. "Detective Silva, we have to take a chance, but I've got an idea. Most systems are focused on the first floor—that's windows, doors, and motion detection. But the second floor is not as protected, and it can save the owner money to focus on the first floor." She pointed to the corner of the house and whispered, "There's a tree next to what looks like a bathroom window. I could open it or break it and climb in."

"You could be wrong and the system will go off anyway. If Berman's inside, you'll be trapped. I can't let you risk it."

She sighed. "Okay, what's your idea?"

Silva leaned against the redwood exterior and thought a moment, then passed the beam back and forth through the window panel again. "I don't see a keypad. There's usually a red night-light to indicate its location. If the panel's there, the light's not on." His jaw tightened. "I'm going in. Don't follow me until I give you a clear signal. If something happens, here are the car keys. Do not go inside. I've got my communicator." He tapped his shoulder. "Backup will be here in seconds; you get out of the way. All right?"

"Got it," she said.

From his jacket pocket he took a small round suction unit and a glass cutter. He applied both to the window by the door knob, gingerly made the cut, and lifted out the glass.

He turned to Hollis, smiled, and put his hand through the hole to unlock the deadbolt on the door.

There was silence, except for a clock ticking somewhere in the darkness of the house.

Hollis held her breath as Silva entered. She saw the panel on the wall at the same time he did; it was dark, with a "system off" signal. His fingers formed an "okay" gesture and he walked into the open living, dining, and kitchen area. Hollis followed behind him. He stood to the side of the closed door to what appeared to be a bathroom and pushed it open slowly.

It was dark and empty.

The flashlight beam swept across a small, square hallway. Finding no one, he moved to the bottom of the stairs, motioning once more for her to stay put. He started the climb, a gun in his outstretched hand and a flashlight pointing at the floor.

Hollis's heart was beating double time, and she took a calming breath. She stepped backward into the center of the living area.

Thump.

Silva was already out of whisper range. She put the blanket down and looked for something to use as a weapon. Glancing around the room, she caught the glint of a ski pole and skis leaning against the wall in the entryway. She continued taking backward steps until she could reach out and pick up the pole. She edged slowly around the room, listening for any sound. She stopped.

Thump.

Hollis tilted her head; the sound was coming from her left. She tiptoed down a short hallway. She'd seen Silva check it out earlier, but she was certain the sound came from this direction. There was a door she'd almost missed. It was paneled like that wall that held it. There was no doorknob, only a sliding pocket door latch. Her breathing was rapid, and raising the pole as if it were a bat, she took a deep breath. Standing to the side she opened the door. It was a small under-the-stairs storage room full of boxes and clothing thrown about. She took a step inside and waited for her eyes to adjust to the darkness. She felt something brush against her ankle, and she jumped back, squinting at a bundle of clothing.

It moved.

She bent down and lifted off jackets, pants, and empty boxes. Finally, in the darkness, she saw the shape of a figure stuffed and bound in the corner.

Tony.

She put the pole down and pulled the cloth from his mouth.

"I knew you would find me, dear girl," he rasped, licking his lips. "Help me up. My legs are like wet noodles. I could use some water."

Hollis scrambled to her feet and ran to the kitchen for a glass of water. Running back, she leaned down and put the glass to his lips. He closed his eyes, and that's when she noticed his pallor. She put her fingers to his wrist and tried to hide the alarm she felt at his racing heartbeat.

"Let's go over to the sofa." She lifted him from under his arm and held on to his waist. They stumbled into the living room and onto the sofa. "Let's sit down, Tony. You're going to be okay. Can you hear me?"

He appeared dazed and didn't respond.

Hollis stood and called up to Silva. She heard him running down the stairs, and he came over to her, kneeling next to Tony.

"Tony was in that room under the steps." She pointed. "I think he's fainted. He's dehydrated and his heart is beating faster than mine."

Gently as she could, she pulled the duct tape from Tony's bare wrists and legs. He moaned.

Silva bent down and lifted Tony's legs with care onto the sofa. "Let me see if I can find some brandy around here." He walked over to what appeared to be a bar and returned with a shot glass. "Give him this."

Hollis tilted his head and put the glass to his lips. Tony accepted the liquid and his eyelids fluttered open.

"Didn't mean to give you a scare," he whispered.

"Tony, I was so worried." She hugged him. She hadn't realized the delicacy of his frame. He felt so fragile.

He touched her cheek then tried to lift his head. "Is he gone?"

"He's gone," Silva said. "But we need to get you out of here. I've called 911. They'll be here shortly."

Hollis lifted the glass of water, but Tony waved her aside and motioned for the shot glass. Silva smiled with understanding and passed her the liquor. She raised Tony's head and let him sip. Color returned to his face.

"Who's he?" Tony said, motioning his head toward Silva and seeing his gun.

"A friend, a police detective," Hollis responded. "Tony, where's Berman?"

"When he threw me in the closet, he said he'd be back in the morning. I didn't know if I could take another night of cold like that. Let's get going." He tried to raise himself, but the movement was too much for him and he fell back onto the pillows.

Hollis could hear the sound of an ambulance.

Silva bent down and picked him up like a baby. "The EMTs are here. I've got you, sir."

Tony fell back onto Silva's arms. The EMTs rushed in with a gurney and helped Silva settle Tony onto the wheeled cart, throwing blankets over him, and starting an IV. Silva stood off to the side, speaking with one of the aides. Hollis noticed Tony's eyes signaling her to come closer. She stood next to his side and bent her ear down to his mouth.

"Don't let this thing that happened to me keep you from doing the right thing," he said weakly. "I want you to get that bastard. I don't know what's going on—you'll have to tell me once this is all over—and don't look so forlorn. I'll be all right." His lips curled into a courageous smile. "Besides, you owe me lunch."

She smiled, tears in her eyes. "You got it. This time the tuna sandwich is on me."

His eyes glistened and searched hers. After a moment he closed them but held tight onto her hand.

Hollis covered him with the blanket and the EMTs closed the ambulance door and drove off. She and Silva walked quickly to the car and followed them to the hospital. By the time they got him settled in the small regional hospital nearby, Tony's voice, still lacking its old resonance, had strengthened and his quick mind was intact, if a little worse for the wear. Lying on the bed waiting for the doctor to examine him, he told of his two days of captivity.

Berman had left him alone most of the time, taped up and locked in one of the bedrooms. With his legs bound he'd lost most of his circulation and soon was unable to walk. Berman gave him a sandwich and allowed him to use the toilet. Then today, he'd put him in the closet, and though Tony didn't realize it, left him alone.

"Did he use … did he use my voice tape?" Tony was becoming visibly tired from talking.

Hollis smoothed his covers. "Yes, but I didn't know you were a tape; you sounded real to me."

"It's an ol' … old trick. Then he could … could kill me … and no one would …." He fell into a gentle snore.

She sighed. "Good, now he'll rest. The doctor will be here soon. Next stop—home."

Silva took a quick look over his shoulder. "He's tough." He glanced at Hollis. "And so are you. You make a great sidekick."

She ignored the compliment. "Can you catch Berman, now?"

"Oh, yeah, he's cooked," he said. "I'll have fingerprints from the house and I saw papers in the bedroom with his dual identities. You can breathe easier. He won't be able to hide."

Hollis raised a skeptical eyebrow.

But they didn't take Tony home. The Truckee doctor thought he should be checked out by his own physician first, so the pre-dawn hour found Hollis riding in the ambulance to Tony's HMO. While she sat in the hospital waiting room, Hollis put in a call to Phyllis.

Phyllis picked up the phone on the first ring.

"Hollis, is he—"

"He's okay, Phyllis. I'm looking at him right now. We're waiting for his doctor to check him out, then his friend Ritz will take him home. She knew the woman on the other end was trying to keep it together.

Silva had left them hours earlier to return to the Bay Area to get started on tracking and arresting Berman.

An officer took Tony's statement while he waited and offered to take Hollis to her car. She sent a text to Ritz, saying Tony was released to go home.

Ritz responded with, "I'm leaving the restaurant now. I'll meet you there. He's going to want to go home as soon as he can. I can stay to make sure he's settled in."

She punched in another number.

"Phyllis, just wanted to let you know that Tony's doctor says he's going to be fine. He just needs a little rest. Right now he's sleeping it off like a baby."

"Thank you," she said, and Hollis heard her swallow hard. "May I ask a favor? Can you pick me up and take me to see him later on this afternoon? He can have guests, can't he?"

Hollis said, "Of course he can. I will pick you up later this afternoon, but first, I'm waiting for Ritz to get here, so I can retrieve my car. Then I want to see what progress the police are making at capturing Berman."

Phyllis's voice was flat. "Yes, I do not want Mr. Berman to have a good day."

CHAPTER TWENTY-ONE

WHEN HOLLIS WOKE, JOHN HAD already left for work. He'd left a note taped to the bedside lampshade:

> I am so proud of you. I hope you're planning on taking the day off. Let's go out to dinner. Call you later. Love, *John*

She used one eye to squint at the clock. She had slept fitfully, waking often, after tossing and turning and finally dozing off. But she was up now. It was almost eleven o'clock. She stood and put her feet into slippers. If she hurried, she could pick up Phyllis and take her to Tony's condo and still get back to the office. The doctor had given Tony a cautionary clean bill of health. After two days of abuse, he seemed to have come through battered but well. He just needed a little peace and quiet.

An hour later, she snuck a peek at her passenger, who was silent and staring out the window.

"He's going to be okay, Phyllis. I can tell you're worried."

"What? Oh … no, I'm fine." She tapped the window. "We

have him back with us. That's all that matters to me."

Hollis wasn't satisfied. "Then what are you thinking about?"

"I'm thinking of how I lived the last forty years of my life with pride, but without love." She sat a little straighter. "And I don't plan on wasting another day in self-justified righteousness."

HOLLIS LOOKED AROUND THE RESTAURANT. It was crowded, even for midweek dining, but that was the Bay Area—fine eating wasn't a luxury reserved for special occasions or relegated to weekends. Besides, they wouldn't be able to get in on the weekend.

"You okay? You're awfully quiet," John said, taking a sip of wine.

"I'm fine. It was a good day. I got some rest and I did a good deed." She took a last bite at her praline cheesecake. "You should've seen the reunion of Tony and Phyllis; they are so much in love. They were like teenagers."

He reached for her hand. "What else? There's something bothering you."

"Tony was a totally innocent victim." She slowly shook her head. "He wouldn't have been put in danger except for me. Berman was tracking my movements and found out that I cared about him."

John leaned back in his chair. "What does Silva say about locating Berman?"

"Silva wouldn't tell me anything other than Detective Lee is hot on his trail." She sighed. "Wherever Berman is, he's not looking for me, and Silva must agree. Did you notice I lost my shadow?"

Unless the bad guys were employing underground cameras, Hollis was no longer being followed or having her home watched.

"I noticed." He finished his wine. "Hollis, the chief wants me to go out of town for an overnighter tomorrow. I'll be back

Saturday, late afternoon, but it's not critical. If you'd rather not be alone, I won't go."

Hollis smiled. "No, go. It works out perfectly. I've got to set up an inventory of Rena's gifts. I told her I'd come by tomorrow night to get started. I couldn't be with you anyway."

He waggled his eyebrows with amusement. "I still can't see you as a matron of honor working on the bridal team."

She made a face. "Hey, I've been practicing smiling sweetly all week."

CHAPTER TWENTY-TWO

"Two more weeks, Hollis, two more weeks," Rena practically squealed. "Can you imagine … all this planning and it will be over in two more weeks?"

Hollis looked at the breakfast menu and decided that in the interest of Rena's seemingly irrepressible mood, and in honor of her friend's health-conscious eating habits, she'd take a simple muffin and yogurt. When the server came she ordered for both of them and Rena didn't seem to notice.

"Yeah, in just two weeks you'll be Mrs. Mark Haddon." At the sound of the words, even she smiled. The couple had clicked from the very beginning, and of one thing Hollis was certain: they were made for each other.

Rena beamed. "And you should see little Christopher. He loves Mark and Mark loves him." Tears came to her eyes. "Three years ago coming off parole, I never would have dreamed I'd be happy again, let alone this happy." She took out a tissue and blew her nose.

Hollis looked at her friend dressed attractively in belted gray slacks and a soft yellow silk blouse and sighed. Her long, curly dark brown hair was held back with yellow jade clips that set off her smooth café au lait complexion. Rena was beautiful inside and outside.

"Well, I think we should get to work on this perfect day." Hollis lifted out her datebook. "Do you have the gift tags? Did you bring your wedding tote?"

Rena laughed. "Yes, captain, only look." She reached down to her side and pointed to an oversized tote that resembled a huge shopping bag. At Hollis's amazed look, she said, "I ran out of room, so I had to get a tote for the tote."

She lifted the bundle and slid it across the floor to Hollis. The remaining bag was still almost half full. She handed her a bulging manila folder.

"Oh, my God, Rena, this is your guest list. Who'd you invite, the United Nations delegation?"

Rena gave her a sheepish grin. "I need your help. I don't know anyone who is more organized than you. I've got to get ready for a big buyer's show and I don't have time to plow through this bag. There are receipts in here, invoices, some gift cards that came in early, and I don't know what all else." She squeezed Hollis's hand. "*Puleeeze* organize it for me. I don't care how you do it—I trust your judgment—but I can't lug this thing around any longer."

Hollis bent down and pulled on the handle to test its weight. It didn't budge. "I agree. You could throw out your back."

"So, you'll do it?"

The server slipped in with their order and Hollis took a bite of salad. "Sure, I have a little time."

"Good." Rena smiled then looked down at her food. "Er … Hollis there's just one thing."

"What?"

Rena looked down at her hands. "Could you hurry up?"

HOLLIS POKED HER HEAD IN George's office. He had gone on to his new life and there was a growing stack of moving boxes in the far corner. She sighed and went to her own desk.

Penny was already there, waiting. When she saw Hollis, she asked, "Are you okay? Tiffany told me what happened after you called in yesterday." Her attire today would likely be considered early commune—leather Birkenstocks, a long flowered dress, and some kind of beaded talisman around her neck.

Hollis did a double-take but kept her response specific to the question. "I'm fine, and our clients are fine."

"They really weren't our clients. You're the one who—"

Hollis momentarily forgot her paralegal's lack of humor and penchant for the literal. "Yes, well they're friends, now."

"Of course," Penny said, with a slight blush. "Here are your messages. I went through the mail and there's nothing urgent. Unless …." Her voice drifted as her eyes fixed on the large tote bag next to the credenza. "What's that?"

"*That* is the price of friendship," Hollis said, glancing grimly at the bag. "I'm helping out a friend. Anyway, I'll take care of work first then—"

"No, you won't," Tiffany said from the doorway. "Detectives Silva and Lee want to see you as soon as possible at the station."

Tiffany saw the burgeoning tote and pointed. "What's that?"

Penny turned to leave. "Don't ask."

HOLLIS WAITED IN THE INTERVIEW room only a couple of minutes before Detective Lee came in, holding two steaming cups,—tea for her and coffee for him.

She beamed. "Detective Lee, you are wonderful." She held the cup to warm her hands before taking a sip.

He sat across from her. "Detective Silva will be here in a short while. He got stopped on his way. You've had a pretty harrowing time of it the last couple of weeks." He took a sip from his own cup. "How are you doing?"

"I'm doing … okay." She realized she hadn't really stopped to think about it. She hadn't had the time. "What's the urgency? Did you find Berman?"

"Detective Silva asked that I wait until he gets—"

At that moment, Silva briskly entered the room.

"Ms. Morgan, it's good to see you looking rested." Silva smiled and put his phone and a notepad in front of him as he sat down. "Not too traumatized, I hope?"

Hollis fidgeted. Polite banter had never been her forte. "Detective, have you found Berman?"

He straightened and gave a slight cough. "Yes. He should be in FBI custody," he looked at the time on his phone, "about … now."

Hollis leaned back in her chair and exhaled a sigh of relief. "Where was he?"

"In Foster City, using yet a third identity. He'd rented a car and was on his way to Canada, where he was planning on flying to Dubai."

She raised her eyebrows. "He does think big, doesn't he?"

Just then Silva's phone vibrated. He picked it up and listened then clicked off.

"They got him." He smiled.

"Well, the kidnapping saga is over," Lee said.

Hollis smiled. "So, why am I here—just to be included in the celebration?"

"No celebrations yet. We haven't linked Berman to the murder of Olivia Shur." Silva nodded to Lee, who pulled out a small recorder. "Right now we need your account of the events leading to last night's rescue of Mr. Grueber." He stood. "I've got a small fire I have to put out, but if you would give Lee your statement, we'll turn it over to the feds. You shouldn't be hearing from us again."

She understood. Her interaction would be with the district attorney's office as they prepared the prosecution's case for the court.

"Well then, I shall say goodbye to you, Detective Silva." She smiled. It came to her that the next time she saw him she would be calling him Dan.

"Goodbye, Ms. Morgan, and say hello to our mutual friend." He grinned and left.

"All right, Detective Lee," she said. "Let's get started."

AN HOUR LATER, HOLLIS RUBBED her eyes.

"Only a few more questions, Ms. Morgan." Detective Lee said kindly. He gave her a long look. "You haven't said what happened to the list?"

She looked at him with a question in her eyes. "I don't know. Olivia may have tried to contact me with the list but she was killed before we could make a connection. Or …." She paused in thought.

"Or, what?"

She looked down. "Or, nothing. My imagination is spent."

He looked at his notebook. "Have you had any more texts?"

She picked up her phone and glanced at her message app. "No, none from the killer." She placed it between them.

He smiled. "Well, let's hope we just caught the killer."

She sighed and smiled, but said nothing.

"I can see you're tired. We're done here. Go home and get some rest."

He turned off the machine and put away his pen, but when he started to get up, his elbow caught his cup of coffee and the brown liquid spread across the table. Hollis pulled back as Lee leaned over dabbing up the liquid with nearby napkins. He wiped off her phone and handed it back.

"Maybe I need a break, too," he said woefully. Then he motioned her toward the door. "Ms. Morgan, Detective Silva wanted me to reassure you that you don't have to be afraid. Berman can't hurt you anymore."

"I'm not afraid," she reassured him. "I could just use a little down time, as well." She held out her hand. "Well, Detective Lee, I will be saying goodbye to you, too. Thank you for looking out for me."

He motioned that his hand was full of wadded up napkins. "Goodbye, Ms. Morgan."

*

For once, Hollis took Lee's advice and went home. It was just past noon, but she decided she would return to the office after a nap. The Triple D conference room table would be ideal to spread out Rena's materials, and since it was Friday most everyone would be gone to start their weekend, she could work undisturbed.

The condo was quiet without John, and when she lay across the bed, she fell asleep almost instantly. She woke with a start and looked over at the clock on the nightstand. It was almost five o'clock. Hoping to be finished with the tote before dark, she scrambled to get up and dressed in jeans and running shoes. She was ready to tackle her matron of honor duties.

Using her key to enter the lobby, she noticed light coming from a single office. Only one attorney was working late; everyone else had left.

Hollis knocked on his door jamb and explained she was going to be using the conference room.

The young man looked up from his keyboard. "Not to worry. I'm out of here soon, but I'll let you know before I leave."

For Hollis, it was easier to drag the tote along the floor from her office down the hall to the conference room. She grunted as she lifted it onto a chair then onto the table.

Then, methodically, she began to sort out papers, cloth samples, business cards, and advertisements. The stacks rose by inches.

She raised her head at the sound of tapping on the open door.

The late-working attorney was pulling on his jacket. "Hollis, I'm getting ready to leave. I'll let the security guard downstairs know you're still here."

She smiled. "Thanks. Despite the way it looks, this is going faster than I thought. I won't be here much longer myself. Have a good weekend."

For another fifteen minutes, she continued to excavate materials from the tote. She could almost see the bottom. Her phone trilled.

"Where are you?" Stephanie asked.

"I'm doing good deeds in the conference room at work."

"Huh?"

Hollis laughed. "I'm helping out Rena by organizing her wedding planning information. I still have to set up a spreadsheet for her gift list, but I can do that at home."

"Gee, I didn't know you knew how to do stuff like that." Stephanie sounded amused. "How much longer are you going to be? Dan is on an assignment that's running late, and I'm hungry. Want to meet me out near the house?"

Hollis looked around the cluttered table and the only three-quarters empty bag. "I could eat, too, but I'll need another hour or so here. Even so, I'm still going to have to come back early in the morning and finish sorting the rest of her stuff."

"Good, you gotta eat," Stephanie said. "Say, now that the Berman adventure is over, and Dan has finished working the case, did they ever find the list?"

"Not that I know of," Hollis said. "Olivia's list dies with her and I'm glad. Having that list was like having a laser target on your chest. Rena was one of the last people to speak with her—besides Berman, I mean. Olivia told her she was ready to make a trade in order to go legit and start over. It's kind of sad, really." She paused in reflection, then added, "Well, let me get to a good stopping point with my task. I'll meet you at seven thirty at the pizza restaurant. I may even beat you there."

"Fine. I'm going to take a shower. See you then."

They clicked off.

Urged on by a growling stomach, Hollis skimmed through the next handful of envelopes and receipts. She placed them on the appropriate stacks in front of her, except for one of the last envelopes—it had her name across the top.

She frowned. She didn't recognize the handwriting and the envelope was sealed.

What was Rena doing with her correspondence?

Hollis reached for a letter opener and slid it across the top. A single sheet of paper was inside.

It was a list.

She froze for a moment, staring but not seeing. These weren't names but initials, followed by numbers, amounts in dollars, and finally dates. She counted eight entries. "Oh, my God, it's the list," she said out loud and sank into her chair.

This time she scanned the paper more deliberately, but no identifying notation jumped out at her. The initials could be anybody, but clearly for those who would kill for the list, they meant something.

What was Rena doing with the list?

She sat in stillness, considering her next move. Finally she picked up her phone and punched in a number. The recorded voicemail message left her frustrated.

She couldn't keep the excitement out of her voice. "Detective Silva, I think I have what you've been looking for. I'm in my office. Please call me as soon as you get my message."

She looked at the time—almost six o'clock. She was about fifteen minutes away from the restaurant. She punched in another number; it too went to voicemail.

"Stephanie, you're probably taking your shower. Call me when you get this message. I think I found … never mind, just call me. If we don't connect, don't worry. We're still on for dinner."

Hollis sat with her chin in her hands, then an idea came into her head. She dashed down the hall, to the copy room, and turned on the machine. It roared as its motor churned on. It would take another three or four minutes to warm up. She returned to the conference room and mindlessly started to put stick-on labels on the various stacks. Then she went back to the copy room. The machine flashed "ready" and she slipped the single sheet onto the glass platen, making two copies. As the pages spit out, she folded them and put them in her pocket. She walked back to the conference room, where she lay the original on the conference table.

It was only then she noticed her shaking hands.

Her head felt a vague throb. She refused to believe that Rena had set her up. It was impossible to conceive that Rena, her closest of friends, could be a killer. No, this she knew for sure: Rena was not a killer—she could not kill.

But what was she doing with the list?

Hollis thought about it a moment—no, Rena only had a sealed envelope with Hollis's name on it. She had not opened it. The list was too valuable; if Rena was the killer she wouldn't give access to the proof of her guilt to Hollis. It was more likely Rena didn't know she had the list; her tote had been a dumping ground and catch-all for weeks.

How did she get it?

Hollis chewed her bottom lip, trying to sort out the circumstances of the list in front of her; then she remembered the last conversation Rena had with Olivia Shur. Rena said Olivia had given her a squeezed hug; maybe she had given her something else. Could Olivia have dropped the envelope for Hollis in Rena's bag?

She peered at the first column of numbers. Each was eight digits long except for one that was five. They could be dates, phone numbers, or a possibly a house number. She considered the five-digit number—it was not a date, forward or in reverse. Eight digits were too many for a house number. Phone numbers had seven and social security numbers had nine. The numbers had to link back to a name, some sort of identifying notation. She looked over the numbers, then ran her pen down the column. They all began with one of three digits—four, five, or six. She tapped the pen against her temple, and scrambled for a pad of paper.

That was when she heard the swoosh of Triple D's lobby doors.

She looked over her shoulder to see Detective Lee standing in the doorway.

"Ms. Morgan, hope I didn't scare you." He smiled. "Detective

Silva asked me to follow up on the phone message you left him. He's working a case in Livermore."

Hollis frowned and tensed.

"Detective, how did you get in?"

He entered the room and glanced curiously at the various mounds of papers on top of the table. "I spoke with the security guard in the lobby. He released the lock on the elevator and your lobby door." He pointed at the mess. "What's going on?"

She smiled. "I'm helping out a friend organize her wedding."

"Ah, Ms. Gabriel's happy day." He walked around the stacks. "Is that how you found the list? She had it?"

Her eyes narrowed. "What makes you think I found the list?"

"It was in your message."

"No, I was careful not to say it over the phone."

He held her eyes. "It was in your voice; your excitement came through your message. So, you did find it among Rena Gabriel's things?"

"No ... I mean yes." Hollis rushed, "I must have accidently let an envelope I'd gotten from Olivia Shur slip from my grasp. I didn't realize it at the time, but it contained the list. It wasn't until I was sorting through the wedding material that I found it. Then I realized I had it all along." She knew she was speaking too fast, and she forced a breath to slow down and cover her lie.

Lee stood opposite across the table, nodding affably and reaching out his hand. "Let me have the envelope, and then you can be on your way to dinner with your friend."

Hollis's heartbeat picked up and she froze.

How does he know I'm having dinner with Stephanie?

Scowling, she looked at the stack of papers scattered in front of her. Her eyes caught sight of the envelope with her name on it at the same time Lee's did. He reached across the table, his jacket falling open to reveal his shield. She glanced down, and her eyes widened in sudden recognition.

"Here ... here it is." She passed it to him.

He snatched it from her.

"It's empty."

"Yes, while I was waiting, I was trying to …." She hesitated. "It's in some kind of code and I was—"

"That's our job." He held out his hand. "Let me have the list."

His voice was stern and his facial expression impassive. Hollis flipped the page over to him, where it fluttered before landing. A smile crept over his face as he scanned the entries. He looked over at her and they exchanged knowing glances.

"Well, now you have the list," she said, "let me know as soon as you and Detective Silva get the bad guys." She tucked her hair behind her ears. "Now, I need to get back to work. I promised one of the attorneys I would help him with a brief, so he could go out for dinner." She looked at the clock on the wall. "He should be back any minute."

He gave her a long look and quickly stepped into the lobby, just beyond the conference room door. Then he moved back into the room.

"What's the matter?" Hollis asked.

"What's that noise?"

She could vaguely hear the distant drone of the copy machine humming its mechanical churn. She stiffened.

"Oh, that might be the HVAC system. You don't hear it so much during the day when we're all here, but when it's quiet otherwise, it sounds quite loud." Her voice came off as strained and forced to her ears. "Anyway, like I said, I need to wrap this stuff up. I'm getting tired. It's been a long week."

"Yeah, your finding Grueber … that was pretty impressive." He was still looking at the list. "Your adventure in Tahoe made me tired just hearing about it." He folded the paper and put it inside his pocket, then stepped into the center of the lobby and called back to her. "I'll just go check out that noise and make sure everything is secure. How about showing me the way?"

She got up slowly, grabbing her cellphone and tucking it in her pocket. She walked in front and to one side of his lanky frame as they went down the hallway into the machine room. Lee fumbled for the lights and ran to the copy machine to lift up the copier flap.

"You made copies?" he growled.

Hollis held her arms at her sides, resisting the urge to pat her pocket, and said nothing.

"Ms. Morgan … ah, Ms. Morgan," he began to check all the copy returns down the side of the machine and made sure they were empty. "You don't seem …."

Hollis didn't wait for him to finish. She spun around, turned off the lights and ran down the hall the opposite way they'd arrived. There was a short hallway with a door leading back to the lobby and another to the stairwell. She was opening the door to the stairwell when she heard Lee running in her direction.

The stairwell was low lit with baseboard-level LED lights. She took off her shoes and ran down to the next floor. She tested the door, but it was locked. Of course, security would preclude anyone getting off on an unauthorized floor. Triple D was on the seventh floor; she had five more stories to go.

She heard Lee cursing softly at the top of the stairs. By his pauses, she could tell he was listening for any slight noise as he eased down the steps. She padded down to the fourth floor. He'd stopped to listen for her, then started up again and was slowing coming down the stairs. She hastily ran past the third and second floors. She imagined he wasn't sure she was actually in the stairwell and was debating going forward or turning back.

Hollis had been stuck in the stairwell once during an earthquake drill. She had waited too long to leave with the others. She found herself alone, trying to make her way back to the building's reception desk, which was in the lobby on the other side of the building. Under ordinary circumstances it wouldn't be a problem taking the time to get there, but now it was time she could ill afford. Besides, Lee would expect her to take it. He would overcome her before she could reach security.

She would go to the mailroom.

She gasped in relief when the stairwell door opened to the basement; then she ran full speed down the darkened corridor into the vast semi-darkness of the mailroom. There were no emergency lights here, only the minimal glare from the exit sign. She remembered the long wall that backed a line of narrow tables holding the row of Triple D white plastic mail crates. After bumping into another table, she bit back a curse and slid underneath it with her back to a corner wall.

She could sense more than hear Lee enter the room.

He moved stealthily, nearly silent, but she could feel the mass of his presence and almost anticipate his breathing. She patted the copies in her pocket and listened. He'd stopped trying to be quiet.

"Ms. Morgan, I know you're here." His voice was low and breathy. Evidently taking the stairs had tested his physical exertion. "I know you made a copy—two copies actually, I saw the number on the machine." He gave a small chuckle.

His voice was coming from another side of the room, and from his footfalls, she could tell he was still moving around carefully. In the dark, the mailroom looked like a huge house packed up and ready for the movers. Hollis's phone vibrated, and she slapped at it to turn it off.

Lee stopped in his tracks, listening.

She glanced down. It was a reminder about her dinner with Stephanie in fifteen minutes. He started walking again. She could almost hear his hand sliding along the wall, feeling for the light switch. He would never find it, at least not any time soon. The light switch was located low on the far wall behind a shelf unit that jutted from the wall with just enough space for someone to get their hand in and out.

"I really don't have much more time, Ms. Morgan," he said. I'm not sure what you're waiting for. If it's for someone to rescue you, I'm afraid you're out of luck." His voice was coming from the left.

She'd hoped that security would do its walk-around soon, but if they saw the light in the firm's offices, they would likely walk past. Lights on in the offices wouldn't raise an alarm. They were accustomed to lawyers working late hours, and this time security knew that she and a police detective were in the building. She had to get out of here and make a run for the delivery door to the street. But first she'd hide the copies. They were the only reason she was alive, the only reason she would stay alive.

Lee's footfalls were closing in; he was searching in a grid pattern. Hollis smiled grimly; one of the inside tips she'd learned in prison was about grid-pattern police searches. He was closing her off from an exit and would eventually reach her corner. She slipped the copies out of her pocket and separated them. As quietly as possible, she raised her hand over the table top and placed a copy in the nearest white container. With the second copy in hand, she crawled to her right, still under the table, and after doubling then re-doubling the page, she packed it between the wall and the table edge. She crept back to the corner. Taking out her phone—she hoped her jacket would be sufficient to stifle any light—she punched in three numbers. As soon as she hit send, a beep sounded a few feet away.

She groaned.

"Ah, Ms. Morgan," Lee said, not masking his irritation, "you're raising the stakes, I see. Now you know how I tracked you. You've sent a 911 message. But I won't be here when the police come, and I can assure you … you won't be able to breathe a word."

He no longer tried to hide his whereabouts. Lee knocked boxes to the ground, and taking out his own phone, he turned on the flashlight app. The arc of light went only a few feet but Hollis knew he was closing in. He swept the area in front of him like a large fan. He was less than twelve feet away. Hollis crawled to the edge of the band of light. As he swept it the other direction, she scampered to the right. If she could reach the next intersection of tables, she would stand and run, knocking boxes behind her, blocking his way. He might shoot her, of course, but he was going to do that anyway.

The light beam was on its way back toward her. She reached the intersection, stood, and ran. Bumping into tables slowed her down, but she was still ahead of Lee, who muttered curses a few feet behind her. She turned to assess his position and didn't see the white container that blocked her own path. She slipped and fell.

He grabbed her by the wrist, twisting it as she came to her feet.

"They'll be here any minute," she said, attempting to keep her voice even and trying to block out the pain he was inflicting. "You'd better go."

"Give me the copies," he ordered.

When she hesitated, he put her in a neck hold and roughly went through her pockets.

"You have less than one minute to tell me where they are. Otherwise, I will shoot you in your right arm, then your left, then your leg …. I think you get the idea."

Hollis shuddered and nodded as well as she could. He released his hold on her neck but not on her wrist.

Catching her breath, she stumbled as he shoved her toward the back of the room where she'd been hiding, but he didn't release his hold.

She swallowed. "I put it in a container over there." She pointed to the table along the wall.

"Turn on the lights and take me to where you put it. Hurry up."

"You're hurting me, and I'm going as fast as I can., I can't get my balance," she whined. "The lights are over there."

"Suck it up. I'm not letting you go." He shoved her ahead of him. "I said get the lights on and give me that list. You have thirty seconds."

She reached down to turn on the lights. The room brightened, revealing upheaved bins on tables and the floor. He pushed her toward the corner. When they reached her hiding spot, Hollis looked into the three possible bins where she could have placed the sheet.

"Which one?" Lee growled into her ear.

She flinched.

"I don't know." She went from one bin to another. "It has to be one of these. It would be on top. But I can't look for it because you've got my hand." She tried to pull her hand back.

"Use your other one. I'm not stupid."

She fumbled with her left hand into the first container—no list. In the second container, she pulled out the sheet on top.

It was the list. She handed it to Lee, who snatched it and took a quick glance.

"Where's the other one?"

Hollis took a deep breath. "There is no other one. The first copy was smeared because the machine was cold, and I threw it in the trash bin. You can go see for yourself."

He stared deep into her eyes. "You're lying." He raised his gun. "You're lying, and I can't waste any more time with—"

"Put down your gun, Lee," a blue uniformed officer holding his own gun said from the doorway.

Lee looked at her with profound disgust. Hollis smothered her smile, took a deep breath, and looked away. He dropped her wrist, placed the gun on the floor and held up his arms. She stumbled over fallen bins to stand beside the officer who kept Lee in his sights as a second cop ran up and jerked Lee's wrists into plastic cuffs. He half pushed, half walked Lee out into the corridor. Hollis and the first officer followed.

"Can I say how happy I am to see you guys?" She grinned. "You got here quick. I didn't think 911 could locate me that fast."

He kept his eyes straight ahead as his partner and Lee

boarded an elevator. "We didn't get a message from dispatch. It was a woman named Stephanie Ross. She said you were in danger and alone in this building."

They took the next elevator, and moments later entered the main lobby.

"We knew something was up when the security guard didn't buzz us in. Through the glass doors, we could see his feet extending from behind the reception desk, but he wasn't moving." He pointed to the guard, who had been propped up in his chair, alive but unconscious. EMTs were gently placing him on a gurney. "We called the San Lucian Fire Department and they gained entry. By then your 911 call showing your basement location made sense."

Hollis grimaced. She knew the extra minute or two Stephanie had given her had saved her life. She looked up to see her friend pushing past the police and EMTs.

They hugged, and Stephanie stepped back, still holding tight to Hollis's shoulder.

"This has got to stop." Tears streamed down Stephanie's cheeks. "Don't you want to live a normal life? I can't take much more of this drama."

"Stephanie, this time it wasn't my—"

"Your phone is flashing." She pointed to Hollis's pocket.

Hollis hadn't noticed the vibration. She looked down at the caller's name and tapped to answer.

"Hi, honey," she said, "how's it going?" She listened a few moments. "Me? Oh, nothing … I'm … I'm doing okay. It's been kind of a crazy day. In fact I'm still at the office."

Stephanie's eyes rolled skyward and she gave Hollis a shake of her head.

AN HOUR LATER, HOLLIS AND Stephanie sat on a small sofa sipping tea and coffee across from Detective Silva's desk. He was speaking rapidly into the phone.

"You owe me dinner," Stephanie whispered.

Hollis whispered back, "That and a lot more." She took a sip of tea. "What made you call the police?"

"You were late. You're never late—that, and the fact you said you had found something. I knew it had to be the list." She tucked her feet underneath her. "When you didn't arrive, I didn't wait ten minutes. I figured if I was wrong, I'd beg forgiveness."

They both turned their attention to Silva, who replaced the phone in its cradle. He sat back in his chair and shook his head.

"Well, well, Ms. Morgan, we are definitely going to have to arrange office space for you." He half-smiled but there was a worried look in his eyes. "You want to tell me what happened?"

Hollis looked sheepish and recounted the night's happenings.

"When did you realize Lee was not on the up and up?" Stephanie probed.

Silva gave her a pointed look, and Stephanie immediately found something interesting in the bottom of her cup.

He turned to Hollis and repeated Stephanie's question, "When did you realize that Lee was not on the up and up?"

She smiled. "He knew I had arranged to meet Stephanie for dinner. But Stephanie and I made that arrangement on my cellphone while I was in the office. I didn't pick up on it right away, but something kept nagging at me. Then I figured out he had put a bug on my phone, probably when I was in his office and he pretended to spill a drink."

Silva slammed his fist on the desk.

"That's how he knew you found the list," he said.

"You didn't tell him to follow up with me?"

"No, check your phone. You'll see I sent a text saying: do nothing until I contact you later tonight."

"I had to turn my phone off so I wouldn't be detected. It had already gone off once," Hollis said. She stood and walked over to sit in front of Silva. "Did you figure out the code?"

"I turned it over to one of our savvy analysts," he said.

Hollis smirked. "That's not necessary. I already did."

Silva looked up in surprise and acknowledged her with a tilt of his head. "Hold that thought."

He left the room.

Stephanie came over and took the other available chair next to her friend. "Are you kidding? You figured it out?"

Hollis grinned. "Believe me, it took a minute. But once I narrowed it down to possible combinations, it was simple. But it was the five-digit number that stumped me, until I had a revelation."

Silva returned with a copy of the list and gave it to Hollis. "Work your magic."

"They're phone numbers with a one-digit leader indicating the area code. Let me show you." She took a pen from the holder on Silva's desk and circled what could be seen as a phone number. "Okay, this one has the number four as a leader, that means 4-1-5, that's San Francisco. Let's call it, shall we?"

She took out her cellphone. Silva reached over and held her hand back.

"No, we'll use this toss-away phone. I don't want to alert anyone with your number on their records."

Hollis picked up the phone and tapped in the number. Silva put the phone on speaker.

"This is Phil Norbeck. I'm not available to take your call. Leave a message and I'll get back to you."

Silva clicked off.

Stephanie's eyes widened. "Phil Norbeck? He's with Norbeck Industries. They make electronic devices in Silicon Valley. He's worth mega millions. He's got some big factory construction project going up in Canada."

"It looks like he might also be a crook," Hollis murmured. "If he answered, I think these must be direct lines."

It took no time at all for Silva to call the other ten numbers. It was late, and all the calls went to voicemail or were answered by an automated voice telling the caller to try again during business hours.

Finally, Silva pointed to a five-digit number. "That's not a phone number. Were you able to figure it out, too?"

Hollis gave him a small smile. "That one took me a while. This is the one where I needed a revelation." She circled the number. "It is with great pleasure that I give you the five-digit police detective shield number of Detective Roland Lee."

If Silva was surprised, he didn't show it. However, he took the sheet from Hollis and she could see his jaw stiffen.

"Wait here," he said and left her and Stephanie alone.

They exchanged looks and used the time to go over the evening's events. Stephanie's facial expression held both concern and admiration for her friend.

Silva returned a few minutes later.

"Lee has already been processed. I just wanted to make sure we had all the proper charges," he said. "He's asking for immunity in exchange for a paper trail of evidence against his fellow culprits. His role in all this was to step in, when needed, to give alerts to the offenders or tamper with the evidence." John's eyes narrowed. "He was a dirty cop. That's one trade this list is not going to make."

"It took me a minute," Hollis said, "to figure out it was Lee who killed Olivia and took the list from her car. He and Berman were working together; at least that's what Berman thought."

Stephanie frowned. "I'm confused. I thought Berman and Olivia were a couple."

"I think they were in her mind, but early on he suggested I might want to take advantage of selling the list for its monetary potential. He was just using her. He was one cold dude, both he and Lee were, and I was their gigantic loose end." Hollis sighed.

"So who left that first text on your phone?" Stephanie asked.

"I'm pretty sure it was Berman. Olivia Shurhad wisely kept the list from him, but she had my old contact information. Berman didn't want my involvement, but he couldn't show his true colors. I don't know if he looked me up on his own, or if Olivia figured it out. Regardless, the text was a mistake on a number of levels."

"How did Lee know you'd found the list?" Stephanie asked.

Silva answered, "From the bug he put in her phone, he could follow her movements and hear her conversations. In his mind it was only a matter of time. He and Berman had already hastened their evacuation plans and would go their separate ways."

Hollis felt all the week's tension slowly descending on her shoulders. "If he gets immunity, will he go free?"

Silva shook his head. "Not a chance. We don't need his evidence; we've got enough without him." He raised the list. "I'll be right back. I need to make a quick report; then I'll take you two home."

He left them sitting on the sofa.

Stephanie raised her coffee cup. "Here's to you, sweetie."

She and Hollis clicked cups.

Hollis smiled. "Here's to both of us."

EPILOGUE

***

THE WEDDING CEREMONY WAS ELEGANT in its simplicity, and Rena was glorious in a floor-length pale mauve gown with a full-length train. Her sheer veil matched the color of her gown and her copious curls were gathered by a simple ornament of enameled jade camellias. Mark and Christopher were dressed alike in tuxedos with cummerbunds in the same mauve color.

"Hollis, I am so happy, happier than I ever thought I could be," Rena confided as Hollis helped put the white jade and diamond studs in her ear.

Hollis was dressed in a slightly darker version of the bride's dress. It complemented her auburn hair, which was brushed up into a contained French roll with a single heavy curl that fell onto her shoulder, held in place with a similar jade clasp.

She smiled at her friend. "I can't believe I was responsible for introducing you two and making something so wonderful happen. You're so lucky to have found each other." She brushed away a tear and added, "Be happy."

Eyes glistening, Rena turned to face her. "We will be." She gave Hollis's shoulders a squeeze. "I still can't believe I had the list all that time. We might not be here today. If only I had—"

"Stop." With a subtle shake of the head, Hollis lifted the skirts of her dress, handed Rena her bouquet, and picked up her own. "The thing is, we *are* here, Rena. Come on, you're getting married."

It was a chilly morning. They had the run of the small Point Reyes hotel since the wedding party and few guests were the only ones in residence. Rena's mother couldn't contain herself; she took picture after picture between dabbing her eyes and blowing her nose. She kept nudging the official photographer to move over. At the start of the ceremony, she had whispered to Hollis, "I don't see why they should pay for pictures when I can take the same shots for a lot less."

Hollis stifled a laugh.

The pace of the service picked up as the minister realized the Bay Area fog was rolling in and they would soon be enveloped in a dense cloud. For the reception, they all dispersed inside the warmth of the modest community room, which had been decorated lavishly with flowers and scattered with candle topped small tables. A single harpist sat in the corner, her fingers strumming the couple's favorite love songs. Mark's parents and his brother mingled easily with Rena's siblings and aunts. The photographer, who fortunately was also a friend, was still being tailed by Mrs. Gabriel. They both flitted in and out of the group, taking formal and informal wedding party poses.

Hollis looked over the scene and smiled at John sitting next to her. He squeezed her hand.

"Isn't it a beautiful day?" she said.

"What's beautiful is you as the matron of honor," he murmured in her ear.

They gazed into each other's eyes.

John smiled and picked up her hand to kiss. "What do you say to us making a day like this?"

Hollis closed her eyes briefly and took a deep breath. Finally she replied, "I say yes."

R. FRANKLIN JAMES GREW UP in the San Francisco Bay Area and graduated from the University of California at Berkeley. Her debut novel in the Hollis Morgan Mystery series, *The Fallen Angels Book Club*, was published in 2013. *The Trade List* is the fourth book in the series. James is married with two sons and resides in Northern California.

For more information, go to www.rfranklinjames.com.

THE HOLLIS MORGAN MYSTERY SERIES

All the members of the Fallen Angels Book Club are white-collar criminals. Hollis Morgan is one, thanks to her ex-husband, who set her up. Now all she wants is to clear her name so she can return to law school. After fellow members start dying in scenarios right out of club selections, Hollis becomes a suspect. Can she identify the killer before she herself becomes the next victim?

While awaiting the results of the bar exam, paralegal and pardoned ex-con Hollis Morgan hopes to clear the name of a friend accused of libel by a philanthropist whose charitable giving looks a lot like money-laundering. Only problem: the evidence has disappeared and her friend Catherine is found dead. Can Hollis exonerate her friend without getting killed herself?

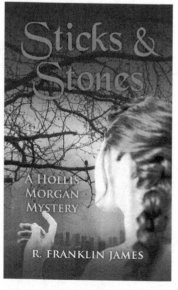

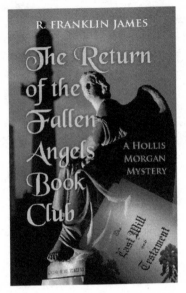

After obtaining a pardon, Hollis Morgan is a new probate attorney in the Bay Area. Her first two cases are trials by fire. The first involves a vicious family dispute over a disinheritance. She is also hired to file the will and family trust of her former parole officer. Jeffrey introduced her to the Fallen Angels, his other white-collar ex-parolees, who unite once again to solve his murder.

70918461R00153

Made in the USA
San Bernardino, CA
08 March 2018